Maureen Peters was born in Caernarfon, North Wales. She is a prolific author whose many novels include *A Child Called Freedom* and *Vashti*.

THE SCENT OF JASMINE

Orphaned at a young age, Melody Craven grew up depending on the charity of kindly relatives, so she had to be reconciled to being treated as second best to her dainty pretty cousin, Mary. But both girls fall in love with handsome young Roger Hallet, an officer serving in the British army in nineteenth-century India, who is briefly on leave in England. It looks as though the girls' friendship might be ruined by rivalry. However, events take an unusual turn when Melody meets Captain Adam Channing, an attractive but mysterious officer.

Books by Maureen Peters
Published by The House of Ulverscroft:

KATHERYN THE WANTON QUEEN
THE VINEGAR SEED
PATCHWORK
THE VINEGAR BLOSSOM
THE VINEGAR TREE
KATE ALANNA
TANSY
A CHILD CALLED FREEDOM
ENGLAND'S MISTRESS
WITCH QUEEN
THE LUCK BRIDE
BEGGAR MAID, QUEEN
TRUMPET MORNING
VASHTI

MAUREEN PETERS

◆

THE SCENT
OF JASMINE

Complete and Unabridged

ULVERSCROFT
Leicester

First published in Great Britain in 2007 by
Robert Hale Limited
London

First Large Print Edition
published 2008
by arrangement with
Robert Hale Limited
London

British Library CIP Data

Peters, Maureen
    The scent of jasmine.—Large print ed.—
    Ulverscroft large print series: historical romance
    1. Orphans—Fiction 2. Love stories
    3. Large type books
    I. Title
    823.9′14 [F]

    ISBN 978–1–84782–404–2

Published by
F. A. Thorpe (Publishing)
Anstey, Leicestershire
Set by Words & Graphics Ltd.
Anstey, Leicestershire
Printed and bound in Great Britain by
T. J. International Ltd., Padstow, Cornwall

This book is printed on acid-free paper

1

The long train of mules and oxen wound its way over the grassy plains. Seated in her canopied palanquin, Melody looked out past the fringed cloth that hung limply in the heat at the sides of her swaying equipage. She would have preferred to have been riding astride one of the mules but Mrs Wilson, who was somewhere towards the rear of the procession, would have been shocked to see her perched on a mule with her hooped skirts flying up behind. Mrs Wilson, on her way to rejoin her husband, was most exceedingly proper.

One of the guides came to the side of the swaying palanquin, water bottle in his hand. Beneath his turban his face was caked with white dust but his smile was as broad as usual.

'Miss Craven, you would perhaps like a drink now? We draw closer now to the fort and soon your journey will be done.'

He spoke in the soft, singsong accent that she found attractive though Mrs Wilson had confided that it irritated her.

'My dear, one hears the voice and turns

round expecting to see a Welshman only to be confronted by a native,' she had murmured as they sat together by the camp-fire during an overnight stop. 'Not that I have much to say for the Welsh actually! Rather sly people on the whole. My husband and I went to Llandudno once during his last home furlough and were charged the most outrageous price for a very mediocre hotel. And they muttered away in what I can only assume was Welsh all the time we were there!'

Mrs Wilson led a simple life, Melody thought, as she drank the warmish water and handed back the bottle with a smiling nod. For the older woman the world was divided into 'them' and 'us'. 'Us' were the English and, at a pinch, the Scottish. 'Them' was the rest of the world with Welsh, Irish, French, Hottentots and Eskimos all haphazardly lumped together.

The woman had been a constant irritation since she had joined the ship at Lisbon, for since then the long voyage, followed by the overland trek, had been punctuated by her ladylike tones expressing disapproval of almost everything and everybody. Melody tried to amuse herself by picturing what Sergeant Wilson was like and how he endured the constant carping.

She leaned back, loosening her tight collar

and mopping her neck with an already sodden handkerchief. How she envied the Indian guides and drovers in their loose tunics and wide trousers! For two pins she would have donned similar garments herself and risked giving Mrs Wilson a heart attack, but since she was going to have a lot of explaining to do when she reached her destination she'd judged it wiser to retain her conventional travelling outfit, the dark-green bodice having a boned collar of white lace, the waist pulled in by whalebone stays, the spreading skirt of green and white silk stretched tightly over its hoops. Now streaks of sweat marked the dress and her straw bonnet was drooping limply.

'Is there very much further to go?' she asked the guide as he began to move away.

'Soon we reach Parakesh, Miss Craven,' he replied politely.

'My dear,' Mrs Wilson had confided, 'the garrison at Parakesh is small, certainly, but we have our social life just as they do in Cawnpore and Delhi. There are card-parties and a very lively sewing-circle and, of course, the regimental dinners and dances. We do try very hard to keep up all the civilized customs.'

'Civilized' meant never displaying one's ankles in public, though in the evening shoulders and arms could be bared. It meant pulling in one's waist to the admired eighteen inches, using a fan to devastating effect in a crowded ballroom, tinkling prettily on the pianoforte and riding side-saddle in the park. Being civilized, Melody reflected, was actually very tedious.

★ ★ ★

She recalled the first ball she had attended three years before. She and Mary were the same age and Aunt Laura had sensibly decided that the two of them should come out into society together and wear very similar dresses, though Mary's was embroidered with seed pearls and frilled with Brussels lace while Melody, being the orphaned cousin, would wear white silk with a rose tucked into her sash.

'It really isn't fair,' Mary said as they sat together in the carriage that was bearing them to the Assembly Rooms. 'You ought to have as expensive an outfit as I have. It isn't your fault that Grandfather left everything to Papa and cut off your father because he made an improvident marriage! Those notions are desperately out of date anyway — we're living in eighteen fifty-four, not in the dark ages!'

It was nice of Mary to mind, Melody

thought, but not tactful of her to remind her of her subordinate status.

Aloud she said placidly, 'Aunt Laura and Uncle Frederick have been very kind to me. Why, when my parents died they took me in at once though I'd no real claim on their generosity.'

'They couldn't leave you to die of the cholera too!' Mary protested. 'Why, Mama had grown so fond of you by the time you recovered that there was never any question about your continuing to live with us. We are more like sisters than cousins! When we marry we must coax our husbands into living very near to each other and then life can go on as it always has.'

Like sisters but not real sisters, Melody thought, as the carriage slowed and stopped and a footman put down the steps and assisted the two girls to alight. They shared lessons and a bedroom and went riding together in the park, but Mary had the first choice of mounts and the velvet habit and it was Mary who went to most of the parties while Melody stayed behind to keep her aunt company.

Aunt Laura had been in feeble health since the birth of her only child and spent much of the day reclining on the sofa, though when word of her niece's dangerous illness had reached her she had forgotten about being delicate and rushed off to the funerals of her brother and sister-in-law before bringing the six-year-old Melody home to be nursed. Mary had been kept away for fear of infection but had accepted her new companion happily when Melody had recovered sufficiently to sit up and take an interest in her new home. After that Aunt Laura had retired to the sofa again, nobly bearing migraines and liver upsets and all the complaints that made it necessary for her to sleep in a separate bedroom from her husband.

Melody thought privately that if she was married to Uncle Frederick she'd develop ill health too. Her late father's elder brother had never been unkind or ungenerous. He was simply always right, in his own opinion at least, and his opinion was that while it had been no part of his duty to assist his younger brother, disinherited for marrying a music teacher of small account, he had a bounden duty to take on his orphaned niece and bring her up in the way all females should be reared — cherished and flattered but never listened to seriously or expected to have much intelligence.

★　★　★

'Miss Craven?'

Another of the guides had ridden up on his mule, inclining his turbaned head politely.

It was the politeness that had impressed her more than anything since her arrival. It was a politeness that seemed bred in the bone of these dark-faced people, having in it no hint of subservience. But underneath she sensed a fierce and ancient pride that made her want to cringe when she heard Mrs Wilson issuing her orders in a loud voice.

'What is it, Ram?'

The swaying palanquin had stopped and she leaned slightly to speak to him.

'A runner brings word there are rumours of bandits in this area,' he said. 'I am sure they are only rumours but as we are responsible for your safety then I suggest the longer route to the fort would be more suitable. It will add no more than an hour to the journey but as the land is not so flat it may be necessary to walk part of the way. I apologize for the discomfort.'

'Bandits?' Melody felt a thrill of excited apprehension. 'I read they were all on the north-west frontier.'

'Bandits do not always stay where they are expected to be,' Ram said, a faint smile curving his mouth. 'I wish to enquire of you whether it might be wise to devise some other reason for our detour since Memsahib Wilson is not as — calm as yourself.'

'Tell her there are rumours of wild buffalo in this area,' Melody said promptly.

'Wild buffalo? An excellent idea! I am grateful to you.'

'Ram!' Melody gestured him back as he began to turn his mule. 'Ram, where did you learn to speak such beautiful English?'

'At the mission school in Lucknow, Miss Craven. I was educated there since my father hoped that I might enter the Civil Service or the military but I prefer an active life where it is not expected of me to tax or kill my fellowmen. When my father died I applied for a post as official guide and have never regretted my choice. I must tell Memsahib Wilson there may be buffalo around. Wild buffalo!'

He smiled at her again and rode off. Melody let the curtain drop and leaned back. So far the long voyage, followed by the train journey until the track had petered out and they had been met by guides with the mule train, had been tiring but fairly uneventful.

Odd that she should have thought of using wild buffalo as an excuse. As she whiled away the time by going over incidents in her past that had marked stages in her growing-up one event leapt as strongly into her mind as if it had occurred the previous day.

She and Mary had been fifteen years old, taking a decorous ride together in the park. Since it was a mild day and the ponies were docile they had dispensed with the services of a groom and trotted down the bridle path without an escort. Since Mary's father was spending the day at his club and her mother was nursing the threat of a sick headache they were safe in the knowledge that no adult relative was on hand to disapprove.

'Let's dismount and explore a bit on foot,' Melody suggested as they reached the wilder reaches of the park, where bushes and trees grew thickly and the paths became narrow and twisted in a beguiling manner towards unseen glades.

'Do you think we ought?' Mary, always the more prudent, looked at her cousin anxiously.

'Why not? Perhaps we shall find some blackberries,' Melody said, putting an end to the discussion by dismounting and catching the reins of her pony.

'We ought to tether them,' Mary said, following suit.

A few moments later they were deep in the woodland, pulling aside trailing creepers, side-stepping half-buried roots as they made their way slowly to the heart of the wood where the trees, their leaves brownish red and gold in the autumn sunshine, formed a ring of dancing branches round what promised to be a small glade.

'I'll wager this is an enchanted place!' Melody said. 'We shall fall asleep here and not wake up for a hundred years!'

'How odd if we really did!' Mary paused briefly as they pushed aside long ferns that grew thickly everywhere. 'I wonder what the world would be like?'

'Oh, women will rule and men will stay at home to embroider and crochet,' Melody joked.

'Well, I hope a handsome prince wakes me with a kiss — and I don't want one who knits and sews!' Mary said with a giggle, forcing her way through a tangle of autumn-crisped creeper. Suddenly she stopped dead as she reached the inner circle.

Melody, a step behind her, flung up her hand to her mouth as she saw what Mary was staring at in horror.

A bull, eyes gleaming redly above a ringed nose, stood in the space, its sides heaving and flecked with sweat, a snorting sound issuing from its nostrils as it realized their presence.

'It must've escaped from somewhere,' Mary whispered in a thread of a voice.

'It's a bit like the Minotaur in that classical

story we read last week,' Melody breathed.

'Never mind stories!' Mary hissed, irritable with fear. 'It's getting ready to charge.'

'Pawing the ground,' Melody nodded. There was a raw power in the heavy black body and horned head which fascinated her as much as it frightened her.

'If we start walking backwards,' Mary was whispering frantically, 'we can hide among the trees or in the bushes.'

'Right,' Melody murmured uncertainly, casting a hasty glance over her shoulder to the bushes behind them which looked uncompromisingly thick and thorny.

Keeping her eye on the animal she took a couple of cautious steps backwards, tripped on a root and went down, a couple of low branches cracking beneath even her light weight.

A bellow shook the glade and as she struggled dizzily to her feet she saw her cousin dart forward, waving her arms and yelling loudly.

Distracted, the bull turned its heavy head, shifting its ground, perhaps confused by the flash of sunlight that arrowed down on to the silver handle of Mary's whip. Whatever the cause it was checked in its headlong rush and then Mary was gripping Melody's arm and pulling her along the overgrown, twisting path to where their ponies were tethered.

'There's a bull got loose in the market!' a loud voice shouted as two thickset men burst through towards them. 'Best get back in the park, young ladies! He's in an ugly mood!'

'Through there!' Melody pointed gaspingly to a gap in the tangle of leaves and branches.

The ponies were straining at their tethers, clearly sensing danger. Melody untied her mount with shaking fingers and followed her cousin who was stumbling ahead with her own pony.

They reached mown grass and decorous hedges of autumn blooms with benches set near them. Mary leaned weakly against her pony's side, her face white.

'I shall be perfectly all right in a moment,' she said gaspingly.

'You saved my life,' Melody said, equally shakily. 'I'm sure it was going to charge.'

'I probably did,' Mary said, regaining her composure and straightening her hat.

'They are taking it back to the market through one of the other gates,' Melody said.

'As long as they don't bring it through the main park and frighten all the nursemaids and the old ladies,' Mary said with a nervous giggle.

'There aren't many people here today.' Melody said, collecting her scattered wits. 'I suppose the poor beast sensed the fate waiting for him and broke free.'

'And you owe me a favour,' Mary reminded her. 'I saved your life.'

'I'll save your life next time,' Melody offered. Now that the danger was past she could feel relief coursing through her.

'Swear that if ever I ask you to save my life you'll do it,' Mary said.

'We're not supposed to swear,' Melody said doubtfully. 'Oh, very well then! If ever you ask me to save your life I'll do so at once. I swear!'

'And we'd best not mention at home what happened,' Mary warned, brushing bits of twig from her velvet habit.

'It would only agitate your mama,' Melody agreed solemnly, as they began to lead the ponies towards the stables.

Her aunt would have a fit of the vapours at the mere thought of their riding without a groom to chaperon them, she reflected. If she ever learned of today's episode they would be confined within the garden for an uncountable number of years!

★　★　★

'I haven't the slightest intention of walking anywhere!' Mrs Wilson's shrill voice shattered the past.

'Memsahib, the path ahead becomes somewhat precipitous,' Ram was coaxing.

'I'm going to walk, Mrs Wilson,' Melody interrupted, stepping down as the palanquin was halted. 'A little air will refresh us, don't you think?'

'What will refresh me,' Mrs Wilson said with a bad grace as she clambered from her own palanquin, 'will be the sight of Parakesh! Buffalo indeed! Most herds avoid human travellers anyway. I shall definitely complain when we reach our destination. And Sergeant Wilson will have something to say! Well, if we must walk then we must. I suppose. Where is my parasol?'

She unfurled a frilled pink one which hardly suited her broad red face and stamped ahead up an incline that grew rapidly steeper.

And, there being no adequate retort to that, Melody meekly followed, not daring to catch Ram's dark eyes.

The sun blazed down, penetrating the silk of her parasol, though its dark-green colour gave her a little shade. Behind her the laden mules were being coaxed over the spurs of gleaming stone that rose at every twist in the path ahead. The palanquins were being hoisted aloft and carried up. Overhead, black against the sky, a large bird was circling.

At least the heat and the increasing

steepness of the path as they left the grasslands below prevented Mrs Wilson from talking beyond the occasional indignant matter.

It was with relief that Melody felt the first shades of evening discourage the fierce glare of the sun and the sky throw out its final rainbow of colour before the stars appeared.

They had reached a large stony plateau with a patch of yellowed grass that had somehow managed to survive in the shade of a tree.

'We shall make camp here and start again at dawn if that contents you, ladies?' Ram announced, bowing before them as if they were at a court ball.

'It appears we have little choice,' Mrs Wilson said ungraciously. 'I trust there will be tea and a fire? The nights here become very cold.'

'It would be better not . . . ' Ram began.

'Why not?' Settled rather clumsily on a blanket produced by one of the muleteers Mrs Wilson tilted back her head and looked at him sharply. 'Are the buffalo likely to climb up here and demand some supper? We have a clear view of the plains below and so far, apart from the domestic buffalo, I've not glimpsed a single hoof!'

'You had much better tell her,' Melody said.

'Tell me what, pray?' Mrs Wilson fixed her with such an accusing eye that she felt any wild animal would be more likely to turn and run than to attack.

'There are rumours of bandits crossing the plains,' Melody said. 'Ram thought it wiser to take a different route but he didn't wish to alarm you.'

'It seems he was less tactful when dealing with yourself,' Mrs Wilson said sharply. 'Bandits indeed! There are always rumours of bandits. India thrives on rumour, the more far-fetched the better! Of course we shall have our tea and a fire! I refuse to be deprived of warmth and sustenance because of a foolish rumour!'

'Yes, memsahib, I will see to it at once,' Ram said promptly, bowing himself away.

'One must be firm with these people,' Mrs Wilson said, not troubling to lower her voice. 'If not they do tend to take advantage. At least the sun has almost gone. The breeze is really quite refreshing though it will turn much colder in a very short while. The view is really rather striking from here.'

This last was voiced somewhat grudgingly as if she was reluctant to bestow appreciation anywhere. Melody murmured an agreement and moved to the head of the path from where she could look out over the plain

16

below, in parts dyed scarlet by the last flares of the dying sun. From this vantage point she could glimpse the wavering outlines of far walls and towers, shimmering in the last of the heat haze.

As Ram approached she asked impulsively, 'Is that a mirage?'

'No, Miss Craven,' Ram told her. 'That is Cawnpore. It is a very fine and lovely city where many Europeans dwell. They have a theatre there and also two hospitals. I fear Parakesh is much smaller, though most agreeable in its own fashion.'

'You must know my fiancé — Captain Hallett?'

'Not personally, Miss Craven, though I believe I have heard of him. Excuse me. I must see to the pegging of the tents.'

He bowed with something less than his usual unhurried grace and moved away into the gathering dark.

★ ★ ★

If he had ever seen Roger Hallett, Melody thought, he would not have so easily forgotten him. Even after three years she didn't need to close her eyes to see him clearly in her mind, his graceful bearing and handsome face blotting out the actual scene

17

she might be watching.

'You both look very pretty, very pretty indeed,' Aunt Laura had approved, surveying her niece and her daughter when they presented themselves for inspection. Her glance towards her own child was certainly a trifle warmer than her look towards Melody but that was merely to be expected.

'I am so very fond of you, my love,' she had once confided to Melody. 'There are times when I can almost imagine that you are twins, though my Mary has the more fragile features.'

Melody, saying nothing, had merely smiled and kissed her aunt upon the cheek.

'They're a fine pair of girls,' Uncle Frederick said in a tone that dared anyone to try to argue.

Since living in London was ruinously expensive to start with he had ordained that they would not keep a carriage but hire one when the occasion arose.

'If I cared to spend my capital,' Melody had once heard him explaining to a slightly bemused Aunt Laura, 'on horses and a carriage which would be used only on the rarest of outings then Mary's dowry would be correspondingly lower. Poor Melody, of course, has nothing but I hope to settle a small allowance on her should she ever marry.'

'That's a kind thought, my dear,' his wife said placidly.

Uncle Frederick was kind, Melody reminded herself, though there were times when she wished his generosity was rather more muted and his opinions less forcibly expressed.

At the Assembly Rooms, where a string of young ladies were making their first official entry into society, all was bustle and glitter. Anxious mothers, trying not to look anxious, were already seated where the chaperons clustered; proud fathers escorted their daughters to the seats reserved for them or stood together, punch-glasses in hand, trying not to eye the young ladies too openly.

Most of the girls wore white with flowers and jewels to provide touches of colour. Some of the girls looked rather mature for eighteen and Melody suspected that this wasn't the first year they had sat among the younger hopefuls, trying not to mind that they were not yet engaged.

'There are a great many officers here,' Mary whispered, squeezing Melody's hand.

'You sound like Lydia Bennet,' Melody said, amused.

Mary, who had skipped Jane Austen's novels, regarding them as dull, brightened.

'There is Timothy Drake,' she whispered. 'Now he would look splendid in uniform!'

'He'd also look rather ridiculous in his father's office,' Melody retorted, sinking into the obligatory curtsy as the pleasant-faced young man came up to them.

'Miss Mary, Miss Melody, I was hoping — '

'That I would accept your invitation to dance,' Mary said daringly.

'If Miss Melody will excuse us?'

Looking pleased and slightly flustered he was borne off by a triumphant Mary.

Melody began to skirt the walls of the ballroom. She had no great expectation of attracting many partners since, though she was pretty, there were many who had commented to her aunt that 'dear Melody' always looked extremely healthy — healthy meaning, she guessed, that she lacked the fashionable 'lady in decline air'! She knew also that her position as Frederick Craven's orphaned and practically dowerless niece was also known. It was only too likely she would end her days as her aunt's loyal and devoted companion. She had never considered the prospect too deeply before but now, hearing the music strike up, she felt a little pang of regret.

She was very fond of Aunt Laura and grateful for the kindness she had been shown but inside her something yearned for an independent life of her own.

'Here is a partner for you, Roger!' An imposing matron was bearing down upon her with a tall officer in tow. Melody recognized her as an acquaintance of Aunt Laura's but she promptly forgot all about her as she raised her blue eyes to the fair-haired young man in scarlet and heard him say:

'I would welcome an introduction, ma'am.'

'Miss Melody, may I present a friend of mine?' the matron said promptly. 'Captain Roger Hallett of the East India Regiment. Miss Melody Craven.'

'I'm honoured to make your acquaintance, Miss Craven.' He bowed, his grey eyes frankly admiring. 'May I solicit the pleasure of a dance, unless you are already fully engaged?'

'My card is empty, sir,' Melody said with the devastating honesty that often shocked her aunt.

'The gentlemen must be blind,' he murmured, taking the velvet-backed card with its small tasselled pencil.

Watching him write his name against three of the dances she protested.

'Captain, two dances are customary!'

'The third is the supper dance which cannot count,' he returned. 'In any case I am on furlough after three years' service and so have lost touch with conventional customs. Shall we dance?'

He led her on to the floor. Melody, whose previous partner had been Mary when they had attended the weekly dancing-class held by Miss Lavinia Thomas, found that dancing with a man roused quite different emotions in her. He held her lightly, smiling down at her with something at the back of his grey eyes that made her feel unaccountably fluttery.

'I believe it is for the gentleman to lead?' he said.

'What? Oh, I'm sorry!' She recollected herself with a blush. 'The truth is that I nearly always take the role of the gentleman at dancing classes since I am a couple of inches taller than my cousin, Mary.'

'This evening,' he said, smiling at her, 'you may relax and be yourself. So you and your cousin attend the same classes?'

'I live with my aunt and uncle,' Melody told him. 'My parents died when I was a small girl and Aunt Laura and Uncle Frederick have been my guardians ever since.'

'I am an only son,' he informed her. 'I have often wished for a sister or brother — that cannot be the end of the measure!'

'I fear it is,' Melody said, wanting to smile at the disappointment in his face.

'But I shall soon claim you again,' he comforted himself.

'Who was your partner?' Mary whispered

when, having escorted her back to her seat, he bowed and moved away.

'Captain Roger Hallett of the East India Regiment,' Melody returned. 'He is home on furlough.'

'Oh, I believe that Papa knows the Halletts,' Mary said. 'Mr Hallett, the father, has investments in Papa's banking concerns. It looks as if you've netted quite a catch. Has he engaged to stand up with you again?'

'Twice,' Melody whispered back.

'Oh my!' Mary rolled her eyes and was promptly all blushing shyness when a partner came to claim his dance.

'Miss Melody, have you this dance free?'

'With pleasure, Mr Drake.'

Allowing him to lead her into the set she noted with amusement the somewhat wistful glance he cast towards Mary. Timothy had adored Mary since they had attended children's parties together, but she recalled now hearing a vague rumour that his father's affairs were not flourishing.

It would be some years before the son was in a position to support a wife handsomely. As for Mary — she was certainly fond of him but how deeply her feelings went was impossible to say.

That evening passed in a rosy blur. Melody found herself partnered in half the dances, which was gratifying for a girl whose engagement-card had been empty, but she rather suspected that some of the young gentlemen asked her merely in order to oblige their mothers! It made no difference to her enjoyment. She was content to sit and watch for part of the time but she felt the colour rise in her face when Captain Hallett came to claim the supper dance.

It was a shorter dance than the others since many were already making their way to the tables in the other rooms, but the measure was spirited and she ended feeling somewhat out of breath.

'I have reserved a place in a quiet corner,' Roger Hallett told her. 'Let me see you seated and then I shall turn waiter with amazing speed!'

He was as good as his word, not only guiding her to a table in an alcove where one could sit comfortably without being jostled, but bringing Aunt Laura over with the gallant remark.

'Two lovely ladies seated together are much better than one, don't you agree, Miss Melody?'

'Captain Hallett was kind enough to rescue me from quite a crush at the centre table,' Aunt Laura said, sinking into the chair and fanning herself. 'Your uncle has vanished into

24

the card-room and Mary has been squired goodness knows where!'

'I'll bring refreshments at once,' Roger Hallett said, and departed, suiting action to words.

'Such a personable young man and so young to be a captain,' Aunt Laura murmured as she adjusted the lace on her bodice. 'Dear Frederick knows his father very well, I believe.'

'I think they have business dealings together,' Melody told her.

'Oh, thank heavens, I never have to deal with that kind of thing!' her aunt said feelingly. 'The son is certainly handsome.'

'And also kind,' Melody agreed. 'He has danced twice with both the Simpson twins.'

She didn't mean to be unkind in her remark. The Simpson twins were so distressingly plain that it was taken for granted, even by themselves, that they would never marry, but Captain Hallett had stood up with both of them with every appearance of enjoying himself.

'Here we are!' Returning, he deposited refreshments on the small table. 'I think you will find the wine nicely chilled. Mrs Craven, I have been wondering . . . '

He hesitated.

'Yes, Captain Mallett?' Aunt Laura said encouragingly.

'Hallett, Aunt dear,' Melody whispered, wondering with a twinge of amusement how often her aunt had been at the punchbowl.

'Hallett!' Aunt Laura said brightly. 'Hallett. Of course!'

'I don't wish to be forward,' he said, 'especially on such short acquaintance, but my furlough is limited so I skip over the usual formalities. May I call upon you and your niece tomorrow? Also your charming daughter, of course, with whom I've not had the pleasure of dancing yet since she is constantly in demand.'

'I'm sure we shall be delighted to receive you,' Aunt Laura said. Melody sipped her wine with downcast eyes, a blush mantling her cheeks.

★ ★ ★

'Tea?' a voice said.

Still in the Assembly Rooms Melody raised her head and saw Ram holding out a steaming cup decorated with mint leaves.

'Forgive me but I was many miles away,' she said in confusion, accepting the cup and sipping the hot, sweet liquid.

'In England, Miss Craven?'

'Yes, England,' Melody said and heard in the word a foretaste of homesickness.

26

'May I offer a word of advice?' Ram said. 'When one comes to India it is better not to look back, wiser not to compare one with the other. That way can crack the heart.'

'You mistake me,' Melody said with a smile. 'I am very glad to be here! I was only recalling the first time I met my fiancé. It was at a ball — a very special ball!'

'There are balls here too,' Ram said. 'The Europeans who travel always make a little Europe in the places where they settle. At Parakesh there are many social occasions for the ladies to arrange and attend. You will soon recapture the delights of your special hall.'

'I hope so,' Melody said softly. 'Oh, I do hope so!'

2

Roger Hallett had called the following afternoon, presumably having chosen the later time in order that the ladies might be fully rested, after the excitement of the previous night.

He looked as spruce as if he had spent the morning at his toilet and his bow to Aunt Laura was, Melody considered, neither so low as to be obsequious nor so brief as to be casual.

'Mrs Craven, your pardon, ma'am.'

Having greeted the two younger girls, he accepted the chair next to Aunt Laura and gave her a faintly deprecating smile.

'You did not dance last night, Mrs Craven. I had recklessly engaged myself for every measure else I would have rescued you from among the chaperons.'

'My dancing days are over, Captain Hallett,' Aunt Laura said with a tinge of real regret. 'My husband never really cared for dancing and my health is not what it was.'

Since her aunt had been gently ailing for the past twelve years Melody permitted herself to wonder how she could possibly remember what it was like to be perfectly healthy.

'Rearing two young ladies must be a great responsibility,' the captain said sympathetically. 'My own mother has often said that she is glad she had only the one child and that a boy.'

'My husband would have liked a son to follow him into the business but he would not be without his daughter — or his niece,' Mrs Craven answered. 'Your own parents must miss your company now that you are so long stationed in India?'

'Indeed they do and I look forward eagerly to home furlough,' he said, 'but it was the one career I had set my heart upon. It is an honour to serve my country, ma'am.'

'In India.' Aunt Laura considered for a moment. 'I have sometimes thought that I would like to travel but the voyage must be so exhausting and, of course, the climate is very hot, is it not?'

'Exceedingly hot, but in the summer season the ladies go up into the cool of the hills and of course the nights are frequently very cold. But the journeying can be tiring. You are right there. My own mother, who misses me greatly, would never venture to visit me.'

'Then your reunions must be all the more

pleasant,' Aunt Laura said.

She looked quite animated, the dying fall gone from her voice and a touch of colour in her face.

The conversation took a more general turn, Mary joining in with her usual vivacity, while Melody sat quietly, contributing only the occasional remark. Inside she felt alive and aware, conscious of Roger Hallett's nearness, of the sheen of autumn sunlight on his fair hair, the one or two swift glances he directed towards her, the cadences of his pleasant voice.

By the time he rose to take his leave Aunt Laura had invited him to tea on the following day and given him leave to escort her daughter and her niece when they next rode in the park.

'Such a charming young man!' she said sighingly when he had gone. 'I used to know the family slightly — his mother's side — many years ago. Sarah Lingford she was before her marriage. Very pretty girl and the son takes after her — the father I haven't met but then I go out so seldom.'

'He seemed very taken with you, Mama,' Mary teased.

'Nonsense! my days as a belle are long gone,' Aunt Laura said, looking pleased. 'He came to see you girls and I'm sure he is welcome to come as often as he likes.'

He would, Melody had few doubts, avail himself of the opportunity. They left Aunt Laura to her nap and went out together. Mary nudged Melody slyly.

'I think he came to see you,' she said. 'His glance just couldn't avoid straying in your direction.'

Melody laughed and changed the subject, unwilling to admit that her own feelings were already warmer than they ought to be after only two meetings.

★ ★ ★

'Miss Craven! Miss Craven!'

She turned, the cup of mint tea still in her hand, as Mrs Wilson sallied forth from the shade of a tree, fanning herself energetically.

'They have erected a tent,' she announced, waving her arm towards it. 'Rather a poky affair but one cannot expect luxury when one is travelling. How long must we expect to rough it here?'

She asked the question impatiently of Ram who took the cup and bowed gravely before replying.

'Tomorrow we reach Parakesh, memsahib. I wish you happiness there. Good night.' He went away to join the other guides round the

31

small fire they had kindled.

'Let me offer you a word of advice, Miss Craven.' Mrs Wilson lowered her voice.

'Yes, ma'am?'

'It does not do,' the older woman said, 'to engage these people with overmuch familiarity. They are apt to take advantage of a friendly manner and become lazy in the performance of their duties. It behoves us to maintain a certain social distance from them, for how else is one to impose discipline?'

'Ram is an educated man,' Melody said, irritated. 'He has beautiful manners and has never tried to presume in the slightest degree!'

'Ah! you are scarcely arrived in India!' Mrs Wilson said with a little smile that made Melody feel more irritated with her. 'You will learn our ways very soon, I'm sure. No sign of those bandits yet!'

'I hope there will be none,' Melody confessed.

'Oh, I believe I can assure you that not a single bandit will show his face,' her companion said. 'The entire story is merely an excuse for the bearers to enjoy a night's rest. You may depend upon it that had there been any danger Sergeant Wilson would have done something about it. As it is we must make the best of things and get some rest ourselves. I have been wondering whether it would be politic to loosen my . . . underpinnings.'

She had dropped her voice further and looked as coy as a portly lady could look.

'Your what?' Melody asked.

'Stays, dear.' Mrs Wilson's voice was now a whisper. 'I generally prefer to remain fully clad but one cannot get a sound sleep when one is in hoops. One doesn't wish these people to see us lower our standards or . . . allow unchecked ideas to enter their minds.'

Melody, thinking privately that Mrs Wilson was hardly likely to be the object of an unchecked idea, said:

'I shall probably take out my hoops. We can close the tent-flap I suppose?'

'Oh, yes indeed! One would not,' said Mrs Wilson with a majestic lifting of her eyebrows, 'dream of doing anything else.'

Melody, watching her return to the tent, sighed inwardly. Mrs Wilson was a kind woman of impeccable respectability but only Mrs Wilson could contemplate lacing herself, with or without underpinnings, into a stuffy tent while all about them an Indian night breathed out its perfumes.

★ ★ ★

At Parakesh Roger would be looking at the same sky. Once during that long-ago furlough they had walked, with Mary lagging behind, along the embankment and he had paused to point across the river.

'How lovely the sky looks as the sun sinks into the river,' he said. 'One forgets how gentle the skies are over England when one has been away for so long.'

'Surely India has beautiful vistas too, Captain Hallett?' Melody queried.

'Spectacular! Vivid and wild and passionate with rainbows exploding in the sky! I wish you could see one!'

He half-turned to include Mary in his remark but his eyes lingered on Melody.

'Such a pretty name,' he had mused one day when taking morning coffee with them. 'Is it a family tradition?'

'My husband's younger brother married a lady who was ... talented in the playing of the pianoforte and their daughter, my dear niece, was named Melody,' Aunt Laura told him.

'My late mother gave music lessons,' Melody said.

'Ah, I see! And you yourself play?'

'Better than I ever did,' Mary put in.

At this very moment, Melody reflected now, he might be standing in some courtyard, watching the brilliant clusters of stars appear to herald the moon. It was exciting to realize that in all probability they were both looking at the same moment at the same sky.

On the dark plains below a first flare of white moonlight glinted along the rim of the grasslands and a breeze sprang up, ruffling her fair ringlets and billowing out her crinoline.

'Miss Craven, it is best you step away from the edge,' Ram warned, coming swift and silent to her side. 'The wind could blow you down.'

'For the wild buffalo to trample?' Melody said lightly.

'Let us hope that wild buffalo and bandits are far distant,' Ram said. In the darkness his white teeth gleamed and she sensed his amusement.

'Ram!' Impulsively she held out her hand. 'I fear you may have heard something of that Mrs Wilson said when she stood here with me before. She doesn't mean to be unkind.'

'Memsahib Wilson is a good woman and a brave one,' he answered quietly. 'Her words are lost on the wind and we judge only by deeds. Good night, Miss Craven.'

And that, thought Melody, frowning slightly as she made her way to the tent, has put me firmly in my place!

'Ah, here you are!' Mrs Wilson, her bonnet exchanged for a mobcap of formidable proportions and several clashing colours, was draped over a series of large cushions with a blanket pulled up to her chin. 'I shall bid you goodnight, my dear.'

'Good night, ma'am.'

Melody took off her bonnet and undid her hooped petticoat, stepping out of it carefully and sinking on to the pile of cushions obviously meant for her. From outside came the soft muttering of the guides as they squatted on their heels round the camp-fire and above that the high whistling of the wind as it gained strength from the darkness.

She hoped that any bandits in the area would stay away. In coming out to India in the first place she was taking a far more serious risk than she dared confess!

Risks, she mused vaguely as her mind drifted towards sleep. Risks that made a nonsense of the placid, regular, rather dull life she had led.

★ ★ ★

She remembered a day three years before, when she had been walking through the Botanical Gardens with Roger Hallett while Mary lingered tactfully behind to examine some enormous water-lilies with intense interest.

'When do you go back to your regiment?' Melody asked.

'Too soon.' He frowned slightly, a shadow clouding his face.

'How soon is too soon?' she persisted.

'In five weeks. This is the first long furlough I've had. There won't be another for five or six years.'

'You'll spend all that time in India?' It was impossible to keep the dismay out of her voice.

'If we had not met . . . ' He hesitated for a moment, then went on soberly, 'I would have gone back to India with very few regrets but as it is . . . '

'Your family will be sad to see you leave,' she said in a small voice.

'You understand that it's my chosen profession,' he said gravely. 'I always wanted a life based upon honour and courage. Happily my father understood my ambitions and encouraged me to enter the military. And India is a very beautiful country. No description of mine could do it justice.'

'Next month,' Melody said again. Saying it was like picking at a sore and causing it to bleed afresh.

'We've had a marvellous summer, haven't

we?' He smiled at her. 'Rides in the park, afternoon teas, the ball. I shall carry very happy memories away with me. Melody — may I call you so?'

'Yes, of course.'

'A pretty name,' he murmured.

'My parents liked it.'

'You remember them?'

'Not clearly now,' she said regretfully. 'We lived in a little house with a long, narrow garden at the back that ran down to the river. Mama gave music lessons and Papa worked in an office. He was Uncle Frederick's younger brother.'

'Yet your uncle lives in a large establishment?'

'Oh, my father's marriage was greatly disapproved,' Melody said frankly. 'He was cut off with nothing when Grandfather died, but he worked hard and our home, what I remember of it, was always cosy and full of laughter. They had seven years together and then there was the cholera epidemic and they died of it.'

'You were a small child then?'

'Six years old,' Melody said. 'Uncle Frederick came at once, for I had the infection too, and took me back to his home where I was nursed but that time is muddled in my mind. After that I grew up with my cousin Mary who is the same age as myself.'

'A pleasant girl,' he said.

'Very pleasant,' she agreed. 'She is more like a sister to me. We shared the same governess until two years ago when she left us to marry, which is not, I believe, the usual happy fate of governesses! Since then we have had more or less the disposal of our own time.'

'You must feel the greatest affection for your aunt and uncle.'

'She and my uncle have always been very kind,' Melody said, unconsciously evading the question.

Had she thought about it consciously she might have said that gratitude pushed aside affection. However, at that moment, Mary, feeling evidently that she had been tactful long enough, ran up and linked her arm through Melody's, demanding that they find somewhere they could sit and enjoy a glass of lemonade.

Later that evening as they gave their hair the customary hundred strokes she was unusually silent, so silent that Melody, tying back her own fair hair, looked at her questioningly.

'Are you tired? We did walk rather far today.'

'No, I'm not tired.' Mary gave a rather

forced little smile as she slipped her lace-trimmed nightdress over her own blond curls.

'You're not feeling ill?' Though her cousin never ailed she had her mother's delicate, fine-drawn look.

'No, really! It's only that — I was selfishly wishing that I had a beau like Captain Hallett. So handsome and well-disposed towards the world.'

'Roger Hallett isn't my beau,' Melody exclaimed, a trifle more forcibly than was necessary.

'I certainly gained that impression,' Mary began.

'He's a friend, that's all,' Melody insisted. 'Soon he returns to his regiment in India and won't be in England again for five or six years.'

'But it's plain he admires you greatly.'

'You have your share of admirers too. Timothy — '

'I've known Timothy Drake for ever!' Mary said impatiently. 'He's more like a cousin than anything else. He will go into his father's business and dwindle into middle age before he's thirty. Can you imagine Timothy joining the Army and travelling thousands of miles in search of glory?'

'If every young man in England did that

the country would be practically empty,' Melody teased getting into bed.

'It will seem rather empty when Captain Hallett leaves,' Mary said wistfully. 'He has such beautiful manners, don't you think?'

'He is certainly a gentleman,' Melody agreed.

'And the manner in which he so kindly included me in the conversation on our way back from the Botanical Gardens — that was most genial of him.'

'Of course he included you! We both did,' Melody protested. Privately she resolved to be more considerate in the future and not allow her cousin to feel in the least degree slighted.

Certainly it wasn't like Mary to display the slightest hint of jealousy. It ought, Melody reflected, carefully keeping to her side of the wide double bed, to be the other way round.

★ ★ ★

Although her aunt and uncle had been kindness itself to her throughout her childhood it had been a kindness that advertised itself at every turn.

'The dress is of silk, Melody dear, exactly the same as Mary's though with a narrower frill on the skirt and smaller hoops. We wish

41

you to appear to the very best advantage so that nobody ever compares you unfavourably with your cousin.'

'Melody, my dear, I have increased Mary's dress allowance slightly for now that she has passed fourteen she has developed quite a fancy for those gewgaws in which women seen to take such pleasure. I intend to increase your allowance by precisely the same amount. I have always said that I would treat my daughter and my niece in the same way, being absolutely fair. I hope you will agree that I have largely succeeded?'

'Thank you, Aunt Laura. My new dress is very becoming. You have always been the soul of generosity, Uncle Frederick. I can never be sufficiently grateful to you.'

Grateful. Grateful. Grateful. The words had echoed in her brain as she composed herself to sleep.

★ ★ ★

A series of loud cracks roused her from her dreaming slumber. For an instant she fancied she was still in bed in her uncle's house and wondered why the mattress felt so lumpy. Then the loud braying of the mules and the shouting of the drovers brought her back to present reality.

'What in the world is happening?' Mrs Wilson was struggling up on her own cushions, nightcap perched over one eye as her hands scrabbled to straighten it and reach for her stays, hidden modestly under a towel, at the same time.

'I believe the bandits are here,' Melody whispered.

She raised the tent-flap cautiously and peered. The camp-fire had burned very low and the moon had withdrawn behind a cloud but she could see dark figures milling about and hear voices.

'I believe the bandits are here,' she whispered again.

'I knew we should have kept to the level route,' Mrs Wilson muttered, feeling around for her bonnet. 'Buffalo indeed! Sergeant Wilson would never have submitted to the change of route. It has always been an iron-clad rule of his that a direction once fixed upon ought not to be altered unless one has a clear reason with authorization from higher authority to change anything.'

'Mrs Wilson, we cannot remain here,' Melody whispered urgently. 'If we stay here we will be discovered very quickly. If I leave the tent I can reach the cluster of rocks below. Give me a count of ten and then make for the higher ground. If we separate one of us is more likely to be overlooked.'

'Miss Craven — !'

Melody shook her head, bunched up her skirts and wriggled beneath the tent-flap, seeing with some relief, as she strained her eyes through the darkness, that the figures had their backs to the tent and seemed to be arguing hotly about something.

She lowered her head and began to crawl over the grass towards the path that dipped down between the rocks to the grasslands below. Crawling was difficult since her foot kept catching in the trailing material of her unhooped skirt and, since she had not even thought of putting on her bonnet, the wind which made a low moaning sound as it gusted up the valleys kept blowing her hair across her mouth and eyes to obscure her vision further.

The black shadows of the overhanging rocks at last fell across her. She had passed the dying embers of the camp-fire without risking more than a brief glance towards the figures still milling about and the re-emerging moon faintly illumined the tips of the stone and the rough track twisting downwards.

She hoped that Mrs Wilson had had the sense to follow her advice and make her way to the higher ground without dislodging any loose pebbles. Mrs Wilson could be sadly irritating but she meant well and to think of her in the hands of bandits was an alarming prospect.

'Not,' Melody breathed, 'to mention myself!'

The shadow of the tallest rock hovered above her. She twisted into a sitting position, pressing her back against a spur of stone and raised her head again cautiously.

A tall figure, legs spread wide, blotted out the sky.

'And where might you be going, ma'am?' a voice enquired.

'You're English?' She could distinguish a sword hilt which protruded from the flared skirts of a military coat.

'Captain Adam Channing, at your service, ma'am.'

His voice was crisp and businesslike as if they'd just met on market day in London, she thought, a bubble of hysterical relief rising and bursting in her throat.

She heard herself say in a small voice.

'Oh, my goodness!'

It was, she thought, one of the silliest phrases she had ever uttered!

3

The newcomer reached down and, grasping her hand, pulled her to her feet.

'We were informed that a small party was on its way to Parakesh,' he said. 'I undertook to ride out and provide a few reinforcements — there have been rumours of bandits in the area. Unlikely, but rumour is sometimes the forerunner of truth so I judged it wiser to provide some extra protection should it be necessary. I apologize for startling you, Miss . . . ?'

'Craven. Miss Melody Craven.'

She was rapidly regaining her self possession.

'Captain Hallett's fiancée. I thought — '

'Do you know Roger?' she asked.

'Slightly but not well. I heard he was expecting his bride-to-be shortly. Ram Singh tells me there are two ladies in the party.'

'Mrs Wilson is returning to join her husband — oh, good heavens! I told her to hide further up the hill. She will be terrified!'

'I think Mrs Wilson can survive the occasional fright,' he said drily. 'Let me escort you back to the tent where you can recover your hoops.'

There was amusement in his voice. Hitching her trailing skirts higher Melody said defensively, 'I didn't have time to dress fully.'

'Oh, a gentleman ought not to notice such things,' he said. 'I apologize if I've caused you any embarrassment. You were clearly in a hurry to be out of the tent.'

'I thought you were the bandits.' Feeling thoroughly silly she took refuge in indignation. 'Why were you shooting at us?'

'Three bursts into the air with two beats between — the usual signal that is exchanged between the army and the official guides. It saves a lot of misunderstanding.'

'Not if the bandits get to hear about it. They could use it themselves and lure you into a trap!'

'The signals are changed from time to time. Ah, here comes Mrs Wilson. I know of her by repute but not yet personally.'

Mrs Wilson, clutching what looked like a blanket around her, was emerging from the higher ground.

'It's Captain Channing, is it not? My husband, Sergeant Wilson, has often spoken of you. Perhaps you know Sergeant Wilson?' she panted, arriving before them in a bulkiness of blanket.

'Indeed I do, ma'am. A fine soldier and a

thorough gentleman,' he replied.

'Well, Charlie'll be pleased to hear that, I'm sure,' Mrs Wilson said. 'They tried at first to tell us there were wild buffalo around but I had my suspicions.'

'We would be well advised to continue our journey immediately,' said the captain. 'My own house is less than an hour from here and you can rest there until daybreak and then continue your journey. Ladies!'

He bowed gravely and walked towards the guides who were still talking and gesticulating with the newcomers.

'Miss Craven, your hoops!' The older woman hissed the reminder as Melody hitched up her skirt and prepared to follow her companion back to the tent.

'I'll make myself respectable again directly,' Melody promised, trying not to laugh.

'It is so vital to keep up appearances and not allow one's standards to drop.' Mrs Wilson was scolding as they rearranged their attire.

'Yes, of course,' Melody said, feeling, when she emerged hooped and bonneted, that she still cut a somewhat discomposed figure.

The moon shone softly when they began the last leg of the climb up the steep hill with its scattering of rocks and loose scree on the narrow winding paths.

Behind them the drovers tugged at the mules, and the palanquins, carried now on the shoulders of the bearers, dipped and swayed from side to side.

The hill fell away below them, the faint moonlight illuminating a tangle of trees and bushes with the outlines of a stone building a good way off.

'Is that Parakesh already?' Melody panted.

'No, of course not!' Mrs Wilson sounded slightly scornful. 'That's part of an old residence of some sort. I believe that Captain Channing uses it sometimes when he's not on duty. This is not the usual route to Parakesh.'

'An old friend of my father's lived there,' Captain Channing said, leading a mule as he joined them, having apparently heard part of their conversation. 'When he died he willed it to me, having no family of his own, so I like to think of it as home. Mrs Wilson, we have only a couple of miles to go now. The descent here is gradual but the climb up must have tired you both out. You will find it more comfortable in a palanquin as soon as we get the mules harnessed.'

'Thank you.' Mrs Wilson inclined her head graciously. 'I would advise you to mount into a palanquin also, Miss Craven. There may be serpents in the undergrowth.'

With a stately inclination of the head she

accepted the help of a drover and stepped up into the curtained equipage. Melody, deciding that serpents in the undergrowth wasn't a particularly pleasing prospect, clambered with rather less ceremony into a second conveyance and the party began the slow, winding descent into the valley, the gradient here being gentler.

Serpents or no serpents, the procession wended its way along twisting paths between trees and bushes, the latter starred with pale moonlit blossom, the former dipping leafy branches that scraped the canopies of the palanquins.

Despite her fatigue Melody found herself leaning forward eagerly and holding back the drapes of the shrouding curtain as they gradually approached the stone building that from a distance had appeared no larger than a doll's house faintly illumined by the moon but which now revealed itself as a fairly large building with steps leading up to a covered veranda.

'This way, ladies!'

Captain Channing came up to them as they were helped down to ground level and escorted up the shallow steps and across the wide veranda through double doors that stood invitingly open.

Through her haze of fatigue Melody gained

the impression of several rooms opening off a central hall with what looked like a fountain in the middle of it and several low couches placed here and there, apparently at random. Then she and Mrs Wilson were being shown into one of the rooms, bare save for thick mattresses supplied with pillows and blankets, laid on the floor.

One of the men brought tea scented with jasmine and then Captain Channing was bidding them:

'Sleep well, ladies!'

It was clear, she thought wearily as she pulled off her hooped petticoat and sank down on one of the mattresses, that he didn't have a wife. Her hoops had somehow got bent and twisted during the course of the night and from beneath the brim of her bonnet her fair curls straggled in limp confusion.

Faint silvery arrows were striking her face. She sat up, wincing, and looked over at the other mattress where Mrs Wilson lay in a mound of blankets that rose and fell with each gentle snore.

She pushed her own coverings aside, rose, hitched up her trailing skirts and pulled off her bonnet which she had forgotten to remove, and moved noiselessly to the door.

The central hall was empty but for the

51

couches and silent save for the gentle plashing of the water in the fountain. Some of the surrounding doors were closed but others had no doors, only arched entrances with long curtains tied back to afford glimpses of the dim chambers beyond.

Aunt Laura, she reflected, would be astonished at the almost complete lack of furniture. Two of the rooms contained mattresses, all unoccupied; another room had a long, low table with cushion-topped stools placed along its sides; another completely unfurnished room led through to a further apartment with a view of a courtyard beyond in the centre of which a fire burned.

It was that hour between the dying of night and the birth of dawn when sun and moon bid each other hail and farewell and the last stars glimmer in the lightening sky. As she stood uncertainly on the threshold a slim, sari-clad girl appeared suddenly through a side archway, joining her fingertips in the graceful salaam.

'Please to follow,' she said in a lilting voice. 'Your bath is prepared.'

She didn't look much like an army valet, Melody thought, following the newcomer through two small ante-rooms into a tiled chamber with a bath sunk into the floor. The bath itself was half-filled with water from which a pale, scented steam arose. There were rugs placed on the floor and a stool on which a pile of fleecy towels reposed. One of her own bags had been placed on another stool.

'Please to call if you need anything,' the girl said, placing her hands together and bowing before she glided away.

The water was deliciously hot and silky, the soap perfumed with rose, the loofah giant size. By the time she had dried herself, twisted up her hair beneath a blue scarf which she took from her bag and donned a simple blue dress that matched it, she began to recover her energies. Under the dress her chemise and drawers of cool cotton and her petticoat with its small hoops felt airy and refreshing and her image in a long mirror mounted in the wall reassured her that she looked if not elegant at least respectable again.

She sat down on another stool to draw on clean white stockings and low-heeled shoes with a beaded design, which had been fitted into her bag, and stood up again to look for some further sign of life.

A door in the opposite wall gave on to a long passage with one side open to the elements. As she paced along it, Melody looked over a low wall into a garden sunk slightly below the level of the building and seeming to have grown up by accident rather than careful husbandry.

Trees hung with vividly coloured creepers rose up, with grassy paths twisting around them; great bushes of magnolia and oleander sprayed blossoms of cream and palest rose against glossy green leaves and honeysuckle twined round the stone columns that supported the roof of the corridor.

She stretched out her hand to snap off a piece of the honey-suckle and was abruptly frozen into motionlessness as a furry shape darted over the low parapet and sat, chattering and grinning, a few feet away.

'Kara! Here!'

Captain Channing, looking as immaculate as if he had just spent several hours preparing for a royal inspection, had come through an archway at the far end of the corridor. The monkey turned and scurried along the parapet towards him, swarming up his tunic to hang upon his shoulder; the chattering became little clucking sounds.

'It's tame!' Melody exclaimed, laughing with relief.

'I had her from a baby.' He stroked the silky fur, bowing slightly as he came nearer. 'I mean her babyhood and not my own. Her mother was taken by a mugger snake — more of a small alligator, actually. I found her and reared her. She's good-tempered and never bites.'

'But you're the favourite,' Melody said.

'She considers us to be a couple,' he said solemnly.

'But you're not — not married? I mean to a human being,' she said clumsily.

'So far I've not found anyone of whom Kara approves,' he said with a smile. 'I pay heed to her opinion because she's a great judge of character.'

Melody smiled in return, relieved that an awkward moment was past.

'Are you rested?' he was enquiring.

'Yes, thank you. Is this really your house?'

'When I was a child, before I went to school in England, I spent some of my time here, playing with the animals, listening to the stories that Jaipur Sahib, the owner, told me. When he died he willed the place to me and now when I'm off duty I come here as often as I can. Come and have some breakfast — chapatis and watermelon and the inevitable tea.'

'Thank you. Mrs Wilson . . . ?'

'The good lady is now taking a bath and changing her clothes and will breakfast in her room. Come!'

He turned and, with Kara on one broad shoulder, went ahead through the further archway, and across another small courtyard into a room she vaguely recognized from before. Now a low table was laid with various dishes and a servant was pouring tea into wide cups with a chained pattern of gold running round their rims. The man paused in his task to bow.

'Nana Gobal came with the house,' Captain Channing said; then, indicating a low stool set close to the table, 'Do sit down.'

Being a captain he had, of course, the habit of command but Melody felt a little stir of rebellion as she seated herself.

'You must excuse my abrupt manner,' he said, motioning to the servant to withdraw. 'It is seldom that I have the chance of entertaining ladies here. Make yourself comfortable. I see you have a more manageable hoop on this morning.'

His dark eyes were suddenly teasing, glinting between their long lashes.

Feeling another little stir of something she couldn't quite recognize, Melody said, 'Please don't remind me of how foolish I was! Now that I think about it the bandits could have sniffed me out in two seconds flat. I am only too thankful it was a false alarm.'

'Oh, there are really bandits about.' He passed her a plate on which slices of watermelon glowed red and black. 'Fortunately they generally confine their activities to more densely populated routes. However, it's never wise to take chances. India is a beautiful lady but a savage one under her embroidered robes and her flashing jewels.'

'How soon will we reach Parakesh?' she asked.

'Within a couple of hours. Has Captain Hallett spoken of it much in his letters?'

'Not really,' she hesitated. 'He was stationed at Lucknow when he came to England on furlough.'

'In the three years since then he has been at Cawnpore and in Delhi. Parakesh is modest by comparison, but a pretty place and in a strategic position since it commands a fine view of the plains and the river.'

'What are they hunting for?' Melody asked. 'Bandits or buffalo?'

'Anything that moves.' He broke off a piece of chapati with long tanned fingers and handed it to her.

'Meaning?' She looked at him sharply.

'Meaning that where there are a thousand dialects and four main religions it is as well to have the eyes of a lynx. Also an eye for what others don't notice. More tea?'

'No, thank you.' Melody set down her cup. 'The way you talk isn't meant to be alarming, is it?'

'No, but then you're not a girl who is easily alarmed, are you? Captain Hallett mentioned that you had a great deal of curiosity about life in India but I suspect he painted you a rosy picture.'

'Not really.' Melody rose, smoothing down her skirt, trying to remember exactly what Roger had said. 'He told me about the markets and the spices and silks and the beggars — we have seen some of those on our way here. He said that India was full of Europeans and that once one found one's niche it was easy to settle down for long periods.'

'Captain Hallett seems to have drawn a fair picture,' said Channing, also rising.

'You don't call him by his given name?' she said.

'We are not close friends. Would you like to take a stroll?'

'Yes. Yes, I would.'

She sensed he no longer wished to talk of Roger and wondered briefly why. Now wasn't the time to probe further. She took his arm as he offered it and walked with him to a further archway. Kara, the monkey, had leapt back to his shoulder and clung there possessively.

As they ascended a flight of stone steps at the end of the open corridor Melody couldn't help casting a somewhat nervous glance at the animal but Kara had evidently formed a good opinion of her since she made no chattering noises of disapproval.

They had reached a flat roof with a waist-high parapet all round it. The sun was rising, streaking the sky with gold, sweeping through the arching branches of the trees below, stirring the creepers into living tendrils of bright leaves. From this height she could look down and see the bright plumage of birds perched in the topmost branches where nests swayed in the breeze.

'Over there on a clear day you can see the turrets of Cawnpore,' Captain Channing told her. 'Turn and look northward and you can glimpse the high hills that rise higher until their tips are powdered with snow and above them are higher peaks still and narrow passes through which the merchants travel and beyond that is the land where few Europeans have travelled.'

'It's . . . ' Melody hesitated and then said simply, 'I have no words.'

'Even the greatest poets and artists fail to do complete justice to it,' he said.

What was it that Roger had said when she and Mary sat in the parlour with Aunt Laura sipping her tea?

'Of course India isn't like England but it's an interesting country for all that. One can pick up some lovely materials and jewellery quite cheaply in the markets provided one is prepared to haggle. Haggling is a passion with the natives. I must say the tales of hardship and want with which they regale a potential buyer would fill a good-sized volume and empty his wallet if he hadn't learned a few of the tricks of the trade himself!'

At her side Captain Channing said abruptly, 'Smell the wind!'

'I beg your pardon?' Wrenched back into the present Melody stared at him.

'The wind!' he repeated impatiently. 'Smell it. Close your eyes. Tell me what you can smell!'

She did so, feeling rather than seeing the newly awakened sunbeams making fluttering birds'-wings on her closed eyelids.

'Jasmine,' she said at last, uncertainly. 'I can smell jasmine. Why?'

'Nowhere in these grounds is there a garden planted solely with jasmine,' he told her as she opened her eyes, still breathing in the faint, elusive perfume.

'My imagination . . . ?' she hazarded.

'Then others have an equally fertile imagination,' he said, smiling slightly. 'Somewhere in these woods is a garden planted solely with jasmine, which was made in memory of a loving wife by a prince who

60

lived centuries ago. Nobody since has ever been able to find the exact site of the garden but the scent of the blossoms lingers still on the wind.'

'That's a lovely legend,' Melody said softly. 'Thank you for telling me about it.'

'Something to remember on homesick afternoons,' he said, stepping back slightly as she leaned further over the wall to watch a humming-bird fly past and alight on a sun-gilded branch below.

'Not so far over!' Captain Channing said quickly. 'The wall needs patching in places.'

'Fortunately I've a good head for heights,' Melody told him, nevertheless stepping back obediently.

'Have you so?' There was an indefinable change in his voice. Suddenly he put his hand under her chin, forcing up her head, his eyes steady on her face.

'Captain Channing . . . '

'Call me Adam. It's the name my mother chose for me,' he said. 'What I'm wondering is what I ought to call you. That is if we were on terms of close friendship. Miss Craven sounds so very formal and British, don't you think?'

'Please! Captain Ch — Adam!' She twisted out of his grasp, her heart hammering.

'Not Mary,' he broke in. 'Not Mary Craven,

that's certain. Captain Hallett chanced to mention at some function that we attended together with other members of the regiment that his fiancée was terrified of heights, that he would never be able to persuade her up into one of the native temples on a sightseeing trip. And you announced yourself unwittingly as Melody Craven and didn't notice your slip. Captain Hallett's intended bride is named Mary Craven.'

'Roger is — '

'Very forgetful? He is not a close friend of mine but he is generally reputed to be an able officer with a strong sense of duty.'

'I can explain . . . ' she stammered.

'Please do,' he said with chilling politeness. 'If you're not Mary Craven then who are you and what are you doing here?'

4

Time swung backwards as Melody stared at him. The tall dark-haired officer with the lambent dark eyes merged into the slighter figure of the officer with fair hair and grey eyes who had taken her hand as they strolled in the park one afternoon.

★ ★ ★

Mary had, tactfully as usual, gone ahead to feed the ducks and Roger and Melody had lingered near a bed of dahlias whose vivid yellows and crimsons had obviously awakened memories in Roger's mind, for he said, 'In Parakesh the flowers startle the eye with their colour and size. Their perfume drowns the senses. Here blossom seems to me to be too often overlaid with fog and mist.'

'London is certainly foggy,' Melody admitted. Although she was wearing gloves her fingers tingled beneath the pressure of his hand.

'But it also contains those for whom we long when we are absent,' he said. 'Very soon I go back to India and this time I shall have more to yearn over.'

He had inclined his head slightly. In another moment he would kiss her.

'Do come and see this baby duckling!' Mary called. 'It's riding on its mother's back!'

She had turned and was waving to them.

'Let us,' murmured Roger, 'by all means look at the duckling.'

He tucked her hand through his arm and they walked on to join Mary who was happily tossing broken crusts to the quacking birds.

'You will be leaving us very soon,' she remarked, turning to smile at them.

'Another week and I embark for the East.'

'We shall be dull during the winter, won't we, Melody?'

'Very dull,' Melody agreed.

'And during this past week I must wait upon my parents with rather more filial respect,' he commented ruefully.

'We have never met them,' Melody said.

'They are quiet and retiring,' Roger admitted. 'The prospect of visiting a strange house or of entertaining unfamiliar people would put them out of countenance for a month! They are very shy indeed.'

'And they have never visited India?' Mary queried.

'Never. My paternal grandfather was the nabob of the family and made a modest fortune. My father was brought up in

England and has never travelled. I inherited my grandfather's taste for foreign climes but not as a trader. I always craved the active life as a military man. Miss Mary, if you lean over any further you are liable to join the ducklings!'

He offered her his other arm and the three of them walked on.

Despite Roger's other engagements and the attention he intended to devote to his parents there was a local ball to attend before his embarkation.

'Only a small affair this time,' Aunt Laura regretted. 'Soon there will be all the preparations for Christmas. Time flies so swiftly when one is busy!'

Since Aunt Laura's contribution to the Christmas festivities consisted in admiring the cake and wrapping up a few gifts, Melody could only conclude that her aunt's notion of time flying was somewhat different from her own.

'I shall wear my pale blue I think,' Mary announced when they were dressing for the occasion in their shared bedroom.

The pale gauze skirts and puffed sleeves of the dress made her look fragile and ethereal. The colour against Melody's brighter blond-ness merely made her look slightly washed out. She put on her white dress and twined a little knot of scarlet ribbon in her hair.

'We shall not be among the wallflowers,' Mary whispered as they alighted at the steps of the Assembly Rooms.

'Nor among those who are already promised in marriage,' Melody thought with unwanted cynicism.

Several girls with whom they had mingled at the coming-out ball now sported engagement rings.

Melody hid a smile as Timothy Drake, having spotted them from the end of the room, moved to claim Mary for a dance.

'Here you are!' Roger, trim in his uniform, came to greet them, as usual directing his initial welcome to Aunt Laura, clad in silvery grey with a flower in her hair.

'Ma'am, I positively insist that you stand up for the first dance with me,' he was saying. 'It is a crime against society to immure you among the chaperons. Come!'

'His powers of persuasion are very great,' Mary whispered to her cousin. 'I have never seen Mama stand up before, but then Papa never cared for dancing.'

Roger bowed slightly as the first dance began and Timothy Drake whirled Mary into the set.

'It was an excellent evening,' Aunt Laura said in a contented fashion as the horses of the hired carriage trotted them home. 'Do you realize that I actually stood up three times? It is amazing how well one remembers the steps once the music has begun!'

Melody smilingly agreed with her, her own head still full of the words that Roger had murmured in her ear as they circled in a slow waltz.

'Tomorrow I mean to call upon your uncle. You understand?'

'Yes,' Melody breathed.

'And approve?' His grey eyes smiled down into her blue ones.

'Very much indeed,' she said and felt his arm tighten slightly around her waist as they moved into the closing bars of the dance.

Now, as the carriage neared home, she heard her aunt say, 'You are very quiet, Mary dear. Did the evening fatigue you?'

'No more than usual,' Mary said in a slightly pettish tone. 'One always sees the same faces at these events.'

Timothy Drake it seemed, notwithstanding his eagerness to partner Mary, had not fulfilled expectations.

★ ★ ★

'I'm waiting for an answer,' Captain Channing said.

She was thrust back into present time with dizzying rapidity.

'I scarcely think — ' she began.

'On the contrary,' he said sharply. 'In my experience ladies think very hard before they utter a word! Are you Melody or Mary Craven?'

'My identity really isn't any of your — ' she began, flushing scarlet with rage and something very close to shame.

A voice from below interrupted her.

'Miss Craven, are you up there? I really feel we ought to resume our journey before the full heat of the day strikes! It is ruinous to the complexion!'

'Just coming, Mrs Wilson!' Stifling her feelings with an effort, Melody said in a rapid undertone to her companion. 'Please, say nothing now. I can explain all and so will Captain Hallett when we reach Parakesh! It is not as you imagine.'

'At this present moment,' he returned in a low voice, 'I am trying not to imagine anything, Miss Craven. You had best take my arm on the way down. The steps are uneven in places.'

At the foot of the steps Mrs Wilson, fearsomely bonneted and hooped, spoke in an agitated manner.

'Do come along, my dear! Just because

there were no bandits or wild buffalo around last night there is no guarantee they will not be about this evening and Sergeant Wilson won't draw a tranquil breath until I am safely within the compound!'

In the dry air Melody's hair had resumed its usual glossy appearance, the bright gold of it glinting in the morning sunlight as she removed her scarf and took the straw bonnet that the older woman was holding out to her, aware as she tied the ribbons that the captain's dark eyes were fixed on her, unwilling admiration mingled with intense curiosity in his gaze.

He would have to wait for explanations until she had been reunited with Roger, she decided, and swept past him with her head held high.

The palanquins had been reassembled and the mules obviously fed and watered as they came out into the central courtyard.

'And you are certain there is no danger of any kind?' Mrs Wilson was demanding as she was helped into her gently swaying seat.

'None at all, ma'am,' Captain Channing assured her. 'I will be accompanying the party anyway.'

Within her own palanquin there was at least a measure of privacy. As it swayed between the trees with their ropes of knotted vines Melody held on to the curving sides, trying to ignore the agitated instructions from just ahead.

'Do not lean out, my dear. Serpents often coil themselves in the lower branches and drop down when least expected.'

Faced with Mrs Wilson any self-respecting serpent would surely slither up the tree again, Melody thought, leaning back obediently against the cushions.

* * *

Her thoughts inevitably drifted back to that day three years before when she returned from an errand she had undertaken for her aunt to find Mary looking out anxiously from the parlour window.

'It took for ever to match the silks,' Melody said, going into the small parlour, 'but I hope Aunt Laura is satisfied with — '

'Never mind the silks!' Mary said impatiently. 'Leave them for Janet to take to Mama. She has no interest in her sewing today.'

'What is it? What's happened?' Melody demanded.

'Captain Hallett called upon Papa while you were out,' Mary said.

'Officially?' Melody's fingers paused in the

untying of her bonnet.

'Exceedingly officially,' her cousin told her. 'It was fortunate that Papa was not in his office this morning and so had leisure to receive him.'

'And?'

'He has made an offer,' Mary said.

'An offer?'

'And Papa has approved! Of course we cannot marry yet, but in three years I am to go out to India and be married there. Isn't it exciting?'

'Roger Hallett has made an offer for you?' Melody's voice sounded very small and weak.

'It was the most unexpected thing in the world!' Mary chattered on. 'I thought — honestly believed that you were the subject of his regard. He told Papa that he fixed upon me from the first but feared to press his suit too rapidly. As it is we cannot be married for three years. Papa was adamant that I must be twenty-one before I travel to India.'

'You are going to be married in India?' Melody felt as numb as if her body had been frozen.

'Roger doesn't get another furlough for about five years,' Mary said.

'You accepted Roger Hallett?' Melody said, feeling and sounding stupid.

'That's just what I've been saying!' Mary

exclaimed with an impatient little laugh. 'Is it so astonishing that he should propose? Oh, I admit I thought him very smitten with you but it seems he never regarded you as more than a friend — you did not take his little gallantries seriously, did you?' She spoke on an anxious note, being a good-humoured girl who was genuinely fond of her cousin.

'No, of course not,' Melody said with a slight effort. 'I did think — his attentions seemed at one time to be somewhat . . . but of course he has such a pleasant, easy way with him that one might easily . . . but . . . Mary, what about Tim? I thought that he — '

'Tim has not offered,' Mary said. 'There are rumours that his father's business doesn't prosper and Tim would never speak unless he was certain of his financial prospects. I think now that that's rather dull of him.'

'I always thought you were fond of Tim,' Melody said.

'One can be fond of someone without wanting to marry them,' Mary said, a faint hint of waspishness in her voice. 'Actually I decided some time ago that Tim is more like a brother to me.'

'And Captain Hallett is the one then?' Melody said. She felt as if someone had just poured a bucket of cold water over her.

'Oh, I am sure of it,' Mary said. 'You will come out to India with me when the time comes, won't you? Mama's health would never stand a long sea voyage and Papa would never dream of leaving her! Perhaps you will find a husband out there too! That would be jolly, would it not?'

'Yes,' Melody said through stiff lips. 'Yes, awfully jolly.'

Mary seemed to have caught some echo of despair for she frowned suddenly, biting her lip before she said:

'You are pleased for me, aren't you? I know we thought that Captain Hallett had a definite regard for you and so he has, but as a friend, it seems. You didn't lose your heart to him, did you?'

'My heart,' Melody said, 'is still firmly in my own keeping. I am only sorry that we two will be parted.'

'Not for another three years,' Mary said. 'If you haven't received an offer for yourself by then you will accompany me to India, won't you?'

'Yes. Yes, of course I will,' Melody promised.

At that moment all she wanted to do was bawl her eyes out, but that would spoil her cousin's pleasure and reveal her own disappointment too clearly. To be fair to

Roger, she thought, he had never said in plain words that he loved her, but he had given no indication of being interested in Mary at all.

She drew a deep breath and smiled brightly as her aunt called from across the hall.

'Is that Melody back? Did you obtain my sewing silks, dear? What do you think of Mary's news? I have been all of a dither since Captain Hallett made his offer. We shall have a small but select engagement party — only a few close friends and neighbours — in a week's time, for after that Captain Hallett must return to India — I suppose I must say 'Roger' now since he is to be my son-in-law! How pleasant that sounds! Son-in-law! Though it will be a great wrench to lose Mary, but I flatter myself that you will supply her place and be a companion for your silly aunt, for you must know how highly you are valued, my dear!'

She had lost her languid air and was seated bolt upright, a sheaf of patterns in her lap.

'There will be no time to have new dresses made,' Mary said.

'But some extra trimmings to your best dresses? Melody is so very neat and quick with her needle! No more than six couples can stand up for the dancing in the salon but with the double doors open and the refreshments laid out in the dining room I flatter myself that we won't be too crowded! Miss Trimbell will play the pianoforte — I will have a note sent to her directly! Will you see to that for me, Melody dear?'

'Yes, of course,' Melody said.

'There is a pattern here for a fichu of silver lace,' her aunt was running on. 'Very simple and pretty over your dress, Mary, and fastened with pink silk rosebuds since fresh ones are so scarce now and would wilt in the heat — yes, I think that would look charming.'

'You will be the belle of the ball,' Melody said.

She could not prevent a certain dryness from creeping into her voice.

'And Melody too must look her best,' Mary said.

'A deep flounce of coffee-coloured lace round the skirt of your white dress? And a knot of matching ribbons in your hair?' Aunt Laura suggested. 'You will not wish to outshine your cousin, I think?'

'Of course not,' Melody said.

'She outshines me anyway,' Mary said loyally. 'Her talk is always more sparkling!'

'But sometimes gentlemen prefer the shyer, more modest girls,' Aunt Laura said. 'I know your father, and your uncle, Melody, always did.'

Melody forced a smile, saying nothing. In

her head impossible theories revolved. Had Roger muddled up the two names? It seemed highly unlikely. Had Mary really known all the time that she was the intended bride and said nothing? Surely not! Mary had always been loving and loyal.

What has happened, she thought dismally, *is that I completely misunderstood everything from the start!*

She was grateful that her aunt required a great deal of help before the engagement party and that Roger himself never put in an appearance. Mary was going about in a kind of happy day-dream and could be relied upon for nothing.

On the evening itself she checked the refreshments and the flowers, helped her aunt into the figured satin she had chosen to wear, and admired her cousin's outfit with genuine pleasure. It was not, after all, Mary's fault that Roger had preferred her. Looking back, Melody couldn't think of a single occasion when her cousin had tried to thrust herself forward.

The guests were arriving — Tim, she noticed, not being among them. However the Simpson girls in all their plainness were there and, last of all, Roger himself arrived, apologizing for his tardiness.

'The truth is that my mother is laid low

with one of her migraines and father never leaves her side on these occasions,' he said ruefully. 'They hope to invite all of you to an afternoon tea later on, though by then I will be on the high seas!'

'Bound for India,' Mary breathed.

'For my sins!' Roger said lightly. 'Mary, you are looking particularly fine tonight. I shall have to fight off the competition.'

The entire evening, Melody thought dismally, was going to be a private nightmare. She made a hurried excuse to prevent Roger having to greet her personally and went off into the hall where a few of the selected guests were removing their wraps.

The pianist recruited for the occasion was trying to arrange her music and Melody was glad of the excuse to stop and help her.

There would be only a brief hour for dancing before supper. Already Roger was leading Mary into the set.

'May I have the pleasure, Miss Melody?' One of the principals from her uncle's firm was bowing before her.

'Indeed you may, Mr Watson,' she said graciously.

Mr Watson was balding and rather stout, but standing up with him meant she would not be forced to sit meekly by while Mary danced past.

Roger looked particularly handsome this evening, she decided, having risked a covert glance at him; his blond good looks outshone the other men and drew frank looks of envy at Mary from the Simpson girls. Melody herself kept her eyes fixed firmly on her feet and hummed the tune the pianist was playing under her breath lest she be forced into conversation with Mr Watson who, embarrassingly, was counting the steps in a clearly audible voice.

Supper when it came was scarcely a relief. Seated a couple of places from Mary and Roger, she couldn't help noticing how attentive he was to her cousin's wants and how eagerly Mary responded to him.

'Ladies and gentlemen, your attention, please.' Her uncle had risen and was waiting for the hum of conversation to subside. 'We are gathered here to celebrate the engagement of my beloved daughter, Mary, to Captain Roger Hallett who, as we all know, returns soon to his regiment in India. Roger has asked me to grant my permission for his marriage in three years' time to my daughter and both my wife and I, while regretting that the ceremony will take place in a far-distant land, have agreed to a match which gives us great pleasure. I ask you to raise your glasses to the betrothed couple.'

The champagne stung the tip of Melody's tongue. She saw Roger slipping a ring on to her cousin's finger, caught the glint of a half-hoop of diamonds, heard the genteel applause ripple about the room, and felt utterly wretched.

There was nothing for it but to sip the champagne and tell herself firmly that broken hearts only happened in the novels that Mary and Aunt Laura so enjoyed reading. When the pianist started up again she slipped quietly from the room and stood in the hall, fighting back dizziness and the awful feeling of being left out of all earthly delights.

'There you are!'

To her dismay Roger had come out into the hall and was approaching her. He looked flushed though whether from the wine or not she was far too flustered to tell.

'We must talk,' he went on.

'I came out here for a breath of fresh air,' Melody said, flustered by his abrupt appearance and equally determined not to show her discomfiture. 'Aunt Laura said something about a fan.'

'You have one in your hand,' Roger said.

'Indeed I do. Aunt Laura — '

'Your aunt is fanning herself with a very pretty Japanese fan,' he broke in.

'Oh,' Melody said.

'We need to talk,' Roger said, lowering his voice but speaking abruptly. 'Surely there is some place?'

'It would be quite improper — ' she began but he had taken her hand and was leading her towards the side door which led into a small extension of the conservatory.

'For a few moments only and then I won't detain you. Please, Melody?'

Hearing her name spoken like a caress brought tears to her eyes. She blinked them away hastily and said in a voice that she strove to make light and unconcerned, 'A few moments then, though I cannot imagine what you have to say to me.'

He made no answer but stood aside to allow her to pass into the long corridor-like room with its panels of glass and the potted palms providing a kind of screen that served also as a refuge. There were wicker sofas and chairs here and plants containing bulbs awaiting the spring, and a neat table with hollows in it for cups and saucers.

'I owe you an explanation,' Roger said.

'You owe me nothing,' she said, regaining her composure as she used her finger to whisk an escaping tear from her cheek. 'I've not yet had the pleasure of congratulating you. May I do so now?'

'This isn't what I intended.' His voice was

low and strained. 'Believe me but there has been the most unfortunate misunderstanding — '

'Made only by myself and concerning myself alone,' she said.

'Won't you sit down for a moment? I promise — '

'That you'll not keep me long?' Forcing back another gush of tears she said quietly. 'You gave me some reason to imagine that you were interested in me but I am not experienced in such matters for which I beg your pardon. It was very foolish of me to — '

'To imagine that I was beginning to care for you?' he finished for her.

'You engaged me in conversation, walked with me while Mary sauntered behind or walked on ahead, told me about India — '

'And behaved like a man in love?' he said. 'Melody, I was — still am a man in love, but not with Mary. Lord knows she's a sweet girl but beside you she is practically invisible!'

'Not a very gallant way to refer to your future wife!' Melody said, recovering her tartness.

'I never thought of her as that!' he interrupted. 'Melody, your cousin is very sweet and I am sure she will make an excellent wife but you were the one I craved! I didn't speak about my feelings for you because we were so seldom alone save for a few moments while Mary was tying her shoelace or something before hurrying to catch us up. I ought to have spoken to you first. I simply took it for granted that we understood each other without words.'

'But you offered for Mary,' Melody said flatly, putting out a hand to ward him off as he moved towards her.

'When I called upon your uncle,' he said, 'it was with the intention of seeking his leave to ask you to be my wife but the moment I began he assumed I was asking his permission to wed Mary and immediately gave his blessing before your name could escape my lips. Indeed had I tried to remedy my mistake I doubt if he would've heeded me.'

'My uncle is a most forceful character,' Melody admitted. 'It has made him very successful in business.'

'Before I could say more he was shaking me by the hand and telling me that he would be pleased to entrust his only child to me. He summoned her immediately and went a fair way to take over any proposal I might've intended to make! And Mary was so clearly delighted and pleased that I simply hadn't the heart to say anything then. I hoped to speak to her alone later and explain the dreadful misunderstanding but there was never a moment and — '

'You ought not to be saying these things to me,' Melody said, low and vehement. 'Indeed you ought not!'

'I have wanted to say them and much more besides,' he said. 'There was never a moment when I could even begin to untwist the tangle. These past days have been like living in a bad dream.'

'It's done now,' Melody said.

'If I had spoken to you,' Roger asked, 'would you have given me a favourable answer? Only say that you would and I'll march in there and break off the engagement at once. It will cost me my commission but better that than — '

'Mary loves you,' Melody broke in. 'She will make you a most loving wife. Speaking out now would only blight your career and break her heart — '

'Then your answer would've been a refusal?'

He stood so close that her heart turned over. She had only to speak and her cousin would be an occasion for mock sympathy from gossiping women, herself denigrated as a designing hussy and Roger possibly cashiered for conduct unbecoming to an officer and a gentleman.

'It would have been a refusal,' she said as lightly as she could. 'I admit I was attracted to you and flattered by your interest in me, but I see now it was done to pique my cousin's interest, and for my own part I can think of nothing worse than being stuck cut in India for the most of my days. Yes, it would have been a regretful but very decided refusal.'

Before he could respond she turned and walked swiftly back to the rest of the party.

5

'There you are!' Aunt Laura greeted her niece when Melody returned to the rest of the party.

'Here I am!' Melody said brightly.

'And looking a trifle flushed.' Her aunt regarded her with more than usual attention. 'You have worked hard to make this evening a success, my love. One day it may be your turn for I am not so selfish as to wish you a spinster for the rest of your life. One day you too may meet a gentleman who desires you for his wife but I cannot help hoping that when you go to India with Mary you return to us with an undivided heart. To lose both at one time would be very hard upon my nerves. I need one of you settled, if not here, at least very close.'

'Much can happen in three years,' Melody said stolidly.

'But nothing too exciting, if you please!' Aunt Laura said playfully. 'This engagement has made me very happy, naturally. One pities the Simpson girls whose mother must soon despair of getting them off her hands but one hopes that one betrothal is not infectious!'

'If it is, Aunt dear,' Melody said, 'I assure you that I have a natural immunity.'

The dancing had begun again but to her relief nobody asked her to stand up and she was able to eat a few sandwiches and drink a glass of negus in a secluded corner, though afterwards she would not have been able to tell whether the dainty sandwiches contained cucumber or sawdust.

To her relief Mary was too tired when, the guests having departed and the doors been locked, they went upstairs, to do more than admire her diamond ring audibly two or three times.

The next day Melody made sure that her duties kept her out of sight and when, a few days later, Aunt Laura informed her that she required some last-minute gifts for various neighbours who had been kind enough to send their good wishes, Melody thankfully put on a warm tippet and bonnet and sallied forth to make the required purchases.

The weather was crisp and cold with the scent of snow on the wind. Mary, who disliked inclement weather, had remained indoors, which gave Melody the freedom to stride out at her own brisk pace.

'Melody!'

Her pace slowed and stopped as Roger came across the road to greet her, his expression eager and pleased.

'Melody, I hoped we might meet! I have just bidden goodbye to your aunt and to Mary, for the next three years anyway. Both were very tearful, so it is pleasant to see a happy face.'

'I enjoy walking briskly on a chilly day,' she said, wishing she could think of something more brilliant and wishing also that she was not so apt to change colour rapidly when she was surprised or upset.

'Something I shall soon not have the opportunity of enjoying,' he said with regret in his voice as he courteously relieved her of her parcels.

'You sail tomorrow then?' The thought crossed her mind that Aunt Laura might have contrived the errands on which she had been engaged in order that Mary might savour the poignancy of the leave-taking alone, but another moment's reflection assured her that Aunt Laura had never been so subtle.

'You have been shopping.' He glanced at the packages she held.

'Some extra items for Christmas that Aunt Laura needs. So it is time to bid you Godspeed?' She spoke lightly and rapidly, not slowing her pace.

'Melody, I wish — ' he began in a desperate tone, but she put up her hand quickly as if to block whatever else he had in mind to say.

'As I made clear to you, Captain Hallett,' she said stiffly, 'had my uncle not misunderstood, had you approached me — my answer would have been in the negative. I would not hurt or offend my cousin for the world.'

'That is your only reason?'

'I have to hurry!' She almost snatched the parcels back, glad of the wind that had arisen and bent the brim of her bonnet in such a way as partly to shield her face. 'I wish you a safe voyage.'

'And we meet again in three years . . . ' he began.

'When you wed Mary,' she said and turned abruptly down a side street which provided a short cut to her uncle's house and left Roger Hallett standing somewhat forlornly on the corner.

When she reached the house she found Mary weeping softly over her engagement ring while her aunt vented her own upset feelings on the parlour fire, which refused to burn properly, and on Cook, whose scones were not as light as usual.

'Three years seems such a dreadfully long time,' Mary said woefully when Melody was at last free to join her.

'I daresay it will pass quickly enough,'

Melody said. Too quickly, she thought privately, for in three years she would be a bridesmaid when once she had entertained vague hopes of being the bride.

* * *

'Memsahib, we are within sight of Parakesh!'

Ram Singh had ridden up, pointing through a gap in the trees to where a bridge spanned a river shrunk almost to a stream by the dry season. At the other side of the bridge she could see high stone walls and a huge gateway with soldiers mounting guard and looking from this distance like toys.

'The bridge is quite safe, Miss Craven!' Mrs Wilson's voice sounded from the other palanquin. 'You need not fear to ride over it!'

It was not the bridge that occasioned the sudden nervous tremor which shuddered through her. Soon she would see Roger again for the first time for three years. Since his leaving letters from him had arrived at irregular intervals for her cousin. Mary hadn't shared their contents save to remark as she lifted her head from the page, 'Roger sends his affectionate regards to you as usual, Melody. He never forgets to do so.'

Affectionate regards could mean anything or nothing. She had merely smiled, remarking

89

always, 'When you write to him pray return his greetings.'

Was it possible that in the three years since she had seen him he had conditioned himself to the idea of being Mary's husband? If so then her long journey would end in embarrassment at the least. She traced herself mentally, fixing her gaze on the tall figure of Captain Channing who rode ahead, not once turning to bestow a word or a glance on her.

His coat was a brilliant scarlet under the sun that blazed down as they emerged from the trees and began the slow crossing of the bridge.

Melody looked down and saw the shallow water moving sluggishly below. Then the high gates of Parakesh loomed before them and they passed through into a wide square lined on three sides by two-storey buildings flanked by covered verandas.

'Miss Craven?'

A smartly clad young officer who must surely be feeling the rising heat in his high boots and tight tunic had come to the side of her palanquin and was saluting.

'Yes?' Instinctively she tensed slightly.

'My compliments, ma'am. Captain Hallett was called away to Delhi three days since but we expect him back within the next few days. He has arranged for you and your cousin to stay at the hotel — your cousin is with you?'

'No. She . . . changed her mind about coming,' Melody said. 'Happily Mrs Wilson has been my companion during the greater part of the journey. Why was Captain Hallett called away?'

'On military matters, Miss Craven. Let me help you down. Your luggage will be taken to your quarters directly.'

'Thank you . . . ?' She hesitated.

'Lieutenant Barry Greenacre at your service, ma'am.' He saluted again.

As he helped her down, Mrs Wilson bustled up.

'Sergeant Wilson is seeing to my things,' she said. 'It will only take me a few hours to settle in and then perhaps you will take supper with me.'

'Miss Craven has undertaken to have dinner with me at the hotel,' a voice broke in.

Captain Channing had dismounted and was bowing slightly.

'Oh!' Mrs Wilson looked flustered for a moment but, evidently deciding it was wiser not to make a fuss, said, 'Another time then, my dear.'

In the background a uniformed figure, as tall and thin as Mrs Wilson was short and plump, hovered anxiously.

'Wilson, my dear, come and greet Miss

Craven!' Mrs Wilson called in an imperious manner. 'She is come from England to marry Captain Hallett!'

'Honoured to make your acquaintance, Miss Craven.' The sergeant was saluting her. Melody contrived a slight curtsy though her equilibrium was slightly unsteady after the swaying of the palanquin.

'Miss Craven will be dining with us one day soon,' his wife informed him. 'Now, if there's anything you require you have only to ask, my dear. We have married quarters on Prince Albert Street. Come along, Wilson!'

As they moved away, followed by a couple of bearers with the luggage, Melody couldn't help wondering if she always addressed him by his surname even in their most intimate moments.

'Until this evening then, Miss Craven?'

Captain Channing had raised an eyebrow and was regarding her as if she had FAKE written in bold capitals all over her.

'This evening.' She nodded.

'Will eight be convenient for you?'

'Eight will be most convenient,' Melody said. Obviously he meant to question her. She longed to tell him to mind his own business but he was probably anxious about a fellow officer. He deserved some sort of explanation and telling him would prepare her for the moment when she saw Roger again and explained everything to him.

'I look forward to it,' he said and turned to issue instructions to the guides in what was clearly fluent Hindustani.

'This way, Miss Craven, if you please.' Lieutenant Greenacre was offering his arm politely as they started across the square towards a handsome building somewhat taller than the others with Europa Hotel scrawled across the façade.

'I was quite surprised to learn there is a hotel here,' Melody confided.

'Oh, in Parakesh we have almost everything they have in Delhi or Calcutta,' he answered, 'though on a slightly smaller scale. Indeed we have many travellers coming through from Simla and spending a few days here. Mind the steps, ma'am.'

They mounted on to the veranda and passed through double doors into a foyer with a floor of cool grey marble, and decorated with palms. An open door beyond showed part of what was obviously a handsome dining-room and an archway at one side opposite a long counter clearly led into a saloon bar where several officers were gathered.

'Miss Craven?'

A short tubby man in a formal suit with a

red turban on his head stepped forward to shake hands in the European manner and introduce himself as Mr Patel, the owner of the hotel.

'Where everything will be done to delight your comfort and satisfy your convenience, Miss Craven. The other young lady is not yet here?'

'Our plans were altered,' Melody said.

'Not illness, I trust?'

'No, not illness. Merely a change of plan,' Melody assured him.

'Then your room will appear even more spacious and delightful,' Mr Patel said. 'Your luggage is already there and water will be supplied directly.'

'Your servant, Miss Craven.' Lieutenant Greenacre saluted and took himself off.

A turbanned porter ushered her up the stairs and along a corridor into a large room with a balcony that overlooked the street below. Melody crossed to look down at the scene. The street was paved somewhat irregularly and crowded with people making their way up and down, some with baskets of vegetables and fruit or jugs of water on their heads, others leading mules or driving rickety carts while their voices mingled in a cacophony of languages and accents, all apparently shouted at the tops of their voices.

Mingling with them, darting in and out, a variety of small children, ranging in colour from almost white to nearly coal-black, were playing a game of tag.

'Most exceedingly noisy!' the porter said apologetically, moving to draw lattice screens across the window and indicating the rest of the room with a lordly sweep of his arm. 'The bathroom is there, memsahib. Please to excuse me.'

He bowed again and went out, leaving her to look round at wickerwork furniture, a wide, low bed hung with muslin and a large coloured portrait of the Queen in coronation robes with crown, sceptre and velvet mantle. It looked decidedly out of place.

The noises from the street drifted up more faintly now. Melody sat down and took off her bonnet running her fingers through her hair which was matted with sweat. She must, she thought ruefully, look a perfect fright by now! Perhaps it was a good thing that Roger had been called away on duty for a few days. When she met him it would be with perfect composure and prettily curling hair.

A knock sounded at the door, followed by two girls in brightly patterned saris, carrying pails of water, a third with a pile of fleecy towels, and two older women, one with a tray of various cordials, the other with a salver on which reposed several small dishes covered with muslin.

Melody found herself smiling and nodding as they distributed the various things, some on the table in the bedroom, others in the bathroom, which she could see through an archway in one corner of the room.

Then they bowed themselves out and retreated in a flutter of colour. The door closed very softly behind them, leaving her in a brief tranquillity. She wanted nothing more than to lie down on the inviting bed and sink into sleep but she forced herself to her feet, slowly stripping off her clothes and realizing fully how bone-weary she felt. She had spent weeks being tossed about on the high seas or rumbling along in a train with passengers not only inside it but also clinging to the outside or seated on top. Then had come the swaying of a palanquin, varied by walking over stony hills with the bearers going ahead and the mules being tugged up the slopes. It felt strange to stand on solid ground without the landscape moving past her or the ground moving beneath her. Not for the first time she felt an unwilling admiration for the stout and indomitable Mrs Wilson.

The bath was delicious! Filled with tepid water, sunk into the floor and with everything laid neatly on shelves and small tables within arm's reach, it provided an oasis for aching limbs and sweat-soaked hair.

Melody soaked herself for a long time, feeling the heat and dust drain away from her limbs before she reached for soap and sponge and a small bottle of some deliciously scented oil which made her feel like a pampered princess. Eventually, reluctantly, she wound a long narrow towel about her wet hair, stepped out of the bath on to the striped matting and wrapped the rest of herself in a huge fleecy towel.

The dishes on the low table contained mainly sliced fruits, slivers of cured meat, and the flat bread that she had already grown accustomed to. There was lemonade, a sparkling water tinged with mint and a jug of cold tea to quench hunger and thirst. She ate and drank what she could, then lay down on the bed and felt the warmth of the sunshine peering through the lattice on her closed eyelids as she fell into a deep and refreshing slumber.

★ ★ ★

The noises from the street blended into other sounds: vehicles passing the house where she had sat somewhat anxiously in the parlour, trying to darn a stocking, her ears alert for the sound of the front-door bell.

'I have a great need for a few breaths of fresh air!' Mary had declared. 'You had best stay in and not infect the whole of London with your cold!'

It had been the previous year and the date for their departure for India was coming ever nearer. Mary's trousseau had been made and was laid in lavender in two large cabin trunks; she had begun to sort the books and knick-knacks she intended to take with her.

Spring had rained itself in and there were still patches of frost in the corners of the street and a covering of ice now dripping down the figure of Queen Victoria in the park. Aunt Laura, who rather prided herself on catching cold more easily and rapidly than almost anyone else, had not only caught a chill but most obligingly bestowed it upon her niece which was why Melody sat alone in the parlour, a shawl around her shoulders and an almost undrinkable concoction on the table at her elbow.

'You had best take one of the maids with you,' Melody had said.

'They are all occupied,' her cousin replied, 'and since I am almost twenty-one I see no reason why my footsteps should be dogged in broad daylight by a maid who will make every excuse to start rapidly for home before we have gone three streets. Don't fuss so, dear cousin!'

Was she becoming fussy and old-maidish? Melody bit off the cotton she was using, added the stocking to the pile in the basket and put her sewing implements away. A bright fire burned on the hearth and the curtains were partly drawn but the room still felt chilly.

She crossed to the mirror over the mantelshelf and took a long look at herself. Her face was pale apart from blotchy reddish patches across her cheekbones, her eyes looked slightly watery still and her nose bore evidence at its tip of having been frequently attacked by a huge cambric handkerchief.

'In other words, my dear,' Melody addressed her reflection, 'you look such a perfect fright that it is highly unlikely anyone will ever fall in love with you!'

The words, uttered aloud, seemed to carry a presentiment of a future spent keeping company with her aunt, running errands, winding wool, eventually being demoted to the company of the Simpson girls, who attended every social event with hopeful hearts and made-over gowns.

A tap on the door heralded one of the servants.

'Mrs Craven's compliments, miss,' the girl

said, 'but she's going to take a nap. She says the second edition of the newspaper hasn't arrived and Mr Craven is always particular about having it folded and ironed for him before dinner when he gets home. Could you — ?'

'I'll go to the newspaper stand,' Melody broke in. 'A brisk walk will do me good.'

'Thank you, miss.'

At least she had a definite excuse for escaping from the stifling confines of the house. She went quietly up the stairs, not wishing to disturb her aunt who might change her mind about the intended nap, put on her thick boots and cape with its attached hood and came down the stairs again, already feeling a spring in her step.

Outside she walked steadily, skirting the few patches of icy slush that remained, and saw the news-stand looming ahead, its owner refreshing himself with a hot toddy before he began to cry his wares in the usual manner.

Melody paused to buy her newspaper, folded it carefully inside her immense inner pocket and, unwilling to return so soon to the house, continued on her way, skirting the park. As she reached the open doors of the circulating library she regretted that she had neglected to bring her ticket, since she had run out of new reading matter.

When she glanced in at the door she was surprised to see her cousin's pale blond head bent over a pad on one of the tables ranged below the main counter. Mary was writing busily, her shoulders hunched, her hand moving rapidly, her attitude one of the most intense concentration.

Melody's first impulse to enter and greet her died as she stepped away from the door and went down the steps into the street again. Why Mary should choose to write something or other in the library when she had materials and ample space at home was a puzzle. Surely she didn't suspect anyone of surreptitiously reading the letters she dispatched to India! At any rate, since she clearly wanted privacy she should be granted it.

Melody began to retrace her steps, a faint frown on her face. There was no accounting for other people's whims but a slight uneasiness had gripped her. It was almost a relief to hear the newspaperman's lusty tones.

'Read all abaht it! *Evening Standard*! Native rising in Australia against the white settlers. 'Orrible slaughters! Read all abaht it!'

A native uprising might bring some much needed excitement into her life, Melody thought, her customary cheerfulness beginning to surface. However since she was unlikely ever to experience one she had best forget about Mary's presence in the library and get the newspaper back in time for her uncle's return from the office!

6

'I think one or two warm dresses ought to be included,' Aunt Laura said, frowning over the list she held in her hand. 'They say the nights can get very cold out there.'

Rather to Melody's surprise her aunt had taken a keen interest in the trousseau, even to the extent of looking up Parakesh in the big atlas that usually reposed undisturbed in the old study which the girls had previously used as a place where they could continue their schoolwork, though in Mary's case the labour had mainly consisted of sighing deeply whenever she chanced upon an unfamiliar word in the book she was reading or a request that Melody please sharpen her pencils since she was getting fingers like nutmeg graters.

'And cotton or silk for the rest,' Melody said. 'I've read there are some wonderful materials out in India, all beautifully coloured and patterned. Mary might have some made up there.'

'I hear the native ladies wear garments that cling closely to reveal the shape of the body,' Aunt Laura said, looking faintly worried. 'I trust neither of you would be tempted into such immodesty?'

'We shall uphold the standards of the British Empire!' Melody said playfully.

Her aunt smiled but Mary looked downcast as if her thoughts were miles away from the choosing of garments.

The wedding-gown was already laid in folds of lavender-scented muslin, its ivory silk lit by crystals in a pattern of tiny hearts; her wedding-veil was of Brussels lace with a cap covered with the same sparkling fragments. It was so pretty that Melody felt a pang of envy when she beheld it, though as bridesmaid she would wear a dress of pale blue with a darker blue sash.

'There are bound to be some lovely fresh flowers out there that can be made up into a spray that puts the finishing touches to your ensemble,' Melody said a little later.

Her aunt had retired for a nap before dinner and Mary was curled in the window seat, her eyes scanning the garden though now and then she sighed as if she could find nothing there to please her.

'Are you tired?' Melody ventured. 'It's rather soon to begin feeling homesick.'

'I'm perfectly all right,' Mary said and sighed again.

'And in two or three years' time you will be

returning to England when Roger has his next furlough,' Melody persisted.

'Do you have to go on talking about it?' Mary burst out suddenly. 'India, weddings, silk or cotton, furloughs — I am sick of the subject!'

'I'm sorry — ' Melody began but Mary, in a mood quite unlike her usual placidity, had risen and flounced out, banging the door behind her.

What on earth was the matter? Melody frowned as she pondered out the irony that she had for three years endured talk of the coming wedding — a wedding at which she should have been the bride had it not been for her uncle's leaping to the wrong conclusion and sweeping all before him — with as much enthusiasm as she could possibly contrive to muster, while Mary, unaware of the true situation, had let her first excitement and delight trickle away into long sighs and a complete lack of interest in the preparations for the voyage.

The front door closed and she was in time to see her cousin whisk past the window, wearing her spencer and bonnet, with what looked like a couple of library books tucked beneath her arm.

Mary, it now occurred to her, had been spending a great deal of time out of the house lately, whether feeding the ducks and forgetting to ask anyone to accompany her or changing her library books twice a week when previously she had changed them twice a month.

There was no point in following her, a proceeding that Mary might with justice regard as spying, but she waited in a fever of impatience, and was relieved to glimpse her cousin whisk through the side door a bare five minutes before Uncle Frederick returned from the office.

The evening passed as it always did, though Mary left much of her food untouched on her plate and had hardly anything to say. It was fortunate that the master of the house was too busy in giving an account of his own hard-pressed hours of business to notice that only his wife listened with her usual eager attention, while his daughter and niece sat practically mute.

Not until later was she able to slip upstairs to their shared bedroom where she found Mary, who had come upstairs before her, seated on the end of the bed, a damp handkerchief screwed up in her hand and an expression on her face that veered between misery and resolution.

'My dear cousin, what ails you?' Melody demanded bluntly. 'You haven't been yourself for days! Does the thought of the long voyage disturb you so much or the prospect of leaving your home for a country you have never seen?'

'And a husband I don't love,' Mary said.

'You don't love . . . ? But, Mary, you were wild with delight when he proposed to you!' *Or rather started to ask for my hand and was so completely misunderstood by Uncle Frederick that he ended up engaged to you,* her mind supplied.

'I thought I loved him,' Mary said in a distressed tone. 'I honestly believed that I loved him very much and I was so pleased that he asked for me because, to be honest, I rather thought that he preferred you! I had been nerving myself up to receive the news of your engagement with every appearance of pleasure I could muster, but he had asked Papa for my hand and then the ring is such a splendid one and everybody kept saying how fortunate I was to be chosen by such a gallant officer, and when he left I was genuinely miserable! And he writes the most loving messages! But the truth is that I think now it was the uniform which attracted me and the prospect of seeing a strange land!'

'This is last-minute nerves,' Melody comforted. 'You will feel all the former affection return when you next behold him.'

'You don't know the whole,' Mary said woefully. 'Melody, I am in love with Timothy Drake and he is in love with me.'

'Mary, you said once that you looked upon Timothy as a kind of brother,' Melody argued. 'You cannot possibly have fallen in love with a man because of his uniform. Surely it was the person himself who captured your heart!'

'I thought it was,' Mary confessed. 'I even began to feel a little jealous of you since he was paying you such marked attentions. But Roger told me that he had spoken more frequently with you because he guessed that I would never marry anyone of whom you didn't approve. And I went on telling myself that but the truth is that whenever Mama was indisposed and you were required to attend her — and none of the maids is any company at all! — I took to slipping out for short walks by myself and I went more often to the library because one can read a nice romantic novel there where all comes right in the end, and one afternoon Timothy came in and we fell into the kind of quiet conversation one has to have in libraries and then he often met me when I slipped into the park to feed the ducks. And I realized that I didn't want to go to India at all. I want to stay right here and marry Timothy Drake!'

'Oh my Lord!' Melody said. 'What on earth's to be done?'

'I don't know,' Mary said miserably. 'Papa will never agree to my breaking my engagement and marrying Timothy. Oh, he likes Timothy well enough, but Tim's father has suffered such severe reverses in his business recently and Papa would never agree to my taking a poor husband.'

'But if you explained to Uncle that Timothy . . . then surely — ' Melody began.

'Oh, who could possibly sway Papa to anything once he's made up his mind?' Mary said.

'Mary!' Melody hesitated and then plunged on. 'Mary, you're quite sure you don't love Roger?'

'I've been sure for months but it wasn't until I became friendly with Timothy again that I could admit it even to myself,' Mary said.

'The truth is,' Melody said, hoping she was doing the right thing, 'that when Roger came here to see Uncle Frederick he meant to ask for permission to marry me.'

'What?' Mary's pale blue eyes opened wider.

'He meant to ask for me,' Melody repeated patiently, 'but Uncle Frederick leapt to the wrong conclusion and assumed he was here to ask for your hand in marriage. Roger tried to explain but Uncle Frederick simply went on and on, saying how delighted he would be to entrust his only child to a gallant officer in the East India Regiment and Roger couldn't get a word in until it was too late.'

'And Roger was too kind-hearted to point out the mistake,' Mary said slowly. 'Melody, I felt right from the beginning that Roger preferred your company and so I made a point of hanging back or of going ahead so that the two of you could converse, though I must admit there were many times when I felt jealous of the gallantries he paid you and the way he always sought you out.'

'And you were in love with him yourself,' Melody said.

'I imagined I was,' Mary said. 'Oh Melody, what a dreadful misunderstanding! And how noble you have been to say nothing — Papa has much to answer for!'

'The problem now,' Melody said slowly, 'is what to do next! Uncle Frederick won't take kindly to the fact that his niece was preferred over his daughter and your mother will be dreadfully upset.'

'Actually,' Mary said, lowering her voice, 'I've been thinking about it for weeks and now that I know Roger actually intended to ask for your hand then it makes everything so much simpler!'

'I cannot see how,' Melody said frankly.

'My dearest cousin, since Roger told you that he had meant to ask for you as his bride then surely he had reason to suppose you would have welcomed his proposal?'

Melody hesitated and then said, colour flooding her face, 'I would have welcomed it above anything and the plain truth is that I still would.'

'You still love him, then?'

Melody nodded.

'And these three years you have given no hint of your feelings! Melody, you must have hated it when letters for me arrived from India, crammed with protestations of faithful affection, and I read out the best bits!'

'Of course I didn't hate you,' Melody said, smiling slightly. 'I realized his attentions to me had been only those of common courtesy. But I have felt a trifle despondent at times.'

'And said nothing!'

'I didn't want to spoil your pleasure. You seemed very much in love with him.'

'Until I met Timothy Drake again and realized that he was the one I'd loved all along.'

'Then I cannot think what's to be done,' Melody said. 'Mary, when you reach India and see Roger again you may discover you loved more than his uniform.'

'No.' Mary shook her head decidedly. 'No, I am older and wiser now. I never shall love anyone but Timothy and he feels the same way about me. Melody, you must help us.'

'Talk to Uncle Frederick? He won't take the slightest notice of me.'

'Do you remember when we came face to face with that runaway bull in the park?' Mary asked abruptly.

'That was years ago.'

'And I diverted the animal's attention when you slipped and fell? And you promised you'd repay the debt if it ever came to a matter of life and death? Well, my dearest Melody, it's come to that because I shall probably go into a decline if I am forced to marry Roger. Timothy and I have devised a plan but we need your help. Say that you will help us, please?'

She looked so pleading that Melody felt herself yielding. At the back of her mind too was the knowledge that Roger, like herself, was in an impossible situation, forced to marry one girl when he was in love with another. Or had he, in the three years since, accustomed himself to the idea of Mary as a wife? With pain she recalled her answer to his question as to whether she would have accepted his proposal had he succeeded in making one. She had told him then, lying most convincingly, that he would have received a firm refusal.

She opened her mouth to say something that would please her cousin and answer her own hopes of a happy ending, but the room grew dim and faded. When, much later, she realized that she had fallen asleep while Mary outlined her plans, she wondered how much she had been dreaming. Did Mary really mean to carry out such an audacious plan, or had her own tired brain played tricks with her imagination?

★ ★ ★

The towel had dried on her and through the slats of the lattice the last rays of the day's sun were pouring in upon her. She sat up and reached for the lemonade, finding it tepid but still drinkable, nibbled a few of the snacks that had been left on the other tray and had just decided she had better dress when she realized that her bags and trunks stood open and empty on the floor.

There was no lock on the door. Mrs Wilson had warned her more times than she cared to recall that pilfering was a way of life for the natives, a sentiment Melody had privately doubted, but it looked as if the exasperating woman had been right.

At that moment a light tapping on the door was followed by the entry of two women in saris, who, to her relief, carried various items of her wardrobe on hangers over their arms.

'All clean and ironed now, memsahib!' the elder of the women announced, tactfully averting her gaze from Melody's towel-wrapped form. 'You were sleeping most deeply when we came.'

'Thank you, you're very kind,' Melody said.

'It is part of the service of the hotel, memsahib,' the woman said as she and her companion proceeded to hang the garments in the wardrobe. 'After a long journey garments can be most sadly crumpled. Our apologies for disturbing you!'

They bowed themselves out.

Glancing at the fob watch she had left on the side table Melody saw that it was later than she had thought. Ahead of her lay a most uncomfortable and embarrassing dinner with Captain Channing followed within the next days by an equally traumatic but, it was to be hoped, pleasanter reunion with Roger Hallett, who would soon be returning from Delhi in the expectation of greeting Mary.

She wondered suddenly, and the thought was an unwelcome one, whether Roger's love for herself would be as strong as he had declared it to be during his furlough in

England. He had, of course, sent her no letters for herself alone but had always sent her his best wishes as he did to her aunt and uncle. Now as she began to dress the faint threat of his love not having endured made her feel a little shiver of apprehension.

However, since he was still in Delhi, there was no point in fretting. Now she had the dinner with Captain Channing and an explanation to give.

* * *

At least she was equipped with a new wardrobe! Uncle Frederick had been generous with her dress allowance.

'Who knows but you may catch a husband for yourself once you reach India?' he had teased in his rather heavy-handed way. 'One would wish you to be well dressed, my dear, and so reflect credit on our family, and should you be fortunate enough — '

'To snare a husband, Uncle?'

'How blunt the younger generation are! To attract a suitable partner, then I promise you that despite the fact that my brother made a most unsuitable marriage and was cut out of my father's will I believe I can spare a hundred pounds a year out of my own modest savings as your marriage portion! And of course a new wardrobe so that you may appear to the best advantage when you reach India! I am told many young ladies are going out to India in the hope of finding marriage partners.'

'They call them the fishing fleet,' Melody had said brightly.

'My dear Melody, I hope you will not employ such coarse expressions when you leave the shelter of our home!' her aunt exclaimed.

She sat, idly flicking through the pages of a book nearby, but had clearly been following the progress of the conversation.

'I promise,' Melody had said, 'but I think that after a month or two I will be returning to England without an engagement-ring on my finger.'

'And though one will feel a little disappointed on your account,' Aunt Laura said, 'for my own part I wouldn't be too downcast. You arrange hair much more skilfully than poor Patsy.'

★　★　★

Her wardrobe, second in splendour only to Mary's, had been duly bought. At the time she had been properly grateful, though not for the reasons her aunt had supposed. The notion that Roger might admire her sufficiently actually to jilt Mary had crossed her mind. It was no more than an idle thought, instantly dismissed since Roger, whatever his private sentiments, would keep his word to Mary, but that had been before her cousin had decided she really loved Timothy Drake and had reminded Melody of the pact made between then.

Though Roger wasn't yet expected back from Delhi she reasoned now there was always the chance that he might appear unexpectedly and in any case she wished to appear to her best advantage when she gave her explanation to Captain Channing, though she resented his suspicions. At least he could be convinced that she was not a flaunting adventuress!

'Not,' she said aloud as she studied the final effect in the long mirror, 'that I pay the least heed to his opinions!'

The skirts of her pale-blue dress swayed over their hoops below a tight bodice with a deep fichu of pleated lace. With her ringlets drawn back behind her ears and secured with a twist of matching lace and only a dorothy bag of silver tissue on her wrist she looked, she thought critically, rather charming.

Only the half-hoop of diamonds on her finger gave her pause for thought. But Mary had insisted that she should wear it.

'Everybody will expect you, that is to say me, to be wearing an engagement-ring,' she had coaxed.

Now Melody squared her shoulders, gave her reflection a little nod of approval, and sallied forth to do battle with the overbearing Captain Channing.

7

'Miss Craven?' Captain Channing rose from a seat in the entrance hall and bowed as she reached him.

'Miss Melody Craven,' she said, returning his bow with a stiff little curtsy, her eyes raised challengingly to his tanned face.

'The cousin,' he said softly. 'Of course! Hallett has spoken of you once or twice. Would you like a glass of wine before we begin our meal?'

'Thank you, Captain Channing.'

She allowed herself to be ushered into a side chamber where a waiter took her escort's order as she seated herself in a low chair, spreading her skirts about her and hoping she looked more confident than she felt.

'You accused me earlier of not minding my own business,' he said, seating himself in an adjoining chair a little removed from her, and giving her a keen look.

'I'm sorry. That was rude,' Melody admitted, 'but I fail to see why Roger's private affairs have anything to do with anybody else.'

'Normally I would agree with you,' he said,

waving the waiter away. 'Your health, Miss Craven.'

She sipped her wine and was glad of the brief respite but too soon he was speaking again.

'A regiment,' he said, 'is rather like a family especially when it is stationed in a foreign country. One looks out for one's men and one attempts to keep a certain spirit of loyalty and friendship among one's brother officers.'

'*Esprit de corps*,' Melody said.

'Exactly. However I had another reason. Hallett has, of course, described his bride to be in my hearing: light-blue eyes and hair of an almost platinum blondness. Your eyes are almost violet in shade and your hair is new-minted gold.'

'Some people find accurate description difficult . . . ' she began.

'But a man waiting to be married does not usually mistake the name of his intended and I am certain that that name was Mary Craven.'

'I still don't see — ' she began helplessly.

'My curiosity had a purpose,' he said. 'Hallett has an uncertain temper and might well be justifiably furious if he turned up to greet the young woman to whom he was engaged and found himself presented with a substitute. I am hoping you have some simple explanation to offer. Miss Mary Craven is not ill?'

'Mary is in the best of health,' Melody assured him.

'Then why isn't she here?'

His eyes were probing. She met his gaze with a defiant stare of her own and said, 'My cousin decided that she had been mistaken in her feelings for Captain Hallett. She is planning to marry another gentleman.'

'Without writing to Hallett to ask him to release her from his promise to him?'

'You don't understand!' Melody said impatiently. 'My uncle, who is Mary's father, is a most excellent man but forceful beyond belief. He would never allow Mary to break off her engagement and marry a man who has lower financial prospects than Roger Hallett! We had to resort to subterfuge!'

'So?'

'As you must know,' Melody said, clasping her hands tightly together, 'some ships coming out to India put into port at Lisbon. That was where Mrs Wilson came aboard. The purser's wife, into whose charge we had been placed on leaving England, was to disembark at Lisbon, where she had some family matters to attend to — she is Portuguese. Mary and I had agreed that I would tell Mrs Wilson that my cousin Melody

121

had been taken so dreadfully seasick in the Bay of Biscay that it had been decided she should leave the ship with Mrs Stephens — the purser's wife — who would arrange for her return to England overland. Of course, Mrs Stephens had no idea that Mary intended to go ashore. The gentleman whom my cousin wished to marry was waiting in Lisbon for her, so she will be quite safe. And Mrs Wilson had never met either of us. She was — is — quite unaware that I have taken Mary's place.'

'But her parents will know by now,' Captain Channing observed. 'And what about your cousin's baggage?'

'Well, of course, it has had to come to India with mine. And Mary's parents will not know yet, for Mary intends to remain on the Continent until I have ... ' she paused, seeing his mouth twist wryly.

'Until you have talked Roger Hallett into marrying you instead?' He uttered a short bark of laughter. 'Hallett may not have a reputation for constancy with women, but I doubt that he will be as obliging as you imagine.'

'You don't understand,' Melody said quickly, her face flushing. 'Roger — Captain Hallett has been in love with me from the beginning. When he began to make his offer my uncle assumed that he was offering for Mary and Roger was unable to extricate himself from the misunderstanding.'

'And my mother,' said Captain Channing, 'was Empress of China!'

'That was very rude of you!' Melody flashed.

'But accurate?'

'You don't know my uncle,' Melody said feelingly. 'Oh, he is one of the most respected and well-meaning of men but his way is always the right way and his opinion the correct one. He does not hear opposition. Uncle Frederick immediately jumped to the conclusion that Roger Hallett was asking for Mary's hand in marriage and sent for her the instant he had given his own consent. My cousin was overjoyed, for she had thought that Roger was paying particular attention to me and it had been very hard for her because she was in love with him herself, or at least thought she was! How could Roger destroy all her delight and hurt her feelings so cruelly by telling her it was a mistake on my uncle's part?'

'I take it the person she is in love with now is unsuitable?'

'Timothy Drake has been a friend since our childhood,' Melody said earnestly. 'He would be suitable in every way save that recently his father has suffered some severe business losses which are unlikely to improve in the near future.'

'So! A difficult situation!'

He finished his wine, bestowed upon her another long thoughtful look and said:

'Have you realized the difficult situation you're in?'

'Embarrassing, certainly,' she admitted, 'but when Roger comes back from Delhi and hears what has occurred he will be only too ready to forgive our stratagem since I was his choice in the first place.'

'For your sake,' Captain Channing said, 'I hope that you are right. What I cannot understand is why you or your cousin did not write to let him know of the proposed substitution.'

'Letters often go astray and are read by the wrong people,' Melody told him. 'Apart from Timothy Drake nobody in the world was in on the secret. Mary thought, too, what a wonderful surprise Roger would receive when he found the one he really loved here.'

'We had best go and eat,' was his curt reply.

The dining room was cool with crystal and silver sparkling on the tables and small lamps hanging above each table to give a pleasant glow to the white cloths. Vases holding sheaves of roses and lilies stood round the walls and fine-mesh screens shielded the diners from the open doors leading on to the veranda.

Mr Patel himself came to oversee the serving of their dinner. Chicken in a creamy sauce, a bowl of lightly cooked vegetables, some unfamiliar to her, bowls of golden rice and flat pieces of bread were all served at the same time, along with dishes of spicy chutneys and saucers of nuts.

'We do not have set courses so much over here,' Captain Channing said, having obviously resolved to make himself pleasant to her though the reserve with which he spoke made her suspect the effort was a considerable one. 'Let me help you to some rice. It's flavoured with saffron and sweetened with raisins. The food is generally excellent. The Patels probably had a hotel here shortly after Eve tasted the apple.'

Melody found herself laughing, some of the apprehension going out of her thoughts. It occurred to her that there was no need for her to feel apprehension anyway. Roger would surely be most delighted to see her and as for Uncle Frederick, he was a world away in England and while he might — most probably would — be very angry she had never known him to be spiteful or to bear a grudge.

'Will your uncle disinherit you when he finds out the truth?' her dinner companion was enquiring.

'I was never due for an inheritance really,' Melody told him frankly. 'Perhaps I ought to explain. My late father was Uncle Frederick's brother, his younger brother. My father married against the wishes of his family. My late mother taught music and my father went into the clergy, so they made very little money. When Grandfather died he disinherited my father completely and left everything to the elder son, my Uncle Frederick.'

'Who helped his younger brother?'

'Uncle Frederick felt obliged to keep to the terms of Grandfather's will,' Melody told him, 'but when I was six years old my parents died of the cholera and I was very ill. They had kept in infrequent touch and my uncle went at once to oversee the funerals and take me into his own home. He and Aunt Laura have always been exceedingly kind to me, and Mary, who is my age, is almost like a sister. My uncle told me recently that if I were to find a husband in India he would be pleased to settle a hundred pounds a year on me.'

'Which he will almost certainly withhold once he learns the truth,' Captain Channing said. 'What of your cousin? Will he be unyielding towards her as well?'

'He will be very angry,' Melody said slowly. 'A strong-willed man doesn't relish being thwarted in anything you know, but I think he will eventually forgive her and by then Timothy Drake may have begun to prosper a little.'

'A great deal depending on happenstance.' He was regarding her thoughtfully. 'Will your cousin be married by now?' he asked.

'I understand Timothy had made all the arrangements and since both Mary and I are twenty-one no formal parental permission was necessary.'

'And soon you yourself will he clasped in the arms of your beloved?'

'Yes, and you need not be so sarcastic about it!' Melody said sharply.

'My apologies but I know a little more about human nature than you do,' he said. 'Perhaps you don't know Hallett as well as you imagine.'

'That's hardly your concern,' Melody said coldly.

'You are absolutely right, Miss Craven. Believe me but I do hope that things go as well for you as you anticipate. It is merely that — excuse me!'

He broke off as Mr Patel, the hotel owner, bustled across, bowed with a gesture of apology and bent to whisper something into

Captain Channing's ear.

There was, she noticed, an increasing hardness in the captain's features and he rapped out something in Hindustani that sent Mr Patel scurrying away.

'Is something wrong?' she could not resist asking.

'Nothing that need concern you,' he said shortly. 'There is some trouble in the bazaar at the other side of town. Nothing to concern you but in this heat tempers can flare — please finish your meal. It is, of course, all accounted for and if you require anything further . . . good evening, Miss Craven.'

He bowed somewhat hastily and went out, pausing very briefly to say a few words to Mr Patel. Melody nibbled absently on a sweetmeat and gazed after him.

Surely trouble in the bazaar wouldn't require an officer to deal with it? In any case she had been under the impression that Captain Channing, no matter how reluctantly, had been off duty and ready to devote the entire evening to her — unless he was bored with her company and had arranged a convenient interruption!

'Will the memsahib be requiring anything more?' Mr Patel had approached the table and was bowing before her.

'Nothing, thank you. The meal,' she

hastened to say, 'was delicious.'

'Some fruit perhaps, or cake? Many British ladies are exceedingly fond of cake.'

'Perhaps a cup of coffee?'

'Yes indeed! Coffee is most refreshing. If the memsahib will follow me I will display to her a small room where ladies retire to drink coffee after an ample repast.'

'There is some trouble, I understand, in the bazaar?' Melody remarked as she rose from the table.

'Nothing to speak about, memsahib. The local natives are frequently restless — oh my goodness me, yes! Smoothed over very speedily always! I will have your coffee brought to you directly.'

He bustled off, leaving her to seat herself at the small table he had indicated and look about a room somewhat larger than he had intimated but pleasantly warm and shielded by the usual lattice screens from the night air.

At other tables a few ladies were drinking coffee and nibbling biscuits in a desultory fashion and she intercepted several glances trained in her direction.

'Miss Craven?'

One of the ladies, an elderly woman in a bonnet that framed a reddish face with a long nose and a wide mouth that seemed formed for gossip, was beckoning her with an imperious fore-finger.

Melody rose politely and went over to her where the woman sat with another lady, somewhat younger and rounder in features.

'You are Miss Craven?' the elder of the two said.

'Yes. I arrived today — '

'To be wed to Captain Hallett. Mrs Wilson has acquainted me with the fact. I am Mrs Grant and this is my sister, Mrs Trenton. We like to come to the hotel in the evening to drink coffee or tea. We would have called upon you tomorrow, of course. My sister is leader of our sewing-circle and I incline more to the musical field. Do you sing?'

'Not very often,' Melody admitted.

'Boy! Bring Miss Craven's coffee over here!' Mrs Grant ordered a passing waiter. 'Pray take a chair, Miss Craven. I shall not enquire after the comforts of your journey. They can have been but few.'

'But interesting,' Melody said. 'Mrs Grant, there seems to be some trouble in the bazaar. Captain — '

'Oh, there is usually trouble of one kind or another in the bazaar,' Mrs Grant said. 'The people here are very volatile, you know — rather like the Irish.'

'You are from . . . ?'

'No, my dear! I would never dream of

visiting Ireland, so volatile as the natives are! My sister is in agreement with me on that point. My husband was telling me only the other day that a section of the native troops — the sepoys — is proving restless.'

'It sounds ominous.' Melody privately congratulated herself on getting out a complete sentence without interruption.

'If one listened to every alarming report,' Mrs Gant said, 'one would never settle for an instant! You mustn't permit a few careless words to disturb you, my dear.'

'We never do,' put in Mrs Trenton.

'I merely thought that as Captain Channing was called away . . . '

The two sisters looked at each other.

'Captain Channing speaks fluent Hindustani, my dear,' Mrs Grant said. 'So he is frequently required at such times to calm swelling passions — if one may employ a somewhat indelicate phrase?'

'My dear sister, you could never be guilty of an indelicate phrase,' Mrs Trenton murmured.

'But sometimes it is necessary to call a spade a spade,' the other replied. 'The disposition of the native is very easily excited by the most trivial occurrences and since only a few of us have troubled to learn anything of the language — '

'I never had any aptitude for study,' her sister murmured.

'And indeed one needs only to know a few simple phrases,' Mrs Grant was continuing. 'Just sufficient to keep one's houseservants in check and prevent then from cheating one too outrageously when they go shopping . . .'

'But this particular incident — whatever it was . . .' Melody looked from one to the other, wishing that somebody would come to the point.

'General unrest, most probably,' Mrs Grant said. 'Captain Channing is the very person to deal with it, soothe inflamed tempers and so forth, being who he is.'

'I'm sorry?' Melody looked from one to the other in bewilderment.

'Adam Channing is a Eurasian,' Mrs Trenton said, dropping her already quiet voice still further, 'One of his grandparents was an Indian — grandfather, I believe?'

'Grandmother,' Mrs Grant said decidedly. 'I am certain it was his grandmother. Not that one ever dreams of holding that against him! She was, I understand, of very high caste.'

'You need not scruple to talk with him as to an equal,' Mrs Trenton advised her. 'He is received in the highest society in both British and Indian circles, and his progress in his

Army career has been nothing short of spectacular!'

'So you need not fear to be on friendly terms with him,' Mrs Grant finished.

'And you must be waiting eagerly for your reunion with Captain Hallett,' Mrs Trenton put in. 'I always say there is nothing like marriage to settle a man. Such a pity that he should chance to be in Delhi when — but I declare! Here he comes now!'

Melody turned her head slowly and saw that Roger had indeed just entered the room and was standing in the doorway.

Her first thought was that he wasn't quite as tall as she remembered. He stood staring at her for moment and then, as if recollecting himself, advanced with a smile of welcome on his face.

'This is a private occasion, sister,' Mrs Grant said quite audibly, settling her bonnet more firmly on her head and rising from her seat.

'Of course,' Mrs Trenton said obediently as she gathered her own belongings, which seemed to consist of various beaded scarves and embroidered bags. 'Shall we have the pleasure of seeing you to tomorrow, Miss Craven? One supposes not, when other considerations are taken into account. A meeting after a long absence! How the heart rejoices at such an occ — '

'Good night, Miss Craven! Captain Hallett, I am pleased to see that you have returned safely. Come along, sister!'

Mrs Grant swept herself and her companion out leaving Roger to recollect his manners and come to where Melody stood, taking both her hands as he exclaimed:

'How happy I am to see you here at last! I feared the long journey might have wearied the both of you beyond endurance and it was in the last degree provoking that I had duties elsewhere just at the time your coming was anticipated. Where's Mary?'

'Perhaps we could sit down?' Melody said nervously.

'She is not ill, is she?' He looked slightly alarmed but allowed himself to be motioned to a seat.

'Mary is quite well,' Melody said, 'as far as I know.'

'As far as you know?' He stared at her in frank perplexity. 'Are you saying she isn't here?'

'Roger!' Melody resumed her seat. 'You recall the conversation we had after your engagement was announced? In the small conservatory?'

'Three years ago. Yes, of course.'

'You explained to me how you had wished

to offer for me but my uncle had entirely mistaken your intentions and assumed you were offering for Mary?'

'Your cousin accepted,' Roger said.

'Because at the time she fancied herself in love with you and neither of us would have subjected her to public humiliation. The point is that she — she has found in the three years that have elapsed that — she was mistaken in her feelings. She left the ship at Lisbon in order to marry another gentleman.'

'Without your uncle's leave?'

'My uncle doesn't yet know of it. We could not write to let you know. Letters are so often lost or intercepted. She didn't make up her mind to it until the last possible moment anyway. Of course my uncle will forgive her — apart from his father's business reverses there is nothing against Timothy Drake. Meanwhile — '

'You are wearing the ring I put on Mary's finger,' he said.

'You did say that you had planned to offer for me but my uncle drew the wrong conclusion. You did mean that, didn't you?'

'We had best talk tomorrow, my dear,' he said. 'I have had a long hard ride of it and must beg for a little time in which to assimilate these events — welcome, of course, but quite unexpected. We will talk tomorrow, shall we?'

He took her hand briefly, kissed it, bowed and went out, leaving her to stare after him in some perplexity.

He had made it so clear that he had originally intended to ask for her. Had his feelings altered in the three years since? And why, instead of having Roger's grey eyes and fair skin fixed in her mind could she only see the sardonic gaze of dark eyes in a tanned, strong-featured countenance and recall, even without closing her eyes, the scent of jasmine carried on the wind?

8

Roger, she told herself, when she had gained her room where invisible hands had laid fresh sheets and blankets on the bed and refilled the water jug, had nerved himself during three years of absence to marry Mary. It was only natural for the surprise of seeing Melody to have taken him unaware, so that instead of the passionate embrace her romantic imagination had painted he had seemed altogether ill at ease. By morning he would have realized that all was working out as he had once hoped and then he would be more inclined to forgive the somewhat unconventional plan she and Mary had decided upon. Mary, she reminded herself, had been the instigator though she herself had added the finer details and if their proceedings had been unconventional she was certain that a good night's sleep would convince Roger of the excellent result he might now enjoy.

With this thought comfortably settled in her head she prepared for bed and once beneath the covers fell asleep with very little trouble despite the long siesta she had taken earlier.

In the morning she dressed with particular care, donning a gown of white silk patterned with green leaves. It wasn't one of the new dresses her aunt had kindly insisted she should have but one she had worn on two or three occasions when Roger had been invited to drink tea. She recalled that as he was leaving he had commented in a low voice that the light green against the white had made her look like a personification of spring itself. Now she hoped that when they saw each other again he would feel the same admiration.

In the hotel dining-room breakfast was being served. Mr Patel was supervising the waiters as they circulated between the tables with trays of hot rolls, dishes of chocolate and fruit and piles of buttered scones and toast.

Rather to her disappointment there was no sign of Roger and she had the doubtful delight of eating a solitary breakfast. Not until she had finished her second cup of tea did Mr Patel bustle across to inform her that Captain Hallett awaited her in the room where she had drunk coffee the previous night.

'Good morning! Did you sleep well?'

As she entered the room Roger, dapper in his uniform and looking less harassed than on the previous night, came to greet her, taking her hands and kissing her cheek with what seemed like a return of his former feelings.

'Fairly well,' she said, allowing him to lead her to a seat. 'Roger, you seemed rather less than pleased to see me!'

'I have grown accustomed over the last three years to the prospect of welcoming Mary,' he confessed, taking a chair at right angles to her own.

'But three years ago you intended to ask for me! You did intend to ask for me, didn't you?' Her voice quivered slightly with disappointment.

'Indeed I did,' he said. 'You were the first object of my affections. When your uncle leapt to the wrong conclusion I ought to have made the position clear immediately but when your uncle has a fixed notion in his head it appears that nobody can dislodge it. He was summoning Mary before I could set the mistake right.'

'And Mary at that moment was delighted to accept your proposal. Since then — Roger, she now realizes that her affection for you was based upon fancy. She discovers that she loves Timothy Drake and he loves her.'

'So the two of you contrived this somewhat deceitful scheme to ensure she married this . . . Timothy Drake while you travelled on here? Did it not occur to you that when the truth is known your uncle may disinherit both of you, and that will harm your cousin's future more than your own since I recall your remarking that you were unlikely to receive any kind of dowry from your uncle.'

'You remembered that?' A cold sick feeling of disappointment was engulfing her.

'As an officer,' Roger said, 'I have my career to consider. I have my own way to make in my chosen profession. Mary's inheritance would have been of the greatest assistance.'

'So you really meant to offer for her all along,' Melody said slowly.

'I meant to offer for you,' he said. 'I admired you greatly from the beginning of our acquaintanceship. I would have corrected the error but events overtook me — '

'You realized that my cousin's dowry would far exceed anything my uncle chose to give me. Was that when you set out to fall in love with her and forget any sentiments you might have felt towards me? Was it, Roger?'

Though she kept her voice low her face had flushed with temper.

'Three years,' he said uncomfortably, 'is a long time.'

'Long enough,' she snapped, 'for Mary to realize that she had been attracted to you partly because you paid *me* so much attention and partly because she was attracted by your uniform!'

'But is it certain that she loves this other fellow?'

'By now she will be Mrs Timothy Drake.'

'Will she be disinherited?'

'My uncle will be very angry but he won't disinherit her.'

'And you yourself . . . ?'

'Was promised a hundred pounds a year. It's doubtful now if Uncle Frederick will allow me a penny. He will consider, very rightly, that I have acted dishonourably in allowing this scheme to go ahead.'

'A difficult situation,' he murmured.

'But not if you still . . . feel about me as you felt three years ago! You were not thinking of dowries then — were you?'

'I admired you greatly,' he said.

He spoke warmly but there was a cold reserve in the very words he used. Melody stared at him for a long moment while inside herself feelings and thoughts were hopelessly jumbled.

'Admired,' she repeated at last. 'Admired! When did it dawn on you that my dowry would probably be very small? Certainly it could never compare with my cousin's inheritance! So you took the opportunity given by the misunderstanding my uncle

141

made to switch your affections. And to salve your conscience you made out to me that it had all been a terrible misunderstanding — or was there no misunderstanding at all? My uncle can indeed ride roughshod over the opinions of others but did that really happen as you told me it did, or did you ask for Mary's hand from the start and then, anxious to retain my good opinion of you, invent the rest? Oh, how could I have been such a fool as to believe you?'

'I was never entirely insincere,' he said quickly. 'You were certainly my first choice but a suitor must think of something save affection! I entered the house with the notion of asking for your hand in marriage but your uncle assumed — and it dawned upon me that his assumption might well prove to be in my best interests. All seemed settled and I never dreamed that you and Mary would decide to change places. This is a tangle indeed!'

'Tangles can be untwisted,' Melody said. 'You have every right to call off the marriage now. Nobody would blame you.'

'It would look very bad on my Army record.' He frowned. 'And, what is more important, it would shame you considerably in the eyes of the expatriate community in Parakesh. My own feeling is that we must make the best of things and start preparing for the marriage. I take it that there is no chance of — '

'Mary and Timothy Drake will be married by now,' Melody said in a cool little voice.

'Then you and I . . . ' He frowned again.

'There is no you and I,' Melody said. 'You have felt nothing stronger for me than admiration and I . . . ' She hesitated.

'You told me once that had I proposed to you you would have refused me. Was that true?'

'No.' She drew a deep breath and spoke again. 'No, it wasn't true. It was a stupid lie to save my pride when you were going to marry Mary. Better for you to imagine there had never been any hope than for you to suffer the pain of loss while you were bound to my cousin. I would have said nothing about my deepest feelings had Mary not confessed to me that she had outgrown her affection for you and was in love, really in love, with Timothy.'

He was silent for a long moment. When at last he spoke his voice was decided.

'If Mary is lost to me then I see no sense in repining. My own liking and admiration for you has always been constant and remains so. We shall begin to make preparations for the wedding. I'd not have you pitied as a girl jilted at the altar.'

'But as you say, it would do your career some harm too,' she reminded him drily. 'In any case I am not Mary.'

'We can say the names were muddled or — you prefer to be known by your second name of Melody. All this can be resolved without scandal. Your uncle may in fact relent and allow you more than the hundred a year he promised to bestow, particularly if you make it clear when you write that it was your cousin who talked you into making the substitution.'

'But you don't love me,' she said starkly.

'Love takes many forms, Melody! Respect and liking count for much.'

'And an untarnished army record?'

'That too,' he said, completely unabashed. 'Believe me, but we have as much chance of bliss as almost any other couple.'

But she had wanted something more, she thought, her eyes lowered as she sipped her cooling coffee. She had wanted an equal loving.

'There is no need for you to go through with the wedding ceremony,' she said at last. 'It won't hurt your career or my pride if we mutually decide that the — affection between us has not survived a three-year absence.'

'It will lower us both in the estimation of the neighbours,' Roger told her. 'People do not correspond for three years, prepare for a wedding, and then cancel on a whim. In London such things probably happen from time to time without much gossip, but out here, where the ideals of civilized living are upheld as far as is humanly possible, such a proceeding would cause great scandal. Believe me, it is better to go through with it. My affection for you will only increase while we make the final preparations for the ceremony.'

'Me and my scant hundred a year,' Melody said wryly.

'Which may be increased through the kindness of your uncle once he learns that we are wed.'

He did not, she reflected, know Uncle Frederick very well. Her only hope was that Timothy Drake would recoup his father's losses and add profit of his own. That would soften her uncle's heart towards both her and Mary. Meanwhile she must content herself with knowing that Roger admired and respected her — cold words for a fiancée to hear!

'We shall leave it at that then for the present,' she said at last.

'The hotel is comfortable? It has an excellent reputation.'

'Very comfortable.'

'I have married quarters prepared at Number Four, Wellington Street. In due course you shall see it.'

But they had been prepared for Mary, she thought. For Mary who was an heiress, not for her cousin at all. At that moment she wanted nothing more than to sit down and weep but her common sense came to her rescue. In the interval between now and the wedding it was possible that Roger would find the warmth of his feelings for her increasing despite the loss of the fortune.

'I shall write to my uncle today,' she said, rising.

'You will make it clear that I was not involved in your plans or proceedings? You and Mary — '

'Were the instigators,' she said.

'Until later then, my dear.'

He kissed her cheek, bowed and went out, leaving her to stare into the dregs of her coffee while she tried to make sense of his reactions.

He didn't yet love her — yet — the word came into her mind she clung to it. He was willing to go through with the wedding to save both their reputations from scandal and he hoped that her uncle would forgive her transgression and not withdraw his modest offer of a hundred a year.

It was even possible, she comforted herself, that Uncle Frederick, who was generous under his hectoring manner, might increase her portion. Probably Roger hoped that that would prove to be so. What made her most downcast was that Roger quite clearly did not love her. However, if liking was a sufficient basis for happiness then their marriage could be a contented one. Beyond that, for the moment, she didn't have the heart to go.

'Was your breakfast satisfactory, memsahib?' Mr Patel enquired as she went towards her room.

She wondered what he would say if she replied:

Oh it was wonderful! I found out that Roger Hallett never really loved me at all and almost certainly scarcely gave Mary a thought until he realized she was an heiress. I don't believe any longer that Uncle Frederick misunderstood his intentions. Roger asked for Mary in marriage from the start for the sake of her inheritance and then excused his marked attentions to me by pretending he was in love. Perhaps he is! Whatever the truth I have a letter to write that will convince my uncle that Mary and I are both happy and that Roger Hallett loves me and that there is every chance Timothy Drake will make his fortune!

'It was an excellent breakfast,' she said aloud. 'I am wondering about payment?'

'Your esteemed father, Mr Frederick Craven, forwarded a handsome bank draft ahead of your arrival,' the manager informed her. 'All is duly accounted for in advance.'

'I see. Thank you, Mr Patel.'

As she mounted the stairs she hoped that her uncle would prove equally generous when he learned how the wedding plans had been overturned.

Writing to her uncle and enclosing a shorter note for her aunt occupied the morning. After a light luncheon of cold fish, rolls and a glass of mint tea, she lay down, having shed her hooped skirt, and dozed on and off, feeling an unwanted tiredness as the sun rose higher.

When she roused herself it was still hot but she could hear the clamour of the streets below and, having slept on and off without dreaming, felt fresh energy course through her veins.

There was no point in waiting for something to happen that might reassure her that Roger truly intended to marry her — she already guessed that he would do so in order to protect his own reputation as well as hers — but she wondered very much how a marriage based on respect and admiration on one side and warm affection on the other would work out. As she dressed herself and added a light cloak to her frock she found herself thinking also of Mary and Timothy Drake. They would be married by now and she envied them a little for they were truly in love and, as Mary had confided to her before they reached Lisbon, 'Timothy is determined to succeed by his own efforts. He has already signed a legal document in which he forfeits any claim upon my own fortune. That should help Papa to forgive us the more readily.'

As she went down the stairs and out into the square Melody wondered whether, given the circumstances, Roger would relinquish his wife's fortune so willingly, and closed her mind to the probability that he almost certainly would not.

'You are going out, memsahib?' Mr Patel had followed her into the square.

'For a walk,' she told him. 'I need to find a post office.'

'If you will entrust your letter to my humble self,' he offered, 'there is a private post-box within the hotel. Many guests prefer their mail to go through the private and diplomatic channels.'

'Thank you.' She took the letter from her reticule and handed it to him. 'I have written to my family to announce my safe arrival.'

'How delighted they will be to receive it!' he cried. 'To know you are safely here and all preparations for the nuptials may proceed!'

'Yes indeed,' Melody said, hoping it might prove true.

Despite her wide-brimmed bonnet and light cloak the afternoon heat still struck her like a blow. She had fancied that the long journey here might have accustomed her to it but the very air was searing and though she could see evidence of the watercarts having sprinkled the surfaces, dust rose up thickly.

A signpost at the corner of the square directed her to the streets leading out of it, though alleys might perhaps describe them better. She stood for a few moments to get her bearings and set off down a none too sweet-smelling passage towards Wellington Street. It was perhaps weak and foolish of her but she wanted to see the house where she would live with a husband who might, she trusted, come to feel for her in due course something more than respect and admiration.

The streets became wider, laid out on a grid pattern with regimental precision. Whenever she looked up she saw the encircling walls with their lookout posts reached by flights of stone steps. The streets themselves were crowded. Ladies in large sunbonnets and frequently carrying fringed parasols walked in pairs along the raised pavements or stood chatting at the intersection of each road. Soldiers went past in twos and threes, scarlet uniforms brilliant under the blue sky. Indians of every caste and colour, their garments varying from the tunic and wide trousers of a government official to the rags of an untouchable picking up refuse in the gutter, seemed to merge and blend with the rest.

Some of the low spirits that had settled upon her began to lift as she took conscious note of each small detail of colour, scent and the sounds of various dialects mingled with English and the liquid syllables of what she recognized as classical Hindustani.

Wellington Street was lined with flat-roofed bungalows, each with its veranda and patch of grass. She reached the one with the number 4 scrolled on the front door and stood for a moment or two looking at the low, white building. Then abruptly a corner of one of the white-muslin drapes that hung at the latticed windows was briefly lifted, yielding her a glimpse of a face before the curtain was dropped into place again.

Roger would live in barracks until his marriage. An excellent reason for getting married, she reflected, looking with some pleasure at the small building. Obviously someone came in regularly to clean it against the time when Captain and Mrs Hallett moved in.

Taking a firm grasp of her reticule she walked up the short path to the front door. It was painted green and stood slightly ajar. There was a knocker of brass but she pushed the door a trifle more open and looked into a vestibule, its floor tiled in black and white, doors opening to left and right and an archway ahead which led into a narrow passage.

'Hello! Is anyone here?'

There was no sound from within. Melody frowned and then pushed the door further back and stepped inside. To left and right the doors stood open. She looked into first one and then the other, seeing matting laid over the floors, furniture made of wickerwork, apart from a solid-looking desk in one room and a similar wooden bookcase with some English books in the other. At the latticed windows hung the long white-muslin drapes which stirred now and then in the slight breeze which invaded the vestibule through the open front door.

'Is anyone here?' She raised her voice again into the silence as she stepped through the archway into the short passage beyond.

At the end of the passage two doors

flanked each other. One led into a bedroom with a latticed wardrobe, dressing-table and a wide, low bed, the other into a smaller tiled apartment containing a hip-bath and shelves holding various soaps and items of shaving-tackle. All the colours were cool and quiet; everything looked neat and clean.

Frowning slightly she stepped back into the room at the left of the vestibule and looked again at the bookcase, the table on which stood an onyx lamp, and the chairs plumped up with cushions. On the back wall a heavier curtain lifted up to reveal a small kitchen with copper pans hung round the walls.

It was a house for honeymooners, she thought wistfully. She could imagine herself doing some embroidery while Roger read aloud to her in an off-duty hour, or prettying herself in the bedroom in expectation of his return from duty.

The front door shut with a little bang that made her whirl about in alarm for an instant. The muslin effectively concealed anyone who might have passed the window but she went to the window anyway, lifting the shrouding curtain but seeing only the patch of green at each side of the narrow path.

Useless to peer out any longer! Several youngsters came running past the bungalow, clearly on their way from some game or other since they were chanting what sounded like a victory song and carrying on their shoulders a boy carrying a cricket bat. Whoever had left the building had melted into the crowd.

Melody turned again to survey the room. Married quarters, she thought, were not spacious but this had obviously been carefully prepared for the reception of a bride. For Mary who stood to inherit a pleasantly generous fortune, she reminded herself, not for the cousin who could not even count on a hundred pounds a year.

She sat down on one of the wicker chairs, looking about her for some clue as to who had been here when she had arrived. A thief? She had no way of being certain but nothing one might expect to find in a dwelling of modest proportions appeared to be lacking. There was also the possibility that Roger might return from duty and find her trespassing in the home that had been prepared for another girl!

As she rose, smoothing down her skirt over her modest hoops, the low heel of her shoe caught in something. She bent down, disentangled her foot from a length of red material — silk from the smooth heaviness of it — and a moment later held it in her hands.

It was a scarf, made of red silk with a pattern of golden butterflies embroidered over its surface. An exquisite, expensive scarf, she thought. Perhaps that was what the thief had been after and had dropped in the haste to get away.

After a moment's further thought she draped the scarf over the arm of the chair and went into the vestibule. She opened the front door, stepped on to the path, and closed the door firmly behind her, as she told herself she had had no business to go there in the first place.

The bungalow had clearly been made ready for the fiancée Roger had been expecting — for her cousin Mary. Melody tried to recall the exact expression on his face when Roger had greeted her. Had there been any strong affection in it or merely satisfaction at having one of the two girls he had been expecting there in the hotel? His first question had been to ask where Mary was. Did that denote that he was more in love with her cousin than with her fortune or had it been the kind of natural enquiry anyone might make? Had he learned to love Mary more and herself less in the space of three years or had such romantic considerations always been secondary to the money aspect of it all? And was he serious when he spoke of marriage to herself even though he stood to lose a great deal of money?

For the moment, for whatever reasons, she was now the prospective bride. What would a young lady who was going to be married buy now?

A veil of course, Melody decided, grateful to have shifted her train of thought.

Upon turning a corner she found herself abruptly in the centre of noise and bustle. The street had opened out into a smaller square round which stalls piled with goods and produce were set up. In the spaces between men sat crosslegged, some penning letters for those who obviously were unable to write, others holding trays of jewellery that winked and glittered in the sun, others with bowls of sweetmeats and nuts. In one open booth a man was extracting a tooth from a lad with what looked like a pair of pliers while a fascinated crowd yelled encouragement.

'Lace, memsahib? Silk? Silk from Persia? Very pretty. Very cheap! You wish to buy?' From a nearby stall a man was beckoning her.

'Lace, please,' Melody said.

The wedding dress and veil that had been designed and made for Mary had gone with her to Lisbon where by now she would be married to a different man. As bridesmaid Melody had been intended to wear a blue

156

dress with white rosebuds around the skirt. A square of white lace would turn the ensemble into a bridal outfit.

'Ah! Memsahib is to be married?' The stall-keeper's sharp eyes had flicked to her ring. 'For such a ceremony one must have the finest lace. If memsahib will please to sit and remove her bonnet . . . ?'

He had pulled out a chair. Melody sat down and untied the strings of her bonnet.

'Only sufficient for a short veil,' she stipulated.

'This one — ' he began, enveloping her in it.

'Would veil half the brides in Parakesh!' Melody said. 'A short and simple one is more to my taste.'

Dark fingers arranged a more modest square over her fair hair.

'I have a mirror!' The man darted to his stall, seized a mirror from the display there and held it before her.

'How much?' she asked. Her face in the mirror, framed by the lace, looked ethereal, unfamiliar.

'Alas!' Brown hands were spread wide. 'If I were a rich man I would give you the lace freely as a gift. As it is I have two wives, many children, a mother whose sight is failing, several cousins — '

'I'll give you twenty rupees for it,' Melody said briskly, taking the coins from her reticule.

'It is worth fifteen,' the stall-keeper said in a burst of honesty.

'Have the twenty and wish me good fortune!'

'A thousand thousand years of happiness, memsahib!'

He was folding and wrapping the lace with ostentatious care. No doubt he would tell all his relatives about the crazy foreign lady who bargained the wrong way round.

'Your bonnet, memsahib. The sun is most injurious to a fair complexion!' he reminded her.

She had just tied on the straw bonnet and put the packet of lace in her reticule when the bustle and chatter around her was silenced as if some knife had cut it in two. For an instant, time balanced on a heartbeat and stopped. Melody rose, lips parted to ask a question, seeing the figures around her as motionless as stone.

In the midst of the silence came a series of crashing sounds and then a man in the uniform of a sepoy burst through a gap between two of the stalls, slashing to and fro with a drawn sabre, severing tent strings, sending a tray of glittering brooches and bangles clattering along the ground.

He was not alone. As he opened his mouth, screaming out some imprecation, a solitary shot rang out. For the first time in her life Melody looked at a body sprawled in the white dust.

9

It had happened so rapidly that for a long moment Melody was frozen, staring numbly at the sepoy on the ground, hearing between waves of dizziness the panic-stricken shrieks of the crowd.

'Miss Craven, are you all right?' A mounted soldier had drawn rein and was leaning towards her.

'Yes, thank you. I am quite unhurt,' she managed to gasp out.

Other soldiers on foot were running in, their guns cocked, market-traders and customers were fleeing between the upset booths and stalls.

'You are not going to faint?' The soldier was looking anxious as he looked down at her. A memory and the determination not to lose control of herself steadied her voice.

'Lieutenant — Greenacre,' she managed to say. 'What happened?'

'A sepoy had probably run mad in the heat. It sometimes happens. However it would be wiser for you to return to the European quarter. I can — '

'I will escort Miss Craven myself.' A voice

broke in as Captain Channing, on foot, pushed his way through.

'Thank you, sir!' Barry Greenacre looked relieved. 'One doesn't like to leave a lady but I have orders to — '

'Get the body moved and the rest will soon settle down,' the captain said brusquely. 'This way, Miss Craven.'

He had reached her side and was urging her with scant ceremony through a narrow passage with high walls at each side. At a gap where the stones had crumbled he paused briefly.

'We can take a short cut this way if you can scramble over a few fallen rocks,' he said. 'That's it! Excellent!'

They were out of the bazaar and in a walled expanse of yellowed grass with stone crosses heading mounds of dried flowers. Ahead of them was a small church, its spire and weathercock sounding a curiously English note.

'It will be shady in the porch,' he said. 'We shall sit there for a few minutes. I can offer you a swig of whisky from my pouch or water from the font.'

'I believe I'll take the whisky,' Melody said, sinking on to a stone bench just within the porch.

'Sip it,' he instructed, putting a silver-mounted flask to her lips.

Melody took a sip and a gulp, for a moment choking on the burning liquid until the heat mellowed and spread through her. She sat up straighter and pulled off her bonnet, fanning herself with it as the sick trembling inside her subsided.

'I owe you thanks,' she began.

'You were in no real jeopardy, Miss Craven.'

'Melody, please. One cannot keep up all the conventions in such unusual circumstances.'

'The rest of the British contingent manage to do so very well,' he told her and favoured her with a brief smile. 'Very well, Melody it shall be in moments of stress. My name is Adam. You are feeling better now?'

'Still a trifle shocked,' Melody admitted. 'What happened?'

'There is occasional unrest in the bazaar.'

'And Indian foot soldiers occasionally run mad in the heat? Captain — Adam, I may be a woman and a newcomer out here but I'm not a fool!' she protested. 'Roger spoke of unrest in Delhi and has a report to write on it. Last evening there was unrest here in the bazaar. What's really happening?'

'It started as a rumour,' he said, speaking with evident reluctance. 'Most of our sepoys are Moslems, bound by Islamic laws. They don't eat pork in any shape or form nor touch pigskin. A batch of bread up near Simla was mistakenly fried in pig fat.'

'And?'

'The whole batch was instantly recalled and apologies made. Unfortunately at the same time some idiot in Whitehall dispatched a bulk supply of grease with which to oil the cartridges for the rifles.'

'Go on.' She ceased fanning herself and looked at him attentively.

'The sepoys bite off the ends of the cartridges when loading then. They'd been greased with bacon fat.'

'And the sepoys refused to touch then?'

'As was their right.' He spoke with barely controlled anger. 'Respecting the customs and beliefs of others is fundamental to good government. The matter might have ended there but another idiot — it may have been the same one — decreed that the bacon fat must be used. A regiment of sepoys promptly downed weapons and refused to obey.'

'One cannot blame them,' Melody said.

'Indeed one cannot if one has a grain of sense,' he answered soberly, 'but the Governor of Delhi is sadly lacking in that quality. He ordered the ringleaders to be hanged and the rest flung into gaol. Since then what began as a blunder by the Foreign Office has grown into a full-scale riot with more and more disaffected troops banding together. They are declaring they will drive out the foreigners and settle a few scores with the Hindus and Buddhists along the way. So far it is little more than talk but there are always hotheads who will rush into conflict at the shouting of a slogan!'

'Then the situation is serious?'

'With goodwill and common sense on both sides it can be resolved but at the moment both seem to be lacking, both in the Government and among many of the sepoys,' he said.

'Roger was in Delhi when I arrived,' Melody remembered.

'Sent there to try to calm things down. Had I been in Parakesh I would have been deputed to go there myself but there were reports of bandits along the route to Parakesh and it was deemed a good idea for me to check out the situation and pay a brief visit to my home at the same time. The trouble among the sepoys had scarcely began to fester when I left, otherwise I would have gone to Delhi myself. One cannot however be in two places at once.'

'So Roger failed to get agreement?'

'For which he's not to be blamed,' he said. 'It required more than one officer to travel there and try to cool tempers.'

'Thank you for being honest with me,' Melody said. 'So many men treat women as if they were fools without an idea in their heads!'

'I doubt if many would make that mistake with you,' he rejoined. 'Your head appears to be full of bright ideas!'

'My coming here instead of Mary was actually her idea,' Melody said. 'I went along with it partly because of a promise I once made and partly because I love Roger and Mary no longer does.'

He had lifted an eyebrow at her and, fancying a sarcastic comment was on the way, she rose somewhat hastily and pushed open the door set deeply in the porch, enquiring as she did so, 'What church is this?'

As she spoke she pushed the door wider and looked into a cool stone-lined interior with long benches, each with embroidered velvet hassocks. There was an altar at the far end on which a vase of silver held some drooping lilies. Behind it was a stained glass window.

'The church where you will be married,' he said, laying no emphasis on the words.

'It looks almost like the church at home.'

'We British,' he said with delicate irony, 'transplant our manners and customs with us wherever we settle. What were you doing all by yourself in the bazaar?'

'Buying lace for a wedding-veil.'

'You say that as coolly as if you were married every month. So Roger Hallett approved the substitution?'

'He is explaining the different Christian name away as an administrative error.'

'Not being certain himself whether his intended wife was called Mary or Melody?'

'You sound sarcastic,' she said uncomfortably.

'What I fail to understand,' he said with sudden vehemence, 'is how he could have been bullied into offering for the wrong girl in the first place? Surely a man worth his salt would have made it clear from the start which one he had chosen as a wife! If your cousin had not taken it into her head to elope I suppose he would have gone through with the marriage to her anyway!'

'I ought not to have been so frank with you,' Melody said uncomfortably.

'Oh, I will say nothing,' he assured her, 'though I am entitled to have my own opinion on the subject! Did you get your veil?'

'A square of white lace. Nothing elaborate.'

'And you are happy with the situation?'

She felt his dark eyes probing through her as she stood, a little turned away from him, in the aisle.

166

'Yes, of course,' she said decisively. 'Naturally he isn't anxious for the full story to emerge. It would make me the subject of some embarrassing gossip — '

'And himself an object of ridicule in the mess,' he finished for her.

'Turning slightly, a retort on her lips, she saw that he had moved towards the door and was holding it wide for her to pass through. Even in the dimness of the church she could glimpse the scorn on his features.

'I wouldn't want Roger's standing to be damaged in any way,' she said defensively.

'No indeed! Following his failure to calm things down in Delhi another misjudgement might indeed damage his standing,' he said sarcastically. 'However, unless a lid is placed firmly on this present seething cauldron nobody will be gossiping about anyone!'

'There might then be some danger to civilians?' she asked, as she passed him the doorway.

'I hope not! One cannot always forecast events.' The expression on his face had softened slightly and as she emerged into the open air he took her hand in both of his own, saying in an altered tone, 'Look, I'm sorry! I have a quick temper and sometimes I speak without weighing my words. Indians on the whole are friendly, respectable people but in every society there are rogue elements and those also with legitimate grievances. When a mob becomes inflamed they often act in a way that would shock them in different circumstances. I believe you'll be safe enough but unless this business with the sepoys is rapidly settled there is always danger. As for your private affairs — I ought perhaps not to have pried but Roger Hallett is a fellow officer, somewhat junior to myself, and his behaviour affects the reputation of the regiment. However, it seems that all will end well in a marriage.'

'Will you come to the wedding?' she asked impulsively. 'I know so few people here.'

'If you wish me to be there — do you wish it?'

'I would like to count you as a friend,' she said.

'A friend? That's a cool word under a hot sky! Well, as your friend I'll come and watch you become Mrs Roger Hallett.'

'You don't like him, do you?' she ventured to enquire.

He had dropped her hand and they were strolling between the ranks of silent gravestones.

'We have little in common,' he said after a brief hesitation. 'He's always amiable when we meet. I wish I could believe it's because he's a decent fellow and not because it pleases him to write home and tell his family that he's so tolerant he has a Eurasian as his senior officer.'

'I don't think he ever mentioned your name in any of his letters to my cousin,' Melody told him. 'Mary used to read bits out to me and the name of Channing never occurred.'

'Did he write to you both?'

She shook her head.

'Only to Mary, the though he sent me his good wishes. The letters themselves were not frequent.'

'He was sure of your cousin's affection, then?'

'Her feelings altered gradually over three years,' Melody said.

'And apparently his also since he is now willing to marry you instead of your cousin. How easily some people move through their lives!'

He sounded faintly bitter and she wondered whether his dash of Indian blood had proved a trial during his career. Somewhat hesitantly she said, 'One of the ladies mentioned that your grandmother was a very important lady.'

'So you didn't know?' He turned towards her a smiling countenance with much of the bitterness erased. 'All Eurasians had grandmothers who were princesses! Actually mine really was of high caste. My grandfather came out as a member of the East India Company and did business with her father who was a rich merchant. He fell in love with her and married her and their daughter was my mother.'

'Was?'

'She died when I was born so I never had the joy of knowing her, though my father who was an army officer stationed here often spoke of her.'

'She is buried here?'

'Her ashes lie in the Ganges according to the custom of her people. My father was killed in action when I was nine. He left me here with an old friend of his — Jaipur Sahib. He had no family of his own and had taken an interest in me since my early childhood. A very happy childhood it was too!'

He sounded carefree as if past pleasures in an untroubled boyhood delighted his memory.

'And?' she prompted.

'After a couple of years following my father's death my English relatives claimed me and I was sent to England to be educated. I enjoyed that too. Travel has always stimulated my mind. But India held me still. I took my commission and then returned here.

Jaipur Sahib had died by then and left me his property. I see little enough of the place which has always been home to me but in a month I end my spell of duty.'

'You go to England on furlough?'

'I must decide whether to remain in the military or resign my commission and turn to some other trade or occupation.'

'If you stay in the army you will probably rise to be a colonel,' Melody said.

'Sitting in an office most of the time, moving men around on a map? You cannot believe the idea would appeal to me!'

'I thought gentlemen liked excitement and danger,' she commented drily.

'Most of us do,' he agreed. 'But garrisoning a small town and being the token half-, or to be accurate quarter-Indian in the regiment hardly satisfies the lust for real adventure, even when one takes the present problems into consideration.'

'What would you really like to do?' she asked.

He had, it appeared lost his somewhat suspicious attitude towards her and was talking openly, his voice enthusiastic, his face flushed with energy.

'Do you really want to know?' He had paused in his stride, turning to face her. 'When I was a child I once stood on the roof of Jaipur Sahib's house — above where you stood to smell the jasmine breeze. As I stood there, knowing that I was likely to be scolded for climbing so high without my ayah to guard me, I saw a figure coming down one of the passes. He looked so small that I could have scooped him up in my hand. When he drew nearer I saw him more clearly. He seemed to be aged about fifty, which then seemed ancient to me, though now as I look back I suspect he may have been older. He had bright slanting eyes in a yellowish-brown face and a round cap edged with fur, and he saw me and called to me in a strange lilting tongue. I scrambled down to fetch Jaipur Sahib and he and the stranger sat down and talked for hours together while tea and bread and fruit were brought out. They spoke in different languages but they seemed to understand each other. And then the visitor rose and bowed and went on his way, leaping like a deer over bushes and flower-beds as if the respite had put extraordinary energy into him. I asked my guardian about him and Jaipur Sahib told me he was a traveller from the roof of the world, from the land of Tibet, where few men have ever been. I thought then that one day, far in the future, I would like to travel over the high passes and find the land where old men leapt like deer and had laughing eyes.'

'Tibet . . . ' Melody said slowly.

'You are the first person I've ever told that to,' he said, searing to become aware of her again. 'The very first. Melody — '

'Miss Craven, there you are!' A stout figure was panting towards them, parasol held aloft.

'Mrs Wilson,' Melody said blankly.

She had the curious impression that she had just returned from some far landscape.

'Captain Channing, how are you? I am so pleased to see you both here,' Mrs Wilson was rushing on. 'You will never guess what has happened! An Indian soldier ran amok in the bazaar and had to be shot! I was not present myself but Sergeant Wilson said it was a shocking business! Is there any truth to these rumours of a mutiny?'

'Rumour generally exaggerates a little,' Adam Channing said.

'Perhaps it was rabies, in which case his death was a merciful release! My dear Miss Craven, Sergeant Wilson informs me that Colonel Smith has told him that your wedding is to be very soon. I hope you will allow me to make myself useful with the preparations?'

'Well, I . . . ' Melody hesitated.

'If you ladies will excuse me,' Channing said gracefully. 'I'm due back on duty.'

'Don't you fret, Captain Channing!' Mrs

Wilson beamed at him. 'I'll see that Miss Craven gets safely home!'

'Mrs Wilson. Miss Craven.'

He saluted them and walked away.

'Such a gentlemanly person!' Mrs Wilson said, looking after him. 'All the mamas have pushed their daughters at him at one time or another and he is courteous and charming to all but shows no sign of losing his heart. Of course he has a sweetheart already, I believe.'

'In Parakesh?'

'No, in his house where we stayed overnight on our way here. Of course no other officer would be permitted to engage himself to a native girl without resigning his commission but he, being who he is which is not, of course, of the least consequence to any right-thinking person — the rules, I imagine, would not so strictly apply.'

'You know he is engaged?' Melody asked.

'Not positively no, my dear, but rumour is frequently the forerunner of truth. Her name, I believe, is Meera.'

'I see,' Melody said. She wondered whether one of the pretty girls who had waited upon them had been Meera.

He had talked of his childhood but not of his present private affairs. There had, of course, been no reason why he should, but Melody, as she recalled how fully she had confided in him, felt a little stir of disappointment.

Mrs Wilson had veered off the main path and approached a headstone where she stopped and bent to pull up a few straggly weeds from the yellowing grass.

'My children,' she said as Melody joined her. 'Thomas and Alice. I come here every week to check that the plot is tidy. When Sergeant Wilson retires it will be hard to return to England and leave them here. They never visited there. Of course he has relatives living in Lisbon, whom, you may recall I told you, I was visiting when I joined the ship; it may be possible to come back after some future visit there but the possibility is very slight.'

'I'm so sorry,' Melody said, distressed.

'It was a long tine ago, my dear.' Mrs Wilson straightened up. 'Thomas died of yellow fever when he was eighteen months old. Alice died of the measles two years later. She was fifteen months old. After that there were no more children. Medical knowledge regarding fevers was not so advanced nearly thirty years ago. One mustn't complain but of course one always remembers.'

'To lose two must have been dreadful for you,' Melody said quietly.

'Very hard,' Mrs Wilson said, 'but a

soldier's wife must be a brave comrade, you know. No sense in surrendering to despair!'

How could she bear it, Melody thought? How could she endure losing two children, spending her life in a foreign country with only the occasional visit to her relatives in Lisbon? She felt the irritation that always scratched her when Mrs Wilson was being particularly tiresome begin to warm into a reluctant admiration for the stout little woman who clung so tightly to the conventional way of doing things.

'Actually,' the other said now, her tone determinedly cheerful, 'I have very little to regret. My sister who resides in Lisbon has three children, all grown up, of course, but I am godmother to them all! The girl, Amelia, was married last year but I wasn't able to go an account of Sergeant Wilson having sustained a slight leg wound while on the frontier. That's partly why I'm looking forward to your wedding, my dear. We haven't had a marriage here for almost three years. Lieutenant Greenacre was married last year, but in England, during his furlough. His wife, Chloe, is expecting a baby which is something else to anticipate, isn't it?'

She gave the headstone a little smiling pat and moved on.

Melody hesitated for a moment, longing to

call her back and confide the truth, that she was not the girl that Roger Hallett had intended to marry, that she had taken her cousin's place, believing that he really loved her, but even as she turned to follow the older woman she realized that she wasn't certain of anything any longer.

'You brought your wedding dress with you?' Mrs Wilson enquired when Melody caught her up.

'A very simple one and I have lace for a veil.'

'Then we must draw up a select number of guests. Chloe Greenacre would be very flattered if you were to choose her as your matron of honour. Would you like me to ask her?'

'I . . . I . . . . yes, of course!'

'And if I might be so bold as to include myself and Sergeant Wilson among the guests? As I accompanied you here — not that either of us would wish to intrude!'

'No, of course not,' Melody said.

'And if Colonel Smith has not already been approached then Sergeant Wilson would be most honoured to stand up with you. If not at the ceremony itself perhaps at the rehearsal?'

'Rehearsal?' Melody looked at her in some bewilderment.

'There is always a rehearsal to ensure the

ceremony goes smoothly,' Mrs Wilson said, looking faintly bewildered in her turn. 'Mr Clarkson is our parson here. Not terribly High Church but not uncomfortably Low Church either — you are not a Catholic, Miss Craven?'

'No,' Melody said.

'Because if you were it would be possible to get Father Justin who is really a most amiable man even if he belongs to the Romanists! My own feeling is that all roads lead to the same place though I have my doubts about the Methodists, Miss Craven.'

'Oh, please call me Melody,' Melody said, smiling. 'Miss Craven sounds so very formal!'

'I thought your Christian name was Mary,' Mrs Wilson said, looking puzzled.

'Mary is my cousin.' Melody flushed slightly.

'But I am positive that Captain Hallett referred to his fiancée as Mary.'

'Our names are frequently muddled,' Melody said quickly, 'and gentlemen have such a bad memory for them, don't you think?'

'Yes, I suppose so, my dear.'

Mrs Wilson still looked doubtful as they passed through a side gate which led into the main square.

10

'Everything appears to be going very smoothly,' Roger said. It was a couple of days later and they were drinking coffee in the small room leading off the main hall.

'And very rapidly,' Melody said.

To her secret embarrassment gifts had already started to arrive. They were locked now in the hotel safe but were to be displayed on the day of the wedding.

'Only ten days to go,' Roger said now, as if his thoughts were following her own. 'I take it you have heard nothing from England — or Lisbon?'

'I doubt if my uncle and aunt have yet received my letter,' Melody said.

'One hopes they will not be too angry at the change in plans?' He shot her a questioning glance.

'I am fairly sure all will turn out as I planned,' she said, mentally crossing her fingers. 'Aunt Laura will be pleased to have both a daughter and a niece married. Uncle Frederick will be angry that his plans have been turned upside down, for he likes his word to be the final one on any matter, but he will relent and neither disinherit Mary nor begrudge me my hundred a year.'

'It is a great pity he was not disposed to be more generous,' Roger said. There was chagrin in his voice and he restlessly flicked a minute speck of dust off his tunic.

He was not, she thought critically, behaving like a man who finds he is going to marry the girl he wanted in the first place. Granted that his duties kept him busy, but when he visited her at the hotel he seemed restless and discontented, and his kisses of greeting and farewell held no warmth.

Was it possible, she asked herself increasingly, that Mary had been his chosen one all the time? If so, then why had he paid such particular attentions to herself. The displeasing answer which occurred to her was that by paying court to herself he would arouse Mary's jealousy and make her more inclined to accept his offer when it was made. She disliked having to suspect him of a certain double-dealing but the suspicion lingered in her mind.

Now, impulsively, she said, 'When am I going to see the house where we will live?'

'When everything in it is prepared for a bride,' he answered smilingly. 'It must be a disappointment to you that there will be no honeymoon trip but the truth is that the unrest due to the wretched sepoy affair is rapidly spreading! Normally I would take my bride to Delhi or Kashmir but times are uncertain.'

Everything, Melody thought, was uncertain and that included her own feelings. She had loved Roger in the beginning and had a hard task to conceal her disappointment when Mary, for whatever reason, had been the one chosen, and she had gone on loving him secretly and silently for three years. Or had she merely been clinging to the habit of loving him because nobody else had come along to engage her fancy?

★　★　★

'Being in love,' Aunt Laura had said once when in a reminiscent mood, 'is the most natural and delightful condition for a girl to be in. When I was younger I am sure I was seldom out of love for I was accounted quite attractive in those days and being in love, no matter how lightly, is the most enchanting sensation. Of course when your Uncle Frederick came along all my other beaux went out of my head. He was never fond of dancing or of trivial conversation but I saw at once that his nature would supply what my own lacked. Trust and fellow-feeling last much longer than passionate speeches and vows of undying devotion.'

She had smiled and sighed a little as she ended her homily as if her long-departed admirers still troubled her mind on occasion.

'But, dearest Mama,' Mary had exclaimed, 'undying devotion must be quite wonderful! I am sure I want Roger to be filled with undying devotion for me!'

'Provided he turns out to be steady and stable,' Aunt Laura had said.

* * *

Melody frowned slightly as she looked at Roger who sat, handsome in his coat of scarlet and gold and buff breeches on the chair adjacent to her own. She found herself wondering how far she might expect undying devotion from a man who, having lost the first prize in the matrimonial stakes, seemed only too ready to accept the consolation prize instead.

She said now, in an effort to divert her thoughts from the unwelcome path on which they were entering, 'I imagine we can take a trip somewhere later on when your duties permit?'

She shot him a faintly challenging look, since he hardly ever mentioned the exact nature of his duties. Apart from his abortive mission to Delhi he seemed to occupy his time in drilling other soldiers and presumably polishing his boots.

'Roger, do you mind very much about losing Mary's dowry?' she added abruptly. 'It would have been an immense help to you I know.'

'As I already explained,' he said with barely concealed impatience, 'I meant to ask for your hand until your uncle forestalled me by jumping to the wrong conclusion. Looking back I realize I ought to have corrected the mistake at once. Nevertheless I did my duty as a gentleman and accepted the fact that Mary was to be my wife. One wouldn't wish to hurt the feelings of such a pleasant young lady.'

Especially when the said young lady stands to inherit a fortune, Melody thought but said nothing.

'And since you were my real choice all has worked out well,' he was continuing. 'I wish her every happiness in her marriage to this — Tom . . . ?'

'Timothy Drake.'

'Ah yes! And there is no need to wish him happy since if his financial state is parlous he will be very glad when your uncle relents and grants her a handsome dowry.'

'I'm sure Timothy Drake will recoup his father's losses and make Mary comfortable by his own efforts!'

She bit her lip as the exclamation burst out of her. It was stupid but she felt they were perilously near quarrelling. To her relief he began to rise from his seat, bending to take her hand and kiss the back of it in a gesture that might have meant anything or nothing. Then he was gone, saluting Mrs Grant and Mrs Trenton, who had just entered.

'Here you are, my dear!' Mrs Grant boomed at her. 'I trust we didn't interrupt a private tête-à-tête? The last few days before a wedding are always stressful. I can recall wishing it was all over even while we were buying the trousseau. Mrs Wilson tells us the wedding rehearsal is in the next day or so. That makes it seem very near — the actual nuptials I mean.'

'Yes,' Melody said soberly. 'Yes, it does.'

She wished that it was over, both the rehearsal and the actual ceremony. She wished that she could believe there really had been a muddle on her uncle's part when Roger had spoken to him and she wished that he didn't assure her quite so often that her paltry hundred a year, which might yet be withheld, meant nothing to him.

'It seems a little sad,' Mrs Trenton

184

observed in her languid way, 'that you will have no relatives, no members of your family, at your nuptials. I'm sure I would have been dreadfully nervous had my dear sister not been there to bolster my courage.'

'You'd never have married at all,' the other said, 'if I hadn't insisted that it was a shame to wait for Prince Charming when Bob Trenton was a perfectly respectable and sensible man with a good head on his shoulders!'

'And you were quite right, my dear,' Mrs Trenton said. 'He has proved a most satisfactory husband.'

Melody choked back a nervous giggle, longing to advise Mrs Trenton that if her Bob ever fell short of expectations, her sister would probably send him back and obtain a more worthwhile model.

Instead she said in a placating tone, 'Even though no members of our families will be there I feel we have friends enough to make the occasion a happy one.'

'It is a pity none of the Halletts will be here,' Mrs Grant said. 'I knew them both very slightly during the time we spent in England. Pleasant people! Such a pity Captain Hallett hasn't made up the breach between them yet!'

'Breach?' Melody looked at her, trying to

recall what she had heard Roger say of his parents.

Very shy and retiring and my mother's heart gives her trouble from time to time. If she were stronger — but she never goes into society and my father refuses to leave her side.

'Oh, some business connected with the firm. Small jewellers. I forget the details,' Mrs Gant said, looking suddenly rather flustered. 'Sister, we have detained Miss Craven quite long enough. She has better things to do than listen to a pair of old married women gossiping!'

'And we look forward to the rehearsal,' Mrs Trenton added, beginning to gather up the various bags and purses with which she was festooned.

'I have arranged a small collation for after the rehearsal,' said Mr Patel, bowing his way into her thoughts. 'Not of course for everybody who comes to watch — good gracious me, no! But for the chief participants in this most happy occasion!'

'Thank you, Mr Patel, you're very kind,' Melody said, her thoughts miles away.

Roger had spoken of his parents intense shyness, his mother's delicacy, their avowed intention to keep themselves to themselves. They had never visited the Cravens nor issued an invitation to their own house. He was, she knew, an only son and his father had retired early in order to be able to spend more time with his wife. He had rarely spoken of them, though, she hastened to remind herself, he had always done so with respect.

Everything, she thought, tying the ribbons of her bonnet and stepping out into the main square was muddied and unclear. Even her own feelings seemed to be altering. Mary's sentiments had altered too during the three years' separation from her fiancé. But Mary had been dazzled by his uniform and, Melody suspected, piqued by the nuanced attentions he had paid to herself. Were her own feelings growing cooler, then? She shook her head at the impossibility and the ribbons of her bonnet, somewhat hastily tied, unwound and sent the bonnet itself whirling into the air on a sudden gust of hot wind.

'Oh, for heaven's sake!' she exclaimed in irritation, but a moment later found herself laughing as a small Indian boy, passing the main gate, ran in, seized the truant bonnet and put it on his own black head, tying the ribbons and, to Melody's amusement, parading as he obviously imagined the British ladies did with little mincing steps and much bobbing to and fro of his head as he sauntered along.

'My bonnet!' Melody called. 'Please may I have my bonnet?'

The little boy shook his head and then turned a somersault that dislodged his headgear and sent it tumbling into the dust.

'Odious child!' Melody shouted, still laughing as the boy, clearly not understanding the words, caught up the bonnet and waved it invitingly in her direction.

'One rupee!' he called. 'One rupee for hat!'

'It was mine already!' she called back, sprinting towards him. 'Why should I give you money?'

That he seemed to understand for he immediately took up a position on one knee, his arms outstretched as he wailed, 'Two wives and six children, all starving, memsahib!'

The clattering of hoofs interrupted the comedy. Adam Channing, mounted and looking as spick and span as if he were going to be married himself, rode in, leaned from the saddle to grab the bonnet and tossed a coin to the child who bit it expertly, turned another somersault and then scampered off.

'You seem to make a habit of discarding certain of your garments,' Adam said as he dismounted and came towards her. 'I seem to recall a certain hooped skirt — '

'Oh, pray don't remind me!' she said,

laughing and blushing at the same time. 'Mrs Wilson was very shocked at my free and easy ways!'

'Mrs Wilson is a walking textbook of etiquette,' he said solemnly, handing her the bonnet with a little bow. 'I'm afraid it's slightly out of shape!'

'Never mind! It wasn't a best bonnet anyway,' Melody said. 'Are you on duty?'

'I'm off to recruit some extra men for the defence of the garrison,' he told her.

'Extra troops?'

'In the surrounding villages there are many young men of the right age and calibre who will be willing to enlist if only to ensure that their families have food upon the table.'

'I didn't realize that you were a recruiting officer,' she said lightly.

'Most soldiers can turn their hands to many things,' Adam said. 'Where were you running to?'

'Running from.' She made a little grimace. 'Mrs Grant and Mrs Trenton can be slightly overpowering when they join forces and start to talk about wedding rehearsals!'

'They are highly respected,' he said, a hint of censure in his tone.

'No doubt they are,' Melody admitted, 'but they are both determined to catch me either for the Sewing Group or the Music Society, and I spent a great deal of time sewing in England.'

'And singing?'

'No indeed! I have some compassion on the neighbours.'

'Mrs Grant and Mrs Trenton are only trying to establish some civilized customs in this corner of India,' he said.

'Surely India has an ancient civilization of her own!' Melody protested.

'Of course, but not all ancient customs are to be admired,' Adam Channing said in a tone that suggested he might relish an argument. 'Or do you think that the custom of suttee is worth keeping for the sake of tradition? A widow burning herself alive on her late husband's funeral pyre is one custom that any country could well do without! Neither am I enamoured of the beggars who deliberately mutilate their children in order to excite pity when they go begging in the streets. I have every reason to love India but I see her faults.'

'Yes, I agree with you,' Melody said quietly, 'but it's still a beautiful country for all that.'

'And I'm in a bad humour and ought not to have snapped at you,' he said promptly. 'The truth is that I resent having to ride off and enlist more troops when there's plenty of work to be done here! The perimeter fences and walls need to be strengthened and water supplies brought in lest the wells run dry. Instead of which I have to ride out and talk half-trained peasants into joining our glorious troops in the hope that trouble holds off until they know how to shoot straight!'

'The situation is truly serious then?' Melody felt a tremor though she didn't know whether it was excitement or fear.

'More serious than many are willing to admit,' he confided. 'The trouble over the rifle cartridges has spread and grown in the spreading. There have been skirmishes on the outskirts of Delhi — '

'Where Roger so recently was!' she exclaimed.

'He was not the most effective man to send on what was actually a delicate diplomatic job,' Adam said moodily. 'Roger Hallett has ambition and very little horse sense! He could have calmed things down, instead of which he began patronizing the locals and talking to them as if they were idiots — I beg your pardon! I had forgotten for the moment that you are on the verge of wedding him.'

'Having no knowledge of military matters I cannot comment,' she said neatly.

'But I hope I learnt a modicum of tact during my English education,' he said ruefully.

'Do you ride alone out to the hill villages?'

'I know the people there and I have the advantage of being a quarter Indian with fluent Hindustani at my command. I will persuade rather than presume to order people to enlist. As it is I doubt if my success will be very great. We received a report this morning that the sowars — they are the mounted Indian troops — are supporting the sepoys. I hope that the information is exaggerated. The sowars are superb horsemen and crack troops and we need them on our side. And I have spent far too long talking to you, Miss Melody Craven, when a long ride awaits me.'

'I didn't mean to delay you,' she said contritely.

'My own doing! I hope to return in a few days — or weeks, as the case may be. I am hoping to make time to visit my own house. There is someone very dear to me there and I would wish to ensure her safety if it's at all possible. Goodbye, Miss Craven.'

'Melody,' she reminded him, only to have him say brusquely as he remounted his horse:

'I shall call you ma'am when you become Mrs Roger Hallett. That surname sticks confoundedly in my throat! Keep safe and try not to go wandering alone in the bazaar for a while. Goodbye!'

He lifted his hand and spurred away towards the gates.

So there *was* a woman in his life. Melody felt a little chill come over her as if the sun had suddenly gone cold. And that, she told herself firmly, was foolish in the extreme for what had Adam Channing's private affairs to do with her?

When she reached the hotel again it was to find Mrs Wilson anxiously checking a list of what proved to be wedding-guests.

'Not that mine is the final word,' she said, 'but you will not yet know just who is entitled to sit where or even which people, whether we like them or not, are always invited to these affairs. Where was Captain Channing going?'

'Out to the hill villages.'

'To enlist more men. It begins to look as if the trouble is spreading. I do hope it won't interfere with the wedding arrangements!'

'Perhaps we should cancel the rehearsal?'

'Goodness no! I need to get a clear picture of who is going to sit where,' Mrs Wilson said.

'I shouldn't have thought it mattered as long as the bride and groom and the parson were there,' Melody said.

She felt rather than saw the slightly anxious glance Mrs Wilson cast upon her but the latter only said, 'It's very natural that you should feel some slight apprehension, my dear. It is hardly likely that a young lady

193

would enter matrimony without at least a *frisson* of nerves. I can recall being quite unreasonably anxious lest Sergeant Wilson — he was corporal then — might lose his nerve and not turn up. Of course he was waiting for me when I arrived.'

Melody wondered what her companion would say if she confided that, judging from his present attitude, it was entirely possible that Roger was hoping she herself would cry off at the last minute.

'Ladies, my profound apologies for disturbing you!'

Mr Patel was bowing before them.

'Nothing wrong, I trust?' Mrs Wilson said with a tone in her voice that hinted she was more worried about the developing violence than she cared to admit.

'Nothing in the world, memsahib!' the hotel manager declared. 'More gifts have come for our bride-to-be and the problem is that the hotel safe is now full! If Miss Craven could keep some of the gifts in the bottom of her wardrobe which has a lock upon it then there will be no necessity for the offerings to be pushed in too tightly.'

'Yes, of course I can,' Melody said. 'People hardly know me and yet they are being so kind!'

'Ah! a beautiful bride softens all hearts,' Mr

Patel said romantically, placing half a dozen carefully wrapped small parcels on her lap.

'Do open one,' Mrs Wilson begged.

'Just one then!' Melody undid the string securing the topmost parcel and drew out a scarlet silk scarf with golden butterflies embroidered thickly all over it.

She stared at it wordlessly. The last time she had seen the scarf had been in the small bungalow which would soon be her home. Had Roger bought it for her?

'No card,' Mrs Wilson said. 'Someone wishes to send you a little gift but wishes it to be anonymous. It's very pretty.'

'Our Indian ladies wear red here,' Mr Patel said. 'For us red is the colour of love.'

Then it wasn't Roger who had sent it, Melody thought, and was shocked at her own thinking. 'It is lovely,' she said aloud.

'Why not wear it for the rehearsal, dear?' Mrs Wilson suggested. 'It would be a pleasant compliment to whoever sent it.'

'Yes,' Melody said slowly. 'Yes, I believe I will. I'll take these up to my room now if you will both excuse me.'

'A bride,' said Mr Patel gallantly, 'is excused anything.'

'Except,' Melody reflected as she mounted the stairs, 'marrying the wrong man?'

There was no escaping what ought to have

been clear from the beginning. Roger had probably meant to ask for Mary all along when he had realized that the girl to whom he had been paying particular attention had no dowry to speak of. He had asked for her cousin's hand and made up the tale of the misunderstanding merely to placate her. It was his bad luck that Mary had fallen out of love and that Melody had taken her place.

'And I went along with Mary's plan,' she thought dismally now, 'because I was in love with Roger and because I didn't want to be left on the shelf, tending Aunt Laura for the rest of my life!'

It was obvious that Roger didn't love her. As she smoothed the scarlet silk between her fingers she found herself wondering just how deeply she loved him herself.

11

For the rest of the day she found herself sorting and re-sorting her belongings. Since she had been expected to return to England after Mary's nuptials much of her stuff was still there, waiting for her. She had however contrived to slip into her luggage a poetry book that had been her mother's wedding-gift from her father. She opened it now and read the loving inscription on the flyleaf with a sense of gathering depression.

'To my now and forever sweetheart and dearest wife,' was penned in her late father's strong and upright hand.

That sentiment seemed to her more valuable than the half-hoop of diamonds on her left hand, an engagement-ring that had in any case been presented first to Mary.

She felt incapable of keeping up a bright conversation with any fellow-guests in the dining room as evening approached and so slipped quietly downstairs to ask Mr Patel if it would be possible for her to have a light supper in her room.

'My dear memsahib, for an English lady anybody would give almost anything in the way of a favour!' he declared in his florid manner which nevertheless struck her as being quite sincere. 'For an English bride everybody would give everything that might please her.'

'Just some cheese and fruit,' she said. 'Perhaps some bread. Nothing heavy.'

'Ah!' He gave her an indulgent look. 'Yes, indeed! Something light to induce sleep and calm the nerves before tomorrow. One understands these things!'

Wishing, somewhat sardonically, that she understood them herself she returned to her room. She had half-expected Roger to call and spend a little time with her but she ate her simple supper and sat by the darkening window with the lattice open until a clock somewhere in the hotel struck ten.

If he loved her would he not have spared half an hour to reassure her that the rehearsal would go well, that she was the one he had wanted to marry in the first place? Or was he too in a sadly undecided state of mind?

It was possible that he didn't want to dash her expectations by telling her his true thoughts on the forthcoming marriage between them.

Perhaps it was for the best that he hadn't called round. She might have blurted out some of the gnawing doubts that now beset her.

One of the Indian waiters brought up a tray, the various dishes light and tasteful, a red rose arranged in a small vase at a corner of the salver. She wished it had been Roger who had placed it there but knew that it was the romantically minded Mr Patel.

When she had finished her supper and put the tray outside the door she was seized by a sudden mood of restlessness. Outside the darkness was almost total save for the torches over the lookout posts. She could see the dark shapes of those on duty silhouetted against the flaring lights and hear, when she opened the lattice a little, an occasional remark, too indistinct to be intelligible, used from one to another. There were few other sounds beyond the occasional shriek of a nightjar or the muffled barking of a dog beyond the walls in the bazaar where, she assumed, the stalls had been closed and the goods packed up ready for the next day.

She reached for a shawl, wrapped it about her head and shoulders, left the room and went down the stairs. The bar where the officers drank was deserted save for a couple of waiters and the little coffee-parlour held only a solitary Mrs Grant, who looked up in pleased surprise from her coffee.

'Miss Craven! I am happy to have some company,' she said. 'Will you take coffee? My sister has gone home to look out her second-best dress for tomorrow. For the actual wedding, of course, we shall be decked in our best. When you write to your relatives, my dear, you will be able to reassure them that though your family cannot be present you will be supported by a group of friends who wish you the happiest of marriages.'

'You're very kind,' Melody said and fought to check a sudden sob that rose in her throat.

'You are feeling a little nervous, my dear,' Mrs Grant said kindly. 'For a young girl marriage is often a daunting prospect but one grows accustomed to the whims of one's husband in a very short time. And if loneliness assails you when he is on duty or a trifle occupied with other matters there is always my little Sewing Circle or my dear sister's Musical Society to provide diversion. Will you take a small glass of wine with me? It will settle your nerves before you sleep.'

'Thank you. You're very kind,' Melody said, feeling suddenly ashamed at the private amusement Mrs Grant and her sister had afforded her. 'To be honest I am a little disappointed that Roger hasn't called upon me.'

'Oh, my dear, the wife of a serving officer must be prepared to spend much of her time either waiting for him to be dispatched somewhere or other or waiting for his return,' the older woman said. 'Foreign service is never easy but one can find compensations.

We are few in the midst of numbers and so we cling the more closely together. I would advise you to get a good night's sleep and tomorrow any little problems of protocol can easily be attended to.'

Melody sipped her wine in silence. The few people in the main hall were wrapping themselves up against the night air and being ushered out.

'I must go,' Mrs Grant said. 'My husband is expected to return early tomorrow and he so appreciates one of my very special English breakfasts! Nothing has come from your family yet?'

Her look of enquiry was innocent enough but Melody felt herself flush.

'Everything in the way of gifts was settled before I left England,' she evaded.

'Such a pity your cousin was unable to travel with you!' Mrs Grant said as she rose. 'Friends are no real substitute for relatives, are they? But tomorrow should go well!'

'Until tomorrow then!' Melody said, also rising and preparing to return to her room.

'Sleep well!' Mrs Grant said kindly and swept out, Mr Patel appearing from nowhere to open the door wider.

'Good night, Mr Patel,' Melody said as he began to usher out the very few customers remaining.

'Good night, memsahib. Most happy dreams attend you!' he replied.

Everybody, she thought, was genuinely kind. Everybody seemed to have accepted that there had been a muddle in the names. Only Roger seemed to be holding himself aloof. She had assumed he was on duty or bound elsewhere on military business. Or had he simply decided to neglect her and spend a solitary evening in the bungalow where they would live during their married life?

A side door was still unlocked. Melody hesitated, then approached Mr Patel, who was counting the day's takings at the main counter.

'I need to slip out for a little while,' she ventured.

'I will be present here at your service when you return,' he answered with the usual bow.

'Thank you.'

Pulling her shawl higher to cover her head she stepped into the narrow passage that ran down the side of the hotel and walked briskly across the square towards the married quarters that lay beyond.

It was possible that Roger had been sent somewhere on duty and had been unable to get word to her. It was also possible that he had simply neglected to call upon her. The second possibility struck her as the more likely and as that sank into her mind she stopped short, suddenly and acutely aware that she was in great danger of making a fool of herself.

Turning back abruptly she almost walked straight into Mrs Wilson.

'My dear Miss Craven, what are you about to be here so late?' the latter exclaimed.

'I — I needed some fresh air to clear my head before retiring,' Melody said quickly.

'My dear, nervousness is permissible in a bride,' Mrs Wilson said, 'but it ought not to be indulged to any great extent! Tomorrow is the rehearsal and not the actual ceremony! It is not wise to allow one's feelings to overcome one's good judgement! I am on my way back to my home. Sergeant Wilson comes off duty soon and will be expecting his supper. We generally make a short detour through the cemetery on such occasions — just to say good night to them, you know. I fear you must think the custom foolish.'

'No,' Melody said. 'No, I don't.'

'Do go to your room and try to sleep,' the other urged. 'You will feel better for it in the morning! Captain Hallett is still out on patrol, I believe. Because of the trouble in the ranks of the sepoys the guard has been increased and extra help is being sought from the surrounding villages; it will all blow over in a couple of days as these things generally do so you will be much fresher for the rehearsal tomorrow morning if you cease fretting now.'

'You're perfectly right,' Melody said, sobered by the other's common sense. 'I will see you in the morning, Mrs Wilson.'

As she recrossed the square she glanced back and saw the figure of Sergeant Wilson climb down from the lookout post and fall into step beside his wife.

'I must remember,' Melody reminded herself as she prepared for bed, 'that Roger's first duty must be to the regiment. He cannot be expected to dance attendance on me twenty — four hours a day!'

Yet her last thought as she fell asleep was that had Adam Channing been in Roger's situation he would surely have found a way to see her on this particular night.

Morning dawned hot and bright with no trace left of the evening breeze. Melody prepared herself for the morning's event with care, fixing her thoughts on her dress; after some hesitation she had decided to wear a simple dress of very pale cream with a ruched hem and a small hoop. The scarlet scarf with its butterfly design would add a wonderful touch of colour. She sleeked down her ringlets demurely behind her ears and wished it was permissible to wear rouge since her lips and cheeks were unwontedly pale.

When she arrived in the main hall it was to find Mrs Wilson waiting for her, wearing what was obviously one of her best dresses, its panels of light green a trifle youthful but helping to slim her ample frame.

'As your cousin isn't here,' Mrs Wilson said, 'and you have expressed no preference — though on the actual day you may prefer someone younger — Chloe Greenacre would make a sweet bridesmaid . . .'

'I have been hoping you would agree to be matron of honour,' Melody was moved to say.

'Oh, my dear Miss Craven!' Mrs Wilson had flushed with delight. 'How truly kind of you. Of course my only duty would be to hold your bouquet and keep to one side but I shall endeavour to perform the task with discretion and grace.'

'I'm sure you will,' Melody said warmly, 'and do please call me by my Christian name!'

'Such a pretty one too!' Mrs Wilson flustered. 'I cannot understand why Captain Hallett, on the occasions he mentioned you, called you Mary.'

'It's a name he prefers,' Melody said and wondered somewhat dismally if she had just spoken more truly than she realized.

'Gentlemen can be very unimaginative,' her companion sympathized. 'You have eaten and drunk a little? These occasions require stamina.'

'Some melon and toast and a cup of tea.'

'Then very shortly we can set out for the church. It will be decorated with creepers and little white lilies on the actual day but what is important now is to get the Order of Service right. I saw Captain Hallett as I was coming past the church. People are already making their way there. Even a rehearsal can engender a lot of anticipation!'

'It's very hot,' Melody said, accepting the spray of flowers one of the maids now handed to her.

'If the rains come the air will be cooler,' Mrs Wilson told her. 'They are late this year.'

'One doesn't look forward to wet weather with such pleasure in England,' Melody said, 'but then we get so much of it.'

'Let me drape the scarf over your head, my dear.' Her companion had the scarlet and gold scarf in her hands. 'If you want my opinion I think this is almost certainly a gift from your husband-to-be. Gentlemen can be very romantic at times. Sergeant Wilson, for example, is shy of expressing his feelings in words but many is the time when I've been feeling a trifle low about my lost little ones

206

and he just puts his hand on my shoulder and that's a great comfort. Now, I do think we are ready to walk over to the church!'

Events had assumed a kind of unreality, as if Melody moved in a dream. Outside the hotel a spruce pony-trap waited, the reins held by Sergeant Wilson, who had polished his boots to an eye-shocking brilliance.

Melody stepped up and was followed by Mrs Wilson. The square was almost deserted save for a few people who had stopped to stare, and the guards, still keeping a nominal watch on the lookout posts.

Had Roger sent the scarf? She wondered suddenly if it was his way of expressing apology and affection. Then the trap moved forward with Sergeant Wilson leading the pony, the latter sporting a white cockade on its head, presumably in honour of the occasion.

At the ungated entrance to the churchyard, where a rough path of uneven cobbles wound to the church door, the trap stopped and the ladies descended, Mrs Wilson carefully rearranging her wrap and casting a critically approving eye over her companion.

Though it was only a rehearsal the little church almost overflowed with uniformed men and their crinolined ladies. Obviously any festival was regarded as better when held twice! Melody paused to allow Mrs Wilson to smooth down her pale-cream skirt before they moved up the aisle.

They were joined by a gentleman in full military dress who advanced up the aisle at her side and was obviously going to play the role of an absent father. The whole episode, Melody thought, felt like a play with everybody except herself knowing their lines.

Roger, taller than his best groomsman, Barry Greenacre, turned his head to look at her as she proceeded up the aisle. With a little shock that almost woke her from her dreamlike state she saw that his eyes were like stones and his face had reddened with what looked like suppressed fury.

'Now if the bride will join her groom,' the parson was saying in a high, nasal voice, 'and hand her flowers to her maid of honour — thank you, Mrs Wilson! I assume the groomsman was entrusted with the ring — we shall use a substitute today naturally — I shall begin with the customary opening. Dearly beloved, we are gathered together to etcetera, etcetera — all may now seat themselves. Please take note of exactly where you are seated today and take the same seat at the actual wedding ceremony. I take it that our excellent colonel will stand in for the bride's father or closest relative.'

People stood, sat down, stood again; the organ started up wheezily and there was a brief delay while it was pumped up. The rehearsal continued remorselessly.

Melody wondered if she ought to take matters into her own hands and proclaim that she had decided not to go through with the wedding and that, judging from the expression on his face, Roger was in full agreement with her. Instead she stood numbly, feeling the tight, angry grip of Roger's fingers and wishing she knew how she really felt deep inside herself.

Did she love him still or had the feeling become a habit and the love itself withered?

What was entirely obvious was that Roger didn't love her at all, never had loved her! She doubted if he had ever loved Mary either. He had merely switched his affections, such as they were, from herself to her cousin when he had discovered Mary would inherit a large amount of money, and then he had invented the story of a muddle and misunderstanding to make himself seem like a victim of her uncle's overbearing nature. She had been stupid beyond belief to believe a word of it.

'Then after the signing of the register the bride and groom will walk down the aisle, preceded by the maid of honour and the groomsman and proceed slowly around the square where I am given to understand a three-gun salute will be fired to mark the occasion,' the parson was informing them. It wasn't too late. She could call out that she'd changed her mind and didn't want to be married at all. She half-opened her mouth but the colonel was announcing, 'There are light refreshments at the hotel for the main wedding party and any invited guests.'

Everybody was moving out into the churchyard, chattering and laughing. It was like stepping into an oven, Melody thought, trying to breathe deeply.

Roger had dropped her hand as if it stung him and had half-turned away to mutter something to Lieutenant Greenacre. His fellow-officers were chatting among themselves while their wives reclaimed them and some children who had been watching from the porch began a game of tag amid the grave-stones.

'I think it will all pass off very nicely on the actual day, my dear,' Mrs Wilson came up to say. 'Of course if it rains the air will be cooler and we can add our umbrellas to our ensembles. Now I must just step over to where my little ones sleep — I don't suppose . . . ?'

She was looking rather wistfully at the bouquet she had just returned to Melody.

'Do please take it!' Melody said hurriedly, pushing it into her hands. 'It will be a nice gesture if we do that on the actual day too.'

'Oh no, dear!' Mrs Wilson clutched the sheaf. 'On the actual day the flowers will be yours to do with as you please. The bride's privilege! I will return in a moment.'

She set off across the graveyard, her crinoline swaying in the hot, dry wind. Overhead a bird swooped and dived and soared, spreading black wings against the cloudless blue.

Then without warning a different sound shattered the chattering of the guests and the laughter of the children as they continued their game. The sharp, crisp crack of many rifles fired in unison from the surrounding walls cut into every other noise.

'Are they firing the three-gun salute today?' Melody asked in bewilderment. She had turned to where Roger stood but her words were interrupted sharply.

'Get to the hotel!' Roger told her and then he was gone with a group of brother officers.

Even as she hesitated the graveyard was alive with crouching, running figures, turbanned and swarthy. Some knelt to take aim; others were dashing forward, waving their sabres, their voices raised in screaming hatred.

In the space of a heartbeat the scene had become one of nightmare. Guests and sightseers were fleeing in all directions, though many stood apparently rooted to the spot. Men drawing their swords and cocking their pistols were falling automatically into battle positions. Some of the ladies had fled back into the church. Melody was caught up in another group, the ends of her red scarf fluttering behind her in the hot wind.

Someone had seized her arm and jerked her aside. Through fear-blurred eyes she looked up at Adam Channing.

'Get down and stay down!' he said. 'There are no more than a score of them. It will be over soon.'

She wanted to ask him what was happening, what he was doing there, but he pushed her down and, cocking his pistol, turned back into the fleeing and pursuing crowd.

From somewhere a cannon blasted out, shocking her eardrums, its echoes slowly dying.

And suddenly there was silence. For the length of a few seconds the screaming and the shooting died into nothingness. She was leaning on a headstone, fighting for control, her heart banging against the tight lacing of her bodice.

Adam was at her side again, his voice urgent.

'Melody, get to the hotel! There'll be more coming very soon if my instinct is correct!'

She couldn't move. She could only stand, red scarf blowing in the acrid wind, looking down at the yellowing grass where Mrs Wilson slept at last with her Thomas and her Alice.

12

'Melody! This isn't the time to stand and stare!' Adam was saying urgently. 'Get to the hotel. Now!!'

She straightened up painfully, meeting his impatient frown with an odd feeling of unreality.

'Mrs Wilson — ' she began and shook her head in disbelief.

'She's past her pain! Run in a zigzag direction with your head down towards the hotel! I will see to Mrs Wilson. Go on now!'

He had gripped her hard by her shoulders. She thought irrelevantly that the marks of his fingers would remain for a long time. Then he gave her a little push and she was running, her skirt swirling about her, her head lowered, across the churchyard and through the still-open gates into the square.

The wounded were being carried into the main foyer of the hotel. There were sepoys among them and she wondered briefly whether they were loyal or rebels.

'Miss Craven, here you are! Not hurt? Excellent! I need some help.'

Mrs Grant looked up from a mattress, laid

among many on the floor, where she had just finished binding up the arm of one of the waiters.

'Caught in the crossfire,' she said briefly. 'Flesh wound but rather painful. Are you unhurt?'

'Yes. I think so,' Melody said uncertainly. 'Mrs Wilson is — she died.'

'Someone must tell her husband. Sister!'

Mrs Trenton, scarves and bags still hanging around her ample skirts, came across.

'Someone just called Sergeant Wilson outside,' she said. 'Miss Craven, this is a sad ending to your wedding rehearsal. You are not hurt?'

Melody shook her head. The self-control of the other two ladies was having its effect. She had stopped shaking and the faces around her were coming into focus again.

'Memsahib, it will be wise for you to change your dress and accept a small glass of wine,' Mr Patel said, appearing like a genie at her side. 'You will be relieved to hear that Captain Hallett is unharmed and is marshalling his platoon.'

'Captain — oh yes, Roger.'

Sipping the wine he had just offered her and aware that her hand was not shaking so violently, she wondered how she could possibly have forgotten Roger.

'This has been a most unfortunate episode,' he was continuing. 'The miscreants will be most severely punished. There will be other repercussions, goodness yes!'

'How can you remain so calm?' she burst out.

'We British are renowned for standing firm in the face of dangers, memsahib,' he said proudly. 'If you require anything further . . . ?'

'Thank you but I am almost recovered now,' she told him, giving back the empty glass. 'Mrs Wilson — '

'Indeed she will be a sad loss to our little community,' he said gravely. 'Her husband has been informed.'

'They were so devoted,' she said on a rising sob.

'Sergeant Wilson will pay his respects and then return to his duties,' Mrs Grant said. 'It is men like him who set the example for others to follow. Go up to your room and change your dress, my dear. It looks sadly soiled. I will send Chloe Greenacre up to help you.'

It was on the tip of Melody's tongue to protest that she was feeling herself again but arguing with either of the formidable sisters at this time would have been like trying to hold back the tide. Instead she merely nodded and, holding on to the rail, began to mount the stairs on legs that seemed suddenly to have turned to jelly.

The bedroom was exactly as she had left it. When she opened the lattice the sounds of shooting had given way to high-pitched voices and the hurrying of feet.

Turning she saw herself in the mirror, her face bloodless against the red-and-gold scarf.

'Miss Craven, are you all right?'

A plump pretty young woman whom she recalled having been introduced to had tapped on the door and now entered.'

'Mrs Greenacre, are you and your hus — ?'

'Barry has rejoined his men and we are both unhurt,' the other said. 'Won't you please call me Chloe? I feel formality could be dropped between us.'

'And I am Melody.' She found herself smiling at the newcomer.

'You look to be in need of a restorative,' Chloe said now.

'Thank you but I had some wine downstairs,' Melody said. 'You have heard that Mrs Wilson — ?'

'Yes, just a few moments ago. She will be very greatly missed,' Chloe said. 'She was one of the leading figures in Parakesh, always so helpful and willing to advise!'

Melody nodded, fighting back the sudden weakness of tears.

'Let me give you some sal volatile. I always carry a small bottle in case of emergency,' the other offered. 'I believe casualties are lighter than was expected. Two of the soldiers are dead, and Mrs Wilson, and ten are wounded but some only slightly. The sepoys who attacked suffered the heaviest losses but one cannot feel triumph in the death of anybody. Here you are!'

Melody sniffed the restorative and caught another sight of herself in the mirror. Her colour had begun to return but her curls straggled over her shoulders and her skirt was stained with a splash of drying blood.

'I must change,' she said automatically.

'Yes, of course! This is a dreadful thing to have occurred on the day of your wedding rehearsal,' Chloe said sympathetically. 'We mustn't delay too long. We shall be needed to help calm those below. It's necessary for the officers' wives to set a good example.'

'Yes, of course.'

Automatically she began to untie her sash while her companion opened the wardrobe door.

'Will you wear this cotton dress?' she enquired, taking it from the rail. 'It will be cooler in the heat.'

'I'd like to take off my stays,' Melody said frankly.

'You can't possibly do that!' Chloe looked horrified. 'Mrs Wilson would never — ' She stopped, her hand flying to her mouth, tears filling her eyes.

'Of course you're right,' Melody said quickly. 'It would set a very bad example. I shall join you downstairs in a few minutes. We shall miss Mrs Wilson very much.'

'She is — was always so kind-hearted,' Chloe said. 'Her funeral will be held very soon. In this heat . . . '

She hesitated, then blinked rapidly, lifted her chin and went out.

Melody put on the cotton dress with its narrow stripes of blue and white and changed into a stouter pair of shoes.

The red scarf with its brilliant butterflies lay on the floor where it had slipped from her head as she changed. She put it on the bed and turned to the mirror again to comb her hair into some semblance of tidiness. It struck her as ironic that she could even think of combing her hair at this moment when only a short while since she had been in danger of having her entire head blown off!

When she went downstairs some order had been established. Chloe was marshalling some small children into the dining-room and Mrs Grant and her sister were still administering first aid to the more lightly hurt.

A familiar figure was drinking what looked like a mug of tea near the door. Melody went up to him hesitatingly.

'Sergeant Wilson? I am so very sorry,' she said, feeling all the awkwardness of offering condolences in such a situation.

His boots were rimed with white dust but otherwise he was as smartly erect as usual.

'Very good of you, Miss Craven.' He set down his mug and turned red-rimmed eyes towards her. 'Hard to take it in yet! Hard to take it in! She felt it most kind of you to ask her to be your maid of honour at your wedding. Very proud of that she was on account of — well, she'll have told you already — we lost two little ones. It was a long time since and you can't grieve forever, and right now there's a bit of comfort in knowing they're all together.'

He cleared his throat, saluted and turned away.

The dust still whirled in the square beyond the open doors, but the yelling and firing had ceased. Those who had been only lightly wounded were still receiving attention from several ladies including Chloe, who looked tired and shaky as if the events of the day were just starting to weigh heavily upon her.

'Melody, my dear?' Mrs Grant was beckoning to her.

'Can I be of use?' Melody asked.

'There is not a great deal left to do,' the older woman told her. 'Dr Quinn has taken the two serious cases to the hospital. My sister and I and dear Chloe Greenacre are holding the fort here.'

'Has Roger asked for me?'

'I understand the captains went into conference with the colonel,' she was informed. 'Your Captain Hallett is quite unhurt however. There are no sounds of further disturbances but one likes to make sure.'

'I can go and find out for you,' Melody said, thinking suddenly it would be a relief to have something positive to do.

'Not into the native quarters yet, dear!' the other said. 'My own opinion is that most people who were not involved have very sensibly gone home, but the duty officer at the garrison will know more and inform you of any further measures to be taken.'

'Yes, of course I'll go,' Melody said.

The garrison, which had been pointed out to her on her arrival, occupied a space adjacent to the square with its gates and lookout posts.

'Best borrow my straw hat,' Chloe said, coming to her side. 'This dry heat ruins the complexion.'

'Thank you.'

Suppressing a smile at the incongruity of the remark, Melody tied on the floppy hat and went out into the square where already native porters were sluicing and brushing away the grim traces of the attack.

At the garrison gate a soldier saluted her politely.

'I am here to enquire what is happening now,' Melody began.

'You'll be Miss Craven? I saw a bit of the ceremony earlier in the church,' he said. 'I'm on duty here until someone comes to relieve me but as far as I know everything's under control. Lieutenant Fleming will be able to tell you more. First left down the passage and second door on the right.'

'Thank you.'

Her heels clicked on the stone floor as she went down the passage.

The second door on the right was open and a red-turbanned sepoy bent over a pile of papers on the desk. For an instant she felt the cutting edge of panic, then he turned and stood to attention.

'I am sent to enquire for Lieutenant Fleming,' she said, steadying her voice with an effort.

'I will find him for you, memsahib. Please to enter?'

He stood aside to allow her to pass into the small office with its cluttered desk. Melody did so, reminding herself firmly that what had happened had been perpetrated by a group of malcontents. Most Indian troops were loyal.

There were letters on the desk, clearly in the process of being sorted into names and ranks. Obviously the mail had been delivered earlier in the day. She stepped up to the pile, hoping suddenly that there might be a note from Mary, which had followed her on her journey.

There was one addressed to her in the pile and she took it up, hesitated and then broke the seal with a little qualm, for the flowing hand was that of her uncle.

My dear Melody, the letter ran.
I have just received a letter from Mary in which she informs me that she has eloped with Timothy Drake and has married him, sending you to Parakesh in her place. I need not say how great a shock her news was. Your poor aunt was almost overcome.

In her missive Mary appears to be under the impression that Captain Hallett may be willing to accept you as a substitute for herself. By now you will doubtless have learned that such is not the case. When the captain offered for Mary he spoke at considerable length about her excellent qualities. It was entirely clear to me that he had lost his heart to her and it was with some difficulty that he was persuaded to agree to a three-year engagement.

I have written to Mary, expressing my forgiveness and my willingness to receive both her and her husband in my home, a decision with which your aunt fully concurs.

What has pained us both greatly, what has caused your aunt in particular many tears, is that a young relative we took into our home should have concurred in such a deception which must have angered and humiliated a gentleman so much in love with my daughter. However, duty compels me to assure you that should you wish to return home our doors will never be closed upon you.

Your aunt sends her love and regrets,
Yours etc,
Frederick Craven.

Her uncle, she thought, had been more forgiving than she could have imagined, though it was obvious he laid the full blame upon herself. What was equally clear was that she had been deceived from the start. Roger Hallett, she thought bitterly, had paid her marked attentions while all the time knowing his sights were set on Mary.

She took her uncle's letter and jumped slightly as an officer she didn't recall seeing before entered.

'Miss Craven?' He saluted her smartly.

'There was a letter for me from my uncle in the mail,' she said, the other's hard stare making her feel as if she had just stolen something. 'I hope it was all right for me to take it.'

'Yes, ma'am. The mail ought to have been distributed earlier but we were overtaken by events,' he said stiffly.

'You are Lieutenant Fleming?'

'Yes, ma'am. My apologies for not introducing myself immediately,' he said. 'I know you by sight already but most of my time is taken up with paper work and in consequence my social life is somewhat limited. I did however see part of the rehearsal for the wedding ceremony this morning and thought it well organized. What can I do for you?'

'Mrs Grant wished to know if there was any prospect of further trouble.'

'It grieves me to be unable to reassure a lady,' he said, 'but reports coming in are very far from encouraging. Everything is quiet now in the immediate vicinity, Colonel Smith having had various reports from his scouts, but word from further afield is discouraging. There has been a massacre of many of the garrison at Delhi and serious riots in Calcutta. I'd not want to alarm the ladies unnecessarily but it is unlikely to remain quiet here for very long.'

'Thank you for being so honest,' Melody said wryly.

'It is better to be prepared for unpleasant events,' he answered gravely.

'All over a bit of animal fat!' Melody said, for it appeared that the Hindu sepoys had also been offended, in this case by the use of beef lard.

'That is the immediate cause, but unrest has been brewing among certain sections of the sepoys for some time. The misdirection from the Foreign Office merely precipitated the trouble. You must be feeling very nervous.'

For the first time a slight warmth had entered his tone.

'I must try to conceal it better,' Melody said. 'Mrs Wilson — '

'A very nice lady, ma'am. A stalwart among us. Always prepared to offer a helping hand. I knew Captain Hallett had good reason to be grateful to her, but he will have told you about it.'

'I . . . ' Melody hesitated, wondering what he was talking about.

'Yes indeed!' Having shed his stiffness Lieutenant Fleming was thawing into amiability. 'He had been thrust out by his parents, as you will know — some financial muddle I believe — and Mrs Wilson who is — who was very skilled at eliciting confidences from people — made it her business to write to them explaining the situation in a way that at least partly exonerated him. But she was your chaperon from Lisbon onwards so you will already know her good points and grieve for her loss.'

More lies, Melody thought, her heart sinking. Roger had disappointed his parents and was unwelcome in their home, a far cry from the regrets he had proffered about a delicate mother and a father who shrank from society.

'When you speak to the other ladies regarding the present situation,' the lieutenant was saying, 'it might be wise to understate the possible danger rather than alarm them more than is absolutely necessary.'

'Yes, of course, Lieutenant Fleming. Thank you for your frankness.'

He saluted her again as she went out, her uncle's letter thrust into her pocket.

In the passage she stood for a moment

feeling the weight of the new information she had gleaned like a stone on her heart. There was no longer any point in trying to deceive herself.

Roger had lied to her from the beginning. She had been a credulous fool and it didn't help to remember that Mary had been the first to realize that she had been seduced by a handsome face, a smart uniform and a glib tongue.

There retained only one thing for her to do and that was break off the engagement which had never really been an engagement at all! Yet even as she decided that, something inside her yearned for a genuine loving based on mutual trust and mutual desire.

As she re-entered the square Adam Channing was dismounting from his horse. He looped the reins over his arm and came towards her, frowning slightly.

'I thought you might have taken it into your head to go wandering,' he said. 'Haven't you the sense to stay in the hotel?'

'Mrs Grant wanted to find out what was happening so I went to the garrison,' Melody told him.

'You should have remained in the hotel until information arrived,' he said brusquely. 'The present situation makes it highly improper for lone females to go rambling round the district.'

'You returned early from your search for recruits in the villages,' Melody countered.

'The villages were agog with rumour and out here rumour often turns into fact,' Adam told her, 'I collected half a dozen willing to stand with us and rode back. Melody, what happened today was only a prelude to what is being planned. I feel that strongly but cannot prove it yet. It behoves us to make every preparation and take every precaution. I cannot think what Hallett is about to allow you to go wandering over to the garrison!'

'I've not spoken to him since the rehearsal,' Melody told him.

'Ah yes! the rehearsal.' His mobile mouth curved into a somewhat sour mile. 'Roger Hallett is happy to go ahead with a different bride then? I would be less easy to please.'

'Roger and I will find an opportunity to talk privately and decide what to do,' Melody said stiffly.

'Events have overtaken us,' Adam said.

'Yes.' Sobered, Melody looked at him. 'It all happened so quickly!'

'And we must hope that it will die down just as quickly,' Adam said. 'Because a couple of idiots in the Foreign Office and the Civil Service don't take the trouble to find out anything about the beliefs and customs of the people they're supposed to be ruling we have the beginnings of what could be a very nasty revolt.'

'The local people seem to be so friendly,' Melody said.

'Insult a man's most deeply held beliefs and gentleness can be the first casualty.'

'A letter has come from my uncle,' Melody confided. 'He forgives me the deception and says if I wish to alter my mind his door remains open.'

'And if you return?'

'I shall be companion to my aunt, but I have much to discuss with Roger first.'

'And he is seeing to the sandbagging of the outer defences in case of further trouble. Mrs Wilson's funeral will be first thing tomorrow. You'll be there?'

'Yes,' she said soberly.

'Then you'd best get back to the hotel,' Adam said. 'People are being advised to stay close to their lodgings for the moment. One last thing!'

He had swung himself back into the saddle as he spoke and now looked down at her with a from between his brows.

'Yes?'

'Why the devil did you choose to wear a Hindu bridal veil at the rehearsal?'

'It was — a gift,' she said. 'Why?'

'No reason. It looked unusual, that's all. Also becoming. Excuse me! a couple of my men are coming in to report.'

He cantered across the square, leaving Melody standing there.

13

The star-hung blackness of an Indian night had fallen over Parakesh. Torches flared against the walls at the lookout posts and from her seat in the dining-room where she was eating a late supper Melody could glimpse the gleam of light on a rifle or a cap-badge. The hotel was quiet tonight, those who occupied married quarters having retired earlier than usual for them, and some of the staff having also left for their homes earlier than usual. Melody would have been glad of company but Mrs Grant and her sister were presumably in their quarters and Chloe Greenacre had also departed, presumably to check on her husband for whom she clearly still felt a honeymoon passion.

Only Mr Patel, immaculate as ever, moved about the almost deserted dining room, straightening the corner of a tablecloth here, signalling for a water jug to be filled there.

'Does the memsahib require anything more?' he asked, coming to her table.

'Thank you, no! You have provided an excellent supper despite today's events,' she told him.

'Ah! for all humankind food and drink is the most pressing necessity,' he said. 'We have ample stocks should there be a siege.'

'You think that's possible?' Alarm flashed into her face.

'Goodness gracious no!' he said hastily. 'I merely prepare for the most unlikely, Miss Craven. To be prepared at all times for any eventuality is my motto. I would advise you to obtain a good night's rest. The sad obsequies for Mrs Wilson will begin very soon after dawn.'

'I hadn't forgotten,' Melody said soberly.

'Ah! upon your good self the blow will fall very hard. She accompanied you from Lisbon.'

'Yes,' Melody said, realizing that she was going to miss the kindly, plump little woman who had borne the loss of her children with such touching dignity.

'I will say good evening to you then,' Mr Patel said, bowing himself away.

'Good evening, Mr Patel.'

She heard her own polite, calm tone with faint surprise. To hear me, she thought, one would never guess that this day I saw death close at hand, found out that Roger lied about the interview with my uncle and obviously cares little for me, since he has not, it seems, troubled to make any enquiries.

233

She finished her coffee, rose and climbed the stairs wearily to her room.

The wind outside had risen and she could see the flames of the torches swaying against the walls and hear the occasional dull thud of a rifle as two soldiers changed position.

The red scarf with its pattern of golden butterflies still hung over a chair. There had been no note with the gift and her first supposition that Roger had sent it to her had faded rapidly when she had caught the expression on his face as he half-turned to watch her progress up the aisle. He had been coldly, bitterly furious. His eyes had fixed themselves upon the scarf and, now, looking back she saw again the convulsive movement of his hands as if he had been about to tear it from her head until he remembered where he was and his hands had balled into fists.

Pulling a blanket about herself, she lay down on the bed, not troubling to remove her stays, knowing she would enjoy very little sleep that night but too weary to attend to her usual toilet.

She must have dozed off briefly, returning to full consciousness with a start, aware that she felt cramped and uncomfortable. The candles burning in her room had dwindled into stumps each with its own winding sheet.

She rose, splashed her face with the cold

water in the basin and combed back her hair. Her stays felt as if they were digging into her ribs. She took off her crumpled dress and loosened the stays slightly. The only uncreased dress she could find was a simple black silk with a high neck and long sleeves. It would serve for Mrs Wilson's funeral she reminded herself and pulled it over her hoops carefully, slipped on a pair of low-heeled, dark shoes and tied a black scarf over her head.

The red scarf caught her eye, seeming to hang over the chair like a mute question mark. Roger had clearly not sent it to her as a romantic token. Any idea she had entertained of his loving her had vanished as swiftly as the events of the previous day.

Suddenly making up her mind, she folded the scarf into a small square and opened her door. There would, she guessed, be a porter on duty in the front hall but with Mr Patel's eagle eye removed for a time it was probable the porter was dozing.

She trod softly along the passage and down the stairs, seeing as she descended that her thoughts had been accurate. The porter was slumped in a chair, eyes closed, head reclined on a cushion.

The main door was fitted with several bars which would make a noise when drawn but the side door boasted only one lock and she glided across, turned the key softly and let herself out into the passage beyond.

Only one torch illuminated the end of the passage. She walked swiftly and silently, keeping close to the walls, alert for any challenge from the men on the lookout posts but they were facing outward, obviously looking for any suspicious activity beyond the walls.

Despite the dark the occasional flashing of a torch coupled with the canopy of stars above helped her to make good progress without taking a wrong turning or banging into anything and she gained the married quarters with the rows of neat, verandaed bungalows without difficulty.

Here she paused for a moment, uncertain what she intended to do. If Roger had come off duty then she could make one last effort to find out whether he harboured any affection for her. If he was still on duty or riding beyond the compound she would leave the scarf where she had first seen it.

She reached the bungalow and paused, frowning at the faint radiance that issued through the slats of the latticed windows. Then she walked up the short path and pushed the door which led off the veranda into the building. It yielded easily to her touch and after a moment's hesitation she stepped into the hall where candles in their sconces turned steadily.

Obviously Roger had come off duty with the intention of snatching a few hours' sleep. Any present danger must have passed, otherwise he would surely have locked the door.

'Is anyone there? Roger?'

She called softly, wondering how Roger would react when he saw her. Or was he deeply asleep?

'Roger?'

She had raised her voice slightly but no voice answered and only the faint hiss of a candle as the draught from the door extinguished its flame answered her.

She took up one of the other candles and stepped across to the small parlour. Dried grasses and brilliant sprays of leaves had been arranged in the vases and a half-open book lay on the table. It began to look as if preparations for her coming had already been set in motion.

The room leading out of the parlour was clearly visible through its open door. Melody went in, looking round at the low bed, the dressing-table on which a small lamp burned steadily, the sofa with its tapestry cover.

On the screen-printed silk coverlet of the bed a spray of browning magnolia blossom lay. She picked up the flowers and bent her head to smell them but the blossoms were almost dead and their fragrance was only the faintest whisper of what once had been.

In the stillness her ears caught the soft creaking of the front door and the sound of sandalled feet padding across the hall. Not Roger then, who would be wearing boots as he came off duty.

Swinging round she found herself facing the slim, dark young woman who stood there, her long black hair half-hidden by a scarf of yellowish gold. Beneath the scarf her sari was of a paler yellow against which her skin glowed like dark honey. Her eyes, as wide and startled as the eyes of a fawn, were fixed on Melody.

For an instant the two stared at each other. Then as the Indian girl half-turned as if to flee, Melody found her voice.

'Please don't go!' she said rapidly. 'Can you speak English? My name is Melody. Melody Craven.'

'I am Lalika,' the girl said.

'What are you doing here?' Melody asked.

'This was my room,' the other said. 'Was my room but now no longer.'

'Your room, but — ?'

'Now no longer,' the girl repeated. 'Soon it will be your room.'

'And this?' Melody unfolded the red scarf and saw the girl flinch, as if seeing it brought pain.

'You sent it to me?' Melody took a step nearer. 'You sent me the scarf?'

'A scarf for a bride,' Lalika said. 'Once it was for me. Captain Roger said — but now it is for you.'

'Oh my Lord! I think I begin to understand!' Melody's hand flew to her mouth.

She had heard vaguely that some men took mistresses from among the native girls. She had giggled with Mary without really understanding the meaning since Aunt Laura had never talked to either her daughter or her niece about such unladylike subjects. In the end Melody had purloined the medical dictionary hidden away on the top shelf of the library and they had studied the hitherto unknown facts of life.

'You are Captain Hallett's sweetheart?' she said.

'He promised me that I would one day be wife,' Lalika said simply.

'When?'

'More than three years past. When he goes to England he tells me he will speak to his father and mother who will welcome me. He does not tell his comrades for such marriages, though I am of a good but poor family, are frowned upon, but he makes me a private promise. He buys me the veil as a pledge that he will keep his promise.'

'You live here?' Melody said. Her mind simply refused to grasp the situation.

'I am here when Captain Hallett requires,' Lalika said.

'And he promised you marriage?' Melody repeated blankly.

'Oh yes! I am not a bad girl,' the other said simply.

'Did others know of this?'

'He says not but I believe that others guess, though I come and go quietly. I ask him when we are to wed and he says always — 'Soon, darling. Soon!' But then I hear talk of an English young lady, very beautiful, very rich, who is coming here to be married. At first I am pleased for a marriage is a lovely thing and I have always hoped that one day — but then Captain Roger tells me that he cannot keep his promise.'

'His promise?'

'He spoke of it once or twice,' Lalika said. 'He said that customs were not set in stone, that the day was fast coming when British and Indians might marry without scandal. But then he told me that he was to marry, that his family had made an arranged marriage for him. He was sad about it but there was nothing he could do.'

'And the bridal veil?' Melody asked.

Lalika smoothed the silk between her slender fingers.

'It was for me,' she said simply, 'but now it is to be yours. You are to be the wife and I — you will not see me again, memsahib. I wish you joy and I have left nothing of mine here.'

'I see.'

She saw too much, she thought bitterly. She saw that Roger lied and cheated to suit his own selfish convenience, never caring whom he hurt.

Lalika gave a graceful little bow and went out, her small dark head held high.

Melody looked again at the dying magnolia flowers. Their scent was cloying as the warmth of the room seeped through them.

This then had been Lalika's room. She had been promised marriage and doubtless her family as well as herself had believed the promise. The red scarf with its golden butterflies hung limply from her fingers. She let it drop on to the dying magnolias, turned and went out of the neat little bungalow with its pretty furniture.

A mistress, she thought, as she walked slowly back under the lightening sky, was one thing. Women disapproved of them but gentlemen evidently needed them. But Lalika had possessed grace and dignity and it was clear that Roger had led her to believe that one day he would marry her.

As she entered the main square a bell clanged so loudly that she involuntarily jumped. Streaks of pink catclawed the sky and the first rays of the sun illumined the cortège in front of the hotel. People were emerging from the hotel and the surrounding buildings, most in black, a few clutching what looked like carpetbags.

'Ah! you are already in black, my dear!'

Mrs Grant, sister in tow, came over to her. 'That is so important! To show the proper respect for the dead. At such a time conventions must be observed.'

It was exactly what Mrs Wilson would have said, Melody thought, remembering the older woman's insistence on retaining her stays during the diversion in their journey. But what did convention matter now when it was obvious from the little huddles of the women and the heavily armed soldiers that the troubles were only just beginning?

'We must maintain our standards,' Mrs Grant said, as if she had read Melody's thoughts. 'The occasion calls for it and it would never do to display any sign of panic before our Indian people.'

'The revolt is not then over?' Melody asked.

'From information received it seems that it is spreading and increasing,' the older woman replied. 'We are ordered to make ready for evacuation. Beyond that I have been told very little.'

'I see.'

She saw little beyond the fact that once Mrs Wilson had been buried there was likely to be a general exodus, but where to remained unspoken.

Suddenly with a little shock she saw Roger, in full dress uniform, a black band on his arm, coming towards her, saluting Mrs Grant who said, 'Ah! here is the person with whom you will be longing to exchange a few words. Come, sister!'

She and Mrs Trenton moved away to take their places amid a fairly orderly group of mourners.

'My dear Melody, you must have begun to consider me sadly neglectful!' Roger was saying, bending to kiss her cheek. 'The truth is that I've been forced to neglect you while events overtook us in a most alarming fashion. I did call at the hotel just before dawn but realized that you would probably still be sleeping. This is a sad occasion indeed!'

'Yes,' Melody said briefly.

'I take it that Mrs Wilson was never privy to the — er — substitution?'

'She thought there had been a muddle in the names.'

'The muddle being originally your uncle's fault,' Roger said smoothly. 'However all will be well when the actual ceremony takes place.'

'I bought a lace veil,' Melody said.

'And I hoped you might wear the red-and-gold!' He sighed briefly. 'Never mind, you are almost certainly correct. It does not do to 'go native' as the expression has it! Have you heard from your uncle yet?'

There was a faint shadow of foreboding in the handsome grey eyes.

'Uncle Frederick is quite prepared to continue to acknowledge me as a close family member,' she said.

'So your little inheritance will be safe, and may even be increased through your uncle's good offices once we are happily settled,' Roger said. 'Ah! The funeral procession is forming up. I hope we may speak later!'

He pecked her cheek again and went to take his place among the other officers.

How could she ever have imagined that she was in love with him? Melody stared after him, trying to raise a flicker of feeling for him but she could experience only weary disgust at the lack of scruples with which he had acted, his blatant hypocrisy and the cruel way in which he had deceived the Indian girl who had trusted him.

'Would you like to walk with me?' Chloe Greenacre had come to her side.

'Thank you, yes.'

There was something fresh and wholesome about the young woman, who so clearly loved her husband and was adapting so comfortably to life in Parakesh.

'Lieutenant Greenacre . . . ' Melody began.

'Barry is one of those who will carry the coffin,' the girl answered with a touch of pride. 'Mrs Wilson was very kind and helpful to me when I arrived last year.'

Most people were kind and helpful, Melody reminded herself, as she took her place with her companion in the procession behind the gun carriage on which the coffin had been placed, draped with a Union Jack — which was, she thought, as it should be since Mrs Wilson had wholeheartedly embraced military life.

From the church a bell was slowly tolling and the parson had advanced to the steps to receive the coffin, now shouldered by six soldiers. Mrs Wilson was getting a good send-off, Melody reflected as they moved into the morning cool of the church.

There were red-turbanned figures among the congregation and she felt a pang of unease which was dispelled a moment later as Chloe touched her arm, murmuring, 'Many, probably most of our sepoys are loyal. They understand the whole thing was a sad blunder in the Foreign Office.'

But it was the malcontents who resented the British presence and the fierce sowars on their horses who would agitate to continue and enlarge the revolt, Melody thought, and bent her head as the solemn service began.

Not until they were coming out of church did she see the upright figure of Sergeant Wilson, a black band around his sleeve, his head high. In public, she recalled Mrs Wilson once saying, a good soldier displays no emotion.

'And I,' she thought, fixing her attention on the yellowed grass and trying not to see the square pit into which the coffin was being lowered, will never be a good soldier.

Now that the ceremony of the funeral was over she felt her indignation against Roger Hallett bubbling up like a fiery stream inside her outwardly composed person.

The notes of the Last Post died into the morning air. Chloe, who had been weeping softly, made a hurried excuse and turned away.

'Are you all right?' Adam's brusque voice at her shoulder made her turn abruptly.

She nodded silently but he took her arm and drew her away until they stood at a little distance, from the rest.

'You look very pale!' His dark eyes searched her face. 'Have you spoken with Hallett?'

'Very briefly.'

'So all is sweetly loving again?'

'You must know that it isn't!' she burst out. 'Roger Hallett never cared for Mary or me! He was only interested in her promised inheritance. He paid definite court to me in order to pique her interest in him, and after he had asked my uncle for her hand in marriage he pretended the whole thing had been a misunderstanding on my uncle's part, and that he saw no way of extricating himself from the situation.'

'A pretty feeble excuse.'

'Then three years passed and Mary discovered she loved someone else and I was still — thought I was still in love with Roger, and so we changed places! And now my uncle assures me there never was any misunderstanding, that Roger asked for my cousin from the start!'

'But he is ready to go through with the marriage to you? That surely betokens some feeling on his side.'

'He knows that I am promised a small inheritance,' she said bitterly.

'And will content himself with the prospect of that? Successful marriages have been founded on more shaky ground.'

'Not this one!' Melody said sharply. 'I intend to return to England as soon as it can be arranged!'

'Under present circumstances that may take some arranging,' he commented.

'Adam, will you answer a question honestly?' she asked as they began to move away from the funeral party.

'I generally do,' he told her.

'I know ladies are not supposed to know about such things. Ladies are not supposed to know about a great many things but they generally get to find out. Men keep mistresses before they marry . . . '

'And sometimes afterwards,' Adam said with a faint smile.

'And sometimes men promise marriage without any intention of keeping that promise?'

'Some do.'

'To Indian girls?'

'A few men take Indian girls as brides, as my own grandfather did.'

'Did you,' Melody demanded, 'know about

the girl called Lalika whom Roger was keeping and whom he'd promised to marry?'

'There have been rumours for a long time that Hallett was seeing an Indian girl of good family,' Adam said slowly. 'In a place like this rumour grows like moss on stone, but when your — or rather your cousin's — arrival was announced as imminent and married quarters were assigned to him, there was some talk of an Indian girl being seen about the place. The more charitably minded assumed she was helping him to prepare for his bride.'

'And Roger didn't confide in anybody?'

Adam shook his dark head.

'Hallett hasn't gone out of his way to make friends,' he said. 'He's a good officer but cold and somewhat withdrawn. Ambitious but rather inclined to pull rank when it isn't necessary.'

'I've seen the girl,' Melody said. 'She's very pretty and sweet.'

'My grandmother's race has a certain dignity under trying circumstances,' Adam said with a faint smile.

'Nobody warned me,' Melody frowned.

'Most people probably don't know or, like myself, had heard only the slightest rumours,' he told her. 'So he promised her marriage?'

'She told me so and I believe her. The red scarf with the butterflies on it was supposed to be for her. She sent me the scarf as a sign that she relinquished her claim on him.'

'She told you that?'

Melody nodded.

'Hallett likes to eat his cake and keep it in the cupboard at the same time,' Adam said, his lip curling slightly.

'Meaning he would probably keep on seeing her after he was married?'

'It's possible but prediction isn't my strong suit.'

'I'm not going to marry him,' Melody said evenly.

'Love is often the same as tolerance and forgiveness,' Adam said.

'But I don't love him!' Melody said abruptly. 'I thought that I did but it was just a dream — like the way Mary felt. Just a dream! It never really existed at all!'

Suddenly afraid that she might burst into tears she turned and walked rapidly ahead of him towards the hotel.

14

Some of the mourners had already reached the hotel and were standing about in forlorn little groups as if they weren't quite certain how they were expected to behave. Mr Patel, however, was proving more than equal to the occasion, moving among them, pausing here and there to murmur a few words in praise of the deceased while a trio of waiters offered sandwiches and tea. It was all very British, Melody thought. Had it not been for the heat beyond the lattices just starting to blaze down and the dark complexions of the staff one might almost have fancied oneself back in London.

'And I,' Melody thought bitterly as she climbed the stairs towards her room, 'ought never to have left England.'

What had possessed her to believe Roger Hallett's tale of having been forced to ask for the wrong girl as his bride because Uncle Frederick had misunderstood and overridden with his blustering any attempt to set the matter straight? He had simply invented the story to explain why he had paid her such particular attention And why had she allowed

Mary to remind her of that ridiculous pact they had made so long ago when Mary had saved her from the runaway bull?

Her reflection in the mirror gave her further cause for disquiet. The black dress was limp over its hoops and her fair curls straggled damply over her neck. She would go home and spend the next several years in running errands for Aunt Laura and reading Mary's chatty letters from Lisbon. At which point she felt like bursting into tears!

A tap sounded on the door. As she turned it opened cautiously and Roger stepped inside.

'Here you are!' he said, slightly too heartily. 'Forgive me for venturing into your room but I feared the recent sad event might have disturbed you greatly. Violent death is not something one sees in London, nor indeed here very often.'

'I am quite calm,' she said, surprised to find that she spoke the truth.

There were, she thought suddenly, worse things than violent death. There was the slow withering of a love that had been based on another's lies and vanity.

'Mrs Wilson will be much missed,' Roger said. 'She was well-liked here.'

'Yes.'

She went on looking at him as he stood

there, and wondered how he could still look so handsome and cut such a gallant figure when her own feelings were so radically altered.

'I have been wondering about the ceremony,' he said

'Ceremony?'

'Our marriage. It would seem correct to postpone it for a while but after today's sad event and in view of the worsening situation, which is rapidly becoming rather alarming, but on the other hand a wedding always puts heart into people and — '

'There isn't going to be any wedding,' Melody said coldly and clearly.

'My dear, you cannot possibly mean that!' He looked so astonished that she almost wanted to laugh.

'I mean exactly that,' she continued. 'I have had a letter from my uncle which makes it very clear that you meant to ask for Mary's hand in the first place. The only reason you paid such marked attentions to me was to pique her interest in you and the reason you wanted Mary is because you knew she was the one with the large inheritance. We were both too young and foolish to see the truth, that's all!'

'You really think I could be so devious?' he said, a hurt tone coming into his voice.

'I believed in your honesty,' Melody said. 'Had I not, then I'd never have agreed to take my cousin's place. I was stupid enough to assume it would be a wonderful surprise for you.'

'Rather more of a shock,' he said wryly.

'Then I cannot understand why you said what you did to me,' she burst out. 'You sought me on purpose to lie that my uncle had misunderstood you. Why?'

'Because I never could resist flattering a pretty woman,' Roger said. 'And it wasn't a complete lie. I did prefer you to your cousin when we first met. Had it not been for the dowry — '

'You would probably have whispered to Mary that she was the one you really hoped to marry. You like playing games with women's hearts, Roger, but some of us don't find it so amusing!'

'I would have been a faithful husband,' he said.

'What about Lalika?' Melody demanded. 'Or have you forgotten the Indian girl to whom you also promised marriage?'

'Lalika?' His smile had faded. 'When you came towards me at the rehearsal with that Hindu flummery on your head I thought for a moment — but then I realized that Mrs Wilson had very likely persuaded you to wear such a scarf at the rehearsal as a delicate compliment to the land we rule or some such nonsense! Who told you about Lalika?'

'I found out for myself. How isn't important.'

'I never really considered marrying her, you know,' he said, looking uncomfortable. 'She was an ... entertainment, but marriage? It would have ruined my hopes of promotion!'

'You never loved her?'

Somehow it would have made her feel better had he confessed some abiding affection.

'She's very sweet and biddable,' Roger said. 'Someone with whom to while away a lonely hour.'

'And then when Mary arrived you'd have turned Lalika out of doors? How could you?'

'Most native girls don't aim as high as marriage.'

'And most gentlemen would never lead them on to expect it!'

'She will always be grateful that I took her up and treated her well. One day she will make a more suitable — '

'Or you would have gone on seeing her as your mistress!'

'For heaven's sake keep your voice down,' he cautioned nervously. 'Someone may overhear.'

'Then they will know the sort of person you are,' Melody snapped.

'Oh, the rumours never hurt,' he said carelessly. 'Were I to marry a native then the outcome might be rather different.'

He was as handsome as he had always been, his smile as charming. Staring at him she marvelled at how quickly one could fall out of love. She hadn't imagined such a change possible before.

'Melody . . . ' He had taken a step towards her.

A tap sounded on the door. Melody, moving to open it, was sourly amused to see how swiftly Roger positioned himself out of sight between the wardrobe and bathroom wall.

'If you please,' Chloe Greenacre said, 'there is a meeting downstairs in a few moments. The colonel is going to explain the situation and the course of action he recommends.'

'I'll be down in a moment,' Melody told her.

'I too must go down,' Roger said, emerging from concealment as she closed the door.

Silently Melody opened the door again and allowed him to pass through.

'There was time only to tidy her hair and smooth down her dress before she followed him down into the main hall.

It was crowded but in orderly fashion, soldiers lining the walls, women either seated on chairs and stools or standing in small groups talking quietly. Melody saw that turbanned sepoys were also present, their faces impassive. Mr Patel, standing in one of the window alcoves, was, from the expression on his face, carefully counting heads, presumably with a view to offering some refreshments later.

On a dais between the coffee lounge and the officers' bar stood the moustachioed figure of Colonel Smith, to whom she remembered being introduced briefly on her arrival. Almost instinctively she looked round for Mrs Wilson before she recalled that the redoubtable matron was gone forever.

'It appears,' began Colonel Smith, his voice rasping through the low-voiced chatter and bringing an instant listening hush, 'that the situation is rapidly worsening. Our runners are bringing news of localized conflict spreading very rapidly and of increased killings of Hindus by Muslims, Muslims by Hindus, Christian Indians by Sikhs. What began as an administrative error, quickly corrected, has become a series of excuses to take up arms against one's neighbour.'

'But this is far more serious than any of us expected!' one of the ladies piped up.

Craning her neck slightly Melody saw that it was one of the sergeants' wives, swaddled in a black overgarment which entirely failed to conceal her pregnancy.

'We have endeavoured to keep rumour under control,' Colonel Smith said with a slightly quelling glance, 'but fact now outpaces rumour. I am reliably informed that whole regiments of Indian troops, joined by bandits, are devastating the countryside around Delhi and Calcutta. This has called for some quick decisions on the part of myself and my senior officers. The sad events yesterday made the news we had received more verifiable and the situation is rapidly worsening.'

'But Parakesh is well protected!' Mrs Grant was heard to exclaim.

'Under normal circumstances, yes.' He nodded in her direction. 'Our local people are loyal as are our sepoys and sowars. We work together with very few problems, but when bandits begin to infiltrate, that is like the tide coming in, slowly at first but impossible to stem. For weeks we have been receiving reports of bandits moving into local areas for richer pickings than they can hope to get on the frontier. Parakesh is indeed well-defended but we are accustomed to shop in the local bazaar which is separated only by a wall from our married quarters.'

Melody recalled how easily she had gained access to the bazaar and to Wellington Road where the neat bungalows stood.

'Parakesh,' Colonel Smith was continuing, 'can certainly withstand an unprovoked impulsive attack. However the time when a brief skirmish such as we had yesterday applies to the situation is no longer relevant. We will therefore evacuate Parakesh in an orderly manner and travel overnight to Cawnpore. It is only twenty miles off, has a large garrison, generous supplies of ammunition and weapons and a well-equipped field hospital. Our own supplies will swell those already available at Cawnpore.'

'We might be attacked on the way there!' someone objected.

'Possible but not probable,' the colonel said briskly. 'Travelling by night in a well-ordered convoy, we should have few, if any, problems. Once the rains come, travelling will be well nigh impossible.'

'But will we be safe at Cawnpore?' Mrs Grant demanded.

'Certainly much safer than here,' Colonel Smith said. 'Cawnpore has a large indigenous population of loyal Indians and is very well defended. We will set out in good order when the sun sets. Any questions?'

He looked as if he expected none and apart from some shuffling and whispering among those assembled there was silence for a spell.

Then a voice enquired:

'What of our Indian citizens, sir?'

Adam, who had been seated at one of the small tables, rose to his feet as he spoke.

'What of them?' the colonel asked.

'Will they be coming with us to Cawnpore, sir?' Adam's voice was silky.

'We shall be escorted by loyal sepoys and sowars,' Colonel Smith said.

'I was referring to the non-military personnel, sir. The women and children and the local traders.'

'We cannot overstretch the resources of the Cawnpore garrison,' the colonel said.

'So the rest will be left unprotected, sir?'

'Captain Channing, our first responsibility must be to our women and children and our own defence!' one of the other officers interjected sharply.

'After yesterday's unhappy events we cannot take that for granted,' another remarked.

'So we are going to leave them to be massacred when the rebels reach Parakesh? That sends a harsh signal to those who believe they live under the protection of the British flag,' Adam said.

'Captain Channing has a close personal interest in our native subjects,' Roger remarked. His smooth voice was flavoured with spite.

'I am indeed one-quarter Indian!' Adam retorted. 'It is therefore logical that I should be three times more concerned for our British people. Colonel Smith, sir, may I make comment?'

'You have the floor, Captain Channing.'

The colonel, Melody noticed, looked none too pleased.

'I'll be brief,' Adam said, not moving from his place. 'I also have my runners and scouts to bring back reports, as most of us have. I am positive, after studying these over the past few days, and despite the tragedies of yesterday, that we do best by remaining here in Parakesh. Strategically we are in an excellent position. On a slight hill, surrounded by walls with a bridge, that can be manned constantly to prevent access to the main compound. Any gaps in the internal defence structures can be plugged. In my opinion if the rebels come they won't waste their shot on us but will head due south and attack Cawnpore in force within a couple of hours.'

'Does anyone agree with that estimate of the situation?' Colonel Smith enquired.

'If Captain Channing is mistaken have we the means to defend ourselves here?' Mrs Trenton piped up timidly.

'Yes, provided our native population remains loyal,' the colonel said, 'but we have no guarantee of that.'

'We cannot stop trusting all the Indians because of the actions of a few,' another lady remarked.

'A few? Mrs Ogilvy, there are thousands joining the rebels!' Colonel Smith exploded.

'We have reports of servants murdering their masters in their beds, of ladies being abducted and children mutilated! This is not a subject I care to dwell upon before gently bred ladies but one must take account of it in any decision we make!'

'I'm sure we're all greatly obliged to Colonel Smith for making the matter so clear to us all,' Adam said.

'Sir, you forget yourself!' Colonel Smith glared at him.

'My apologies, sir, but frightening the ladies doesn't seem to me to be the best way of reaching a decision,' Adam said, unrepentant.

'Perhaps we should take a vote on whether to go to Cawnpore or not,' another lady suggested.

'A military garrison is not run on popular

opinion,' the colonel said.

'Colonel Smith, we have the right to a voice!' Mrs Grant said truculently. 'Tell him, Arthur!'

Her husband, thus addressed, tugged furiously at his mutton-chop whiskers and said, at last:

'Sir, I think it might be wise to leave a skeleton force here, in order to provide some security for our native population. Should that be your final decision then I would volunteer to remain behind.'

'Your offer is noted.' Colonel Smith's voice was icy. 'In any event we shall delay our leaving now until just before dawn. Ladies! Gentlemen!'

He stepped down from the dais and stalked out, followed by four of his officers.

A babble of question and comment broke out in his absence.

Above the tumult Adam's voice sounded decisively.

'Mr Patel, I understand you have prepared refreshments for those who are here?'

'Yes indeed, Captain Channing,' Mr Patel assured him.

'Then I suggest we partake of them now before those who are leaving gather up whatever they intend to carry with them.'

'At once!'

Waiters began circulating with sandwiches and coffee.

Roger, a slightly fixed smile on his face, had reached Melody's side.

'You will, of course,' he said, 'go with the other ladies to Cawnpore.'

'Excuse me but I'll do what seems best when the moment arrives!' Melody said sharply. That he should make plans for her struck her as presumptuous.

'I am thinking of your safety,' he said. 'In my opinion the colonel will insist that all the ladies travel to Cawnpore and to wait until near dawn may prove too risky.'

'Yes, of course.' For a moment her indignation wavered and she looked up at him pleadingly. 'I do understand there are more urgent matters to attend to than my personal wishes. I will of course go along with whatever is decided. But, Roger, this whole sorry mess began because you amused yourself by trifling with my feelings. And I was stupid enough to compound the error by coming out here in Mary's place. Can we not now end this with some dignity and tell everybody that we have decided, by mutual consent, not to marry?'

'My dear Melody!' His tone had chilled and for the first time she sensed real impatience and dislike in his feelings towards her.

'I am not,' she said stiffly, 'your dear Melody or your dear anything else.'

'At this moment,' he retorted, 'we are in a situation of the utmost peril. Personal affairs must be laid aside. Surely even you can understand that!'

'What I do understand,' Melody said, low and bitter, 'is that ever since my arrival here we have been living a lie.'

Her voice was low and vehement, her face pale with suppressed emotion. Roger had taken a step back, automatically straightening himself as if he was on parade. When he spoke each word was a little chip of ice.

'You will go to Cawnpore or wherever is decided upon,' he said. 'That is obviously the best place for the women and children to be. In that at least you will oblige me.'

Then with a slight inclination of his head he walked away.

Melody stood, fighting back her anger. In one way Roger was right, she acknowledged. What was happening here transcended private concerns. On the other hand she knew that, from the beginning, Roger's concern had been only to protect his own position.

'Are you all right, my dear?'

Mrs Grant had come to her side, her face full of kindly concern.

'I am a great coward, I fear,' Melody said with assured lightness.

'Oh, when the moment comes you will rise to it magnificently,' the older woman assured her.

'The colonel is returning!' One of the other women made the announcement in a fluttering voice.

He stalked in, jaw set, flanked by his senior officers.

'It has been decided,' he said without preamble, his clipped tones falling like small pebbles into the sudden silence, 'that four officers will remain in Parakesh with a detachment of loyal sepoys to provide protection from any attack from the rebels or from any traitors among the native population. Grant, Osborn, Greenacre and Trenton will remain. The rest, including the women and children, will leave under cover of darkness for Cawnpore. Captain Hallett, you will remain here to oversee the preliminary defence measures and then follow on. We will leave in an hour. Ladies are requested to limit their luggage to one bag each.'

A fluttering of skirts and a hum of voices succeeded his words.

'And there's a fine example of administrative muddle,' Adam said, coming over to where Melody stood. 'Four officers and one detachment of sepoys to hold Parakesh! Not sufficient to make the least difference but sufficient to incite the rebels to attack anyway! And the ladies are to be permitted to take luggage as if this was a holiday jaunt. It will slow everything down.'

'What will you be doing?' Melody ventured to enquire.

'I have leave to go to my own house and then follow on,' he said. 'I have a pressing private matter to attend to.'

'Meera?' she could not avoid asking.

'Meera, yes.' For an instant his dark eyes glowed with some emotion held firmly in check.

Before she could frame another question Mrs Grant billowed up.

'The colonel need not imagine that I will travel tamely to Cawnpore,' she said firmly. 'My sister and I will both stay here with our husbands. We have some nursing experience and will be able to make ourselves useful should the worst come to the worst. The colonel will have to hogtie me before I stir a foot!'

'I pity the colonel if he tries to argue with you, ma'am,' Adam said.

'Shall I too stay?' Melody began but was cut short by Mrs Grant's interruption.

'My dear, your fiancé would never hear of

it! He wants you safe at Cawnpore with the rest.

'What do you think?' Melody asked Adam.

'It isn't my place to advise you,' he said formally. 'However, if everyone bound for Cawnpore comes up with an excuse to remain the colonel may end up going off alone!'

'Captain Channing, what you say hits near the literal truth,' Mrs Grant said, slightly embarrassed. 'We are all, civilians and military, under orders now! I shall ask the colonel for permission to remain behind with my sister. If that permission is not granted we will leave for Cawnpore as ordered.'

'That,' said Adam, looking after her thoughtfully, 'is a formidable lady!'

'Yes.'

Melody looked at him, waiting for him to say something further but he only bowed slightly and walked away, leaving her to wonder if she would ever see him again.

15

The colonel had stipulated one bag for each lady. In her room again Melody looked about her, seeing the dress she had decided to wear to her wedding and the veil she had bought. They mocked her high hopes as she contemplated then.

She would dress warmly, she decided, in dark colours that wouldn't attract attention should they meet rebels along the way. The Indian citizens were being advised to remain in the hotel. Suddenly she thought of Lalika. Had Roger made any provision for the safety of the girl to whom he had promised marriage? Somehow she doubted it.

A few minutes later, drably clad, she went quietly down the stairs, threaded her way through the ladies and children assembling in the hotel foyer and let herself out quietly by the side door.

Outside, the watchtowers were dimly lit by flickering lanterns and she could discern the dark shapes of the guards and hear the occasional mutter of voices. She hesitated, then walked, swift and silent, in her low-heeled sandals, to the narrow passage which brought her into the area where the married quarters had been erected. Married quarters, she reflected wryly, that she had once hoped to occupy.

There were lamps burning behind the lattices of many of the bungalows when she entered the road. Those bound soon for Cawnpore were packing the one bag allowed them and no doubt wishing they could wake up and find it all a bad dream.

She reached the bungalow where she had first seen the red scarf with its tracery of golden butterflies and hesitated. It was possible that Roger had slipped out to ensure the safety of his Indian mistress but even as she hesitated the front door opened and Lalika stood on the step, shielding the flare of the candle she held behind one slender brown hand.

'Please!' The other girl's voice was an urgent whisper. 'Please not to be angry! I return now to my family.'

'Wait a minute!'

Melody went swiftly up the short path and hesitated there.

'You wish to enter. Nothing has been taken,' Lalika began.

'I'm sure it has not,' Melody said soothingly. 'I came to see if adequate arrangements had been made by Captain

Hallett for your safety.'

'I have not seen him,' Lalika said sadly, moving aside to allow Melody to enter the hall.

'Not at all?'

'Not at all,' Lalika said. 'I must return to my family, I believe. They live in a small village only a few miles away. Not far to walk.'

'Will they welcome you?' Melody asked doubtfully.

'Yes, but since he has never paid a bride-price they will be disappointed. They will feel my shame,' the girl said. 'I will explain to them that he has many duties.'

'He wished you to have this,' Melody said, slipping the half-hoop of diamonds off her finger. 'It is his farewell gift to you and your family.'

'It is your jewel — ' Lalika began.

'To be kept for you,' Melody said. 'With the sale of this ring you will be able to give your family many comforts.'

'And be welcomed back with honour,' Lalika said. 'It does not help the loss of love but my people will be glad.'

'Will you be safe going home alone?' Melody asked as the girl reached for a heavy shawl.

'As safe as a white bird in the woods when the serpents sleep,' Lalika said. 'Thank you,

271

memsahib. Thank you!'

She picked up a small bag in which she had obviously packed her few possessions and went past Melody with a small but gracious inclination of her head.

She had, Melody thought, more dignity than Roger Hallett for all his posturing had ever shown. As for the pretty little bungalow where she had once hoped to begin her married life her only wish was that she need never enter it again!

She turned and walked quickly back to the walled enclosure of the main compound.

In the square itself a motley collection of vehicles ranging from canopied palanquins to carts and an ancient sedan chair had been assembled.

Melody went up the stairs to collect the one bag the ladies had been allowed and came down again to where people were bunching into groups, the excitement of starting out muted by the realization that they were almost certainly in great danger.

She moved out into the square again and looked up at the dark bowl of the sky which was unrelieved by either moon or visible star. Lanterns hanging from the sides of the palanquins and fixed to the few shabby carriages that had been drawn up scarcely dented the stygian gloom.

Mrs Grant, followed by her sister, was climbing up loudly and protestingly into one of the few carriages, accompanied by an equally reluctant Mrs Greenacre.

'If my husband had not insisted we were under military orders,' she was saying, 'I never would have agreed to desert the compound!'

'Miss Craven, let me help you up!'

Lieutenant Barry Greenacre was assisting her into one of the shabby carriages where Mrs Grant had been installed with her sister and Chloe Greenacre.

'God grant we meet again,' Mrs Greenacre said softly, her eyes on her husband.

'We will,' he answered staunchly, touching her hand briefly. 'We all will!'

Mules were drawing the carriage; the horses, Melody supposed, had been requisitioned for the military and the sowars considered to be loyal.

Their vehicle was at the tail end of the string that stretched ahead, vanishing into the darkness. Here and there she caught the faint glint of a lantern. As they moved onward, slowly and creakingly, she heard a wailing sound that rose and fell like the waves of the sea.

'Our native people think we are deserting them,' Mrs Grant said. 'Captain Channing was quite correct you know — either all stay or all leave. This exodus sets a very bad example, for how can they trust in British protection in the future?'

They had negotiated the bridge beneath which the river was no more than a swamp of drying mud and were proceeding slowly over the grasslands. The creaking of wheels and the flapping of the canopies on the palanquins mingled with the wind.

At least they had a vehicle to ride in, Melody thought. The wives and families of the soldiers were either jolting along on mules or trudging on foot, many with small children across their backs.

Mrs Grant leaned out towards one.

'Mrs Phillips, give Olive to me. You cannot carry her, and your bag together.'

'Are you sure there is room?' The young woman turned a pale, careworn face up to the carriage.

'Always room for a little one!' Mrs Trenton said sweetly, holding out her arms for the small girl, her mother gladly relinquishing her extra burden.

Melody, making room for the new occupant, leaned her head on her hand and closed her eyes, feeling slumber gaining on her. She needed time to think, to sort out the jumbled impressions in her weary mind, to remind herself that she too had been at fault in not warning Roger that she and not Mary would be coming to Parakesh. All she could recall clearly, however, was the tall figure of Adam Channing walking away with his fellow officers across the hall of the hotel.

He had set out for his home to make sure his Meera was protected. That was as it should be, Roger, by contrast, had deserted Lalika entirely, leaving her without even the brideprice that would have raised her in the esteem of her family.

She must have slept a little for she seemed to be back in the parlour where, by some odd twist of dreaming fancy, she could see Aunt Laura bent over the evening newspaper while Uncle Frederick laboured over a sampler he was embroidering!

She woke, amusement bubbling up in her, and was suddenly painfully back in the real world as cramp shot up her arm.

'Let me hold Olive on my knee,' Mrs Grant was saying.

'Why cannot I go with Mama?' the child piped up.

'Your mama has a heavy bag to carry,' Mrs Trenton soothed. 'She is only just ahead of us. You will see her very soon but she cannot carry you and the bag.'

'I can walk,' Olive insisted manfully. 'I've been walking for years and years!'

'Can you tell how far we have already come?' Melody whispered to Mrs Grant.

'Not in this darkness, my dear.' The older woman was peering at her fob watch. 'Six or seven miles possibly? I really cannot say!'

Chloe Greenacre, starting up suddenly from a doze, said in a low, urgent voice,

'Surely we cannot be too far distant from Cawnpore? I can see lights ahead.'

'A reflection from those with lanterns?' Mrs Trenton suggested.

The man leading the mules as they pulled the ramshackle carriage ahead turned as Mrs Grant leaned forward to tap him on the shoulder with her closed parasol.

'Those lights ahead,' she enquired. 'Are we near Cawnpore?'

He opened his mouth to reply and was silenced before uttering a word by a loud screaming sound ahead of them that rose and fell in a broken cacophony of hatred and revenge.

'Dear Lord!' Mrs Trenton said under her breath.

'Dervishes, memsahib,' the man leading the mules said. In the darkness his eyes were white-rimmed with terror.

'Fanatics!' Mrs Grant said succinctly. 'If

they have joined the rebels we can expect no mercy.'

'And the lights?' Chloe quavered.

'Ambush,' Mrs Grant said. 'Had they waited they could have encircled us but they were too eager to begin the slaughter. Driver, turn the mules and head back to Parakesh at once!'

'Sister, they will see us,' Mrs Trenton said.

'Not if we douse the lantern and act quickly!'

Already she was climbing down, reaching up for the lantern with its tiny blue flame.

The carriage was being turned, the mules swerving reluctantly with snorts of discontent. Ahead of them the screaming had subsided to fainter cries and then Mrs Grant had clambered back into the vehicle and they were returning into the darkness through which they had already travelled.

'They may not follow even if they realize we have retreated,' Mrs Grant said. 'There is a chance that they will slake their blood lust and remain to celebrate.'

Her voice was firmly controlled and Melody, clinging to Olive as they jerked and bounced over the sea of rustling grass, felt a surge of admiration for the older woman.

'What about Mama?' Olive was imploring. 'Let's go back for Mama!'

'Hold on tightly, love!' Chloe said swiftly.

By now, Melody hoped, Mrs Phillips with the heavy bag and the careworn face was past her pain. The darkness was closing in about them again though with a little imagination it was possible to discern a faint and nebulous greyness in it.

The carriage lurched sudenly to one side.

'Wheel is loose, memsahib!' the driver announced.

'And?'

'It is necessary to walk,' he said stolidly.

'Everything ought to have been more thoroughly checked before we set out,' Mrs Grant said, climbing down again.

'How far have we already come?' Chloe asked, huddling her cloak around her and trying to speak as if this were an ordinary excursion.

'Four miles — five miles, memsahib. Very hard to tell,' the man answered, busy unleashing the mules. 'It is best to go cautiously in case there are already rebels at Parakesh.'

'We can ride the mules,' Melody suggested, scrambling after him.

'No, memsahib.' His tone was polite but regretful. 'The mules I must take to my village. My family is also in danger I fear.'

'Those mules are Army property!' Mrs

Trenton cried. 'You have no right to take them. I could have you shot!'

'Sister, the man has already risked his life by helping us,' Mrs Grant reproached. 'Rather than stand arguing here when the dervishes may already be headed in this direction we ought to take his advice and start walking!'

'A thousand apologies, memsahib, but I dare not come further with you,' the man said. 'I am no soldier but a farmer who offered to help the memsahibs but — '

'Get to your village then,' Mrs Grant said briskly but not unkindly. 'We wish you Godspeed.'

She bent down to hoist Olive up to her shoulder, leaving her sister to carry their two pieces of luggage, and she set off into the diminishing dark, the others straggling after her.

'A few hours will take us back to Parakesh,' Mrs Trenton said, evidently determined to follow her sister when it came to a question of courage. 'You can manage a few miles, can't you, Olive?'

'Yes,' said Olive with a sob, 'but I want Mama!'

'Come!' said Chloe, her voice determinedly bright. 'Let's see if any late stars come out as we walk and we can count them as we go!'

There were no stars but the sky was

becoming greyer as they trudged along. Melody, bringing up the rear, hoped they were going in the right direction.

'Let me take Olive for a while,' she said.

'I am awake!' the child protested, struggling down. 'I am ever so awake now!'

'You're a brave little soldier!' Chloe encouraged her as they plodded on.

Melody's spirits lifted as the faint outline of a dying moon arched over them and in the gathering light she saw, eyes blurred with exhaustion, the outlines of the hill with its surrounding walls and the bridge over the dried-up river bed.

Night always made distances deceptive, Melody thought as they went along, their feet now and then stumbling in the dry grass. Vaguely she wondered if any snakes were around but decided it was probably unlikely.

'My feet hurt!' Olive said plaintively.

'Not far to go now!' Chloe encouraged but over the little girl's head her eyes met Melody's with an expression of the deepest foreboding in them.

'I pray there is a sentry from our own people on the main gates,' Mrs Trenton said.

'The bridge appears to be unguarded,' Mrs Grant said, halting to shield her eyes from the silver of the rising dawn as she stared towards the river.

'We've heard no shots from the compound,' Chloe said in a tone she strove to make cheerful.

'Let us hope that's a good sign,' Mrs Trenton began, then paused abruptly, a frown creasing her pleasant features.

'What is it?' Melody asked.

'The watchtowers are unmanned,' the other said. 'A twenty-four-hour watch is always kept even when there is no threat.'

'And it's too quiet,' Chloe said nervously. 'Perhaps Colonel Smith changed his mind and ordered everybody to evacuate.'

'Colonel Smith never alters his decisions,' Mrs Grant said. 'Ladies, I believe we must enter the compound another way!'

Olive had ceased complaining and came along quietly, her small hand dragging at Chloe's, her feet slipping now and then. Perhaps in some part of herself she had already accepted that her mother must be dead, Melody thought with pity, and wondered how the small girl would react when the truth became evident.

Aloud Melody asked, 'Which way can we now enter?'

'We can scramble down into the bed of the river and climb up the old temple staircase at the far end of the bridge,' Mrs Grant told her. 'If we walk under the bridge our moving figures will not be seen should anyone be watching from the walls. My husband showed it to me once.'

'I had forgotten that,' Mrs Trenton said. 'Olive, my love, you must keep as quiet as a mouse and not make a single sound.'

They edged their way slowly down the steep banks into the mud which had formed curious whorls and patterns, mainly hard and dry but under the bridge where the heat had not penetrated so much the mud was sticky and Melody, putting down her foot, tugged it free with a little squelching sound.

'What about muggers?' Chloe had stopped abruptly.

'Small alligators,' Mrs Trenton said, catching Melody's look of enquiry. 'They live in the mud avoiding the sun. Most eat insects and mice but the bigger ones can group together and attack larger prey.'

'I shall lead the way!' Mrs Grant drew herself up and stepped boldly into the thicker mud under the concealing overhang of the bridge, drawing up each foot with a little squelching sound as she made her way across.

Trying not to imagine what could be lurking beneath, Melody put her arm round Olive and stepped after her. The early sky with its glints of silver was concealed by the bridge overhead as the way across became darker and the mud deeper. There was, however, no sign of snapping jaws or the flick of a scaly tail and they reached the far side in safety.

Round to the side, in the lee of the hill, she could discern steps, crumbling and uneven, set into the earth. They looked, even to her inexperienced eye, exceedingly unsafe.

'Barry told me,' said Chloe, pausing to look up, 'that nobody goes there any longer. The natives say there are bad spirits there.'

'We would climb more safely if we removed our skirts,' Melody suggested.

Even in the near dark it was possible to see the shock on the faces of the two older ladies.

'My dear Melody,' Mrs Grant said, 'one of the reasons we have held India for so long is that we have never permitted our standards to slip. Let us climb slowly and breathe evenly as we go.'

'It would be best for Olive to go first since she is lighter than the rest of us,' Mrs Trenton remarked, 'and she can climb more easily since she is not yet in stays.'

'We climbed the lower slopes of the Himalayas last year,' Mrs Grant said, 'and I do not recall any arguments abut shedding our modesty. Up you go, Olive!'

The hill with its unevenly placed steps was no more than a hundred feet high but it was steep and the stone blocks hammered in centuries before were worn and slippery, a few hanging loose, others tilting sideways.

With her hoops squashed flat against the face of the rock Melody pulled herself up hand over hand, trying not to regret the state her nails would be in if she made it safely to the square building whose entrance yawned blackly above her.

Olive gained the topmost step and wriggled over the threshold followed by Mrs Grant, who turned to help the others up as she herself crouched on firm ground.

They were in an enormous stone chamber, partly open to the sky, its floor littered with slabs of rock and the bones of small animals. High overhead bats swooped and glided, and as they stood up something slithered away into the darkness.

'Let us keep to the outer walls while we make our way to the other entrance,' Mrs Trenton whispered, a whisper the echoes caught and sent rippling round the ancient stone in which, as her eyes became accustomed to the dark, Melody could discern huge effigies carved.

Had she been alone she might well have missed the entrance at the far side since it was no more than a narrow slit between two towering surfaces of stone, barely sufficient to allow even a slightly plump person to pass through.

Her hoops, Melody thought, squashing herself through the opening, would be bent out of shape for ever even if they hadn't actually cracked yet. She closed her mind to what, set against their present situation, was no more than a trifling inconvenience and came out on to one of the watchtowers where only hours before she had seen the shapes of guards and guns.

The guns had gone, though pieces of lead shot lay around. Of human life there was no sign at all. Cautiously she moved to the parapet and looked down into an empty square with dark stains on its paved surface.

Even the two fixed cannon were tumbled on to their sides and not a sound came from the latticed windows in the buildings that circled the main compound.

'Something is very wrong,' Chloe whispered, coming to her side.

'Everywhere seems deserted,' Melody whispered back and then wondered why she was keeping her voice so low when there was nobody below them to hear.

'The rebels may be in the surrounding buildings,' Mrs Trenton suggested, joining them. 'There are Government documents that may be of use to them.'

'Sister, you're talking nonsense!' Mrs Grant said, joining them. 'What fanatical dervish is going to stop and read official documents even if one supposes he could read or understand English anyway? One of us must go down to take a closer look.'

'I'll go,' Melody said quickly. 'I've not carried Olive as the rest of you have. Wait here!'

She herself didn't wait for anyone's permission but started down the stone steps. In her mind was the knowledge that her three companions had left husbands behind here and might find them slaughtered.

Without allowing herself to think that someone might be watching her from one of the surrounding buildings, possibly taking careful aim, she ran, zigzagging across the square, and gained the main door of the hotel which hung crookedly on its hinges.

The main hall was a shambles of smashed tables, chairs and glassware, with the same dark stains everywhere that had disfigured the paving stones of the square. The same stains had splashed up the whitewashed walls and her heightened senses told her that the sickly-sweet scent filling her nostrils was blood.

As she hesitated a figure moved from one of the open doors, throwing a shadow across her.

16

For an instant cold terror held her motionless and then the figure resolved itself into the bloodstained figure of Mr Patel, his face drawn with weariness and apprehension.

'Oh, my goodness, memsahib! You are safe!'

'Mr Patel, what happened here?' Her voice shook as she stared at him.

'Very great trouble and most annoying inconveniences, memsahib,' he said. 'After your leave-taking word was brought by a runner that Cawnpore was already surrounded by most wicked rebels. The officers resolved to ride out to bring back the ones who had left for Cawnpore but I fear they did not succeed.'

'We saw nobody on our way back,' Melody said.

'They planned to detour around but what happened I cannot say,' Mr Patel went on. 'After they had left the rebels came. Silently, memsahib, like hyenas in the night, they crept over the walls, swarmed into the houses. Many were killed in their beds and others fled into the forest.'

'They killed their own people?' Melody whispered.

'Hindus and those of their own faith who had not joined them, memsahib.'

'Your own family?'

She dreaded the answer.

'My daughter received a sabre cut on the shoulder but will live. My wife is quite safe, hiding in the cellar with the rest of my staff. I fear that those living near the bazaar did not fare so well.'

'We heard nothing.'

'There was not much shouting,' Mr Patel said. 'When the watchtowers had been taken the rebels used their sabres. Please, memsahib, it would be wiser not to venture into the bazaar.'

'The guards are all killed? The colonel . . . ?'

'I cannot say. I too took refuge in the cellar.'

'There were rebels waiting ahead of us as we travelled towards Cawnpore,' Melody said.

'Here they took the mules and much of the food,' Mr Patel said. 'Memsahib, this is not the most beautiful of welcomes in your life here!'

'It isn't your fault, Mr Patel.'

'That's very kind of you, memsahib.' He bowed with something of his usual formal courtesy.

'I have Mrs Grant, Mrs Trenton, Mrs Greenacre and one of the children across the square,' Melody said, pressing her fingers to her temples as she tried to marshal her thoughts. 'We came up by the steps near the old temple. They will need food, water and shelter.'

'I shall escort them here directly,' Mr Patel said.

'Have you word of Lieutenant Greenacre and the others?' she ventured.

He shook his head.

'I have to change my dress,' Melody said.

'Your shoes also, memsahib!'

Apparently noticing them for the first time he looked as shocked as if she stood there in her drawers.

'Yes,' she said, feeling a bubble of slightly hysterical laughter rise up in her. 'Yes, of course.'

Then she was climbing the stairs, each step a burden, going into her room where sheets and towels and most of her clothes were tumbled about, many with sabre slashes in them as if the rebels, finding no person there, had wreaked their anger on her petticoats.

One plain blue dress had escaped destruction. She pulled off her clothes, donned the blue dress over a small undamaged hoop at the back of the wardrobe, pushed her feet into a pair of low-heeled sandals and seized a length of ribbon to tie back her sweat-soaked hair.

Then she hurried down the stairs again and through the side door which swung now on its hinges and was scarred with deep cuts. As she passed through she could hear Mr Patel's voice just outside in the square.

'All will soon be made most comfortable for you, ladies!'

She stepped out into the narrow passage and, trying not to think of what she might see, walked towards the married quarters.

There were bodies lying in the road, one headless, the other sprawled in a pool of drying blood outside one of the bungalows.

Above in the early morning sky a carrion crow circled slowly.

Melody averted her gaze and walked on steadily.

She had reached the bungalow where she once — how long ago it now seemed — had hoped to live. The front door stood half-open and, without giving herself time to think, she went up the short path and pushed the door wider. She stepped into the hall. Within, the wickerwork chairs had been flung aside and a vase lay shattered on the floor.

Beneath the closed door of the inner room a line of light glowed yellow. Melody avoided the broken shards of glass and opened the door.

They had died together, Lalika throwing herself across Roger in what had clearly been a final, futile attempt to save him. His sword lay on the floor next to the bed and his hand was curled about a lock of his lover's dark hair.

He had deserted his post then, she thought without emotion, had gone to his quarters and coaxed Lalika into remaining with him. The tumbled bedclothes and the splashes of red up the walls told their own story.

A lamp still burned on a side table and someone had flung a red scarf thick with golden butterflies across Lalika's blood-stained back.

Melody stood looking at them, past anger or grief. Had Roger gone at the last moment to help Lalika or had he merely left his post for the sake of an hour's dalliance? It made no matter. At the last he had come to the girl whom he might have loved had he been capable of loving. The half-hoop of diamonds had vanished from the girl's slender finger. Taken by the killers, she supposed, and felt suddenly wary to the marrow of her bones.

'Memsahib?'

A red turbanned figure stepped into the room.

291

Frozen, she stared at him, her eyes blank with terror.

'Memsahib Craven, don't you remember me?'

He took another step forward, lowering his drawn sabre.

'Ram Singh!' Suddenly recognizing the guide she gasped with relief.

'There is brandy here! You need to drink.'

He took her arm firmly, guiding her to one of the few chairs left upright.

Her teeth chattered against the neck of the bottle as the fiery liquid went down her throat.

'I came too late,' he said soberly. 'Much slaughter had already been done. The soldiers had ridden out towards Cawnpore.'

'In the hope of catching up with those already bound there,' Melody said, choking a little as she pushed the bottle aside.

'Too many went,' Ram Singh said. 'Few were left on the watchtowers. They hoped, I think, to make a diversion but others had the same plan and they were ambushed.'

'Our party too,' Melody said flatly. 'We were at the back of the line and heard the dervish yells and so turned back.'

'We?' He looked at her questioningly.

'Mrs Wilson died before the real massacres began.'

'I am indeed sorry to hear it. She was a most excellent lady.'

'Three other ladies and a small girl were in the carriage with me,' Melody explained. 'We were the last vehicle but the wheel was loose and then we heard the yelling and the screaming ahead and turned back, but the driver took his mules and went off to his own village so we walked back here. It was all over when we arrived.'

'You were trapped between two massacres,' he said soberly. 'There is an evil spirit abroad in India today, memsahib!'

'All because some stupid official in London ordered the cartridges greased with animal fat!'

'And would not rescind the order. But there is more than that to these events! It serves as the excuse for Moslem to attack Hindu and Sikh, for those with private quarrels to settle them with a bullet or a sabre slash, for many to seek the opportunity to rid the land of its British masters! Revolution has many heads.'

'Why are you here?' Melody asked.

'Captain Channing asked me to come here to ascertain what had happened,' he said.

'Adam? He left Parakesh yesterday.'

Had it really been such a brief time before?

'I met him in the forest. He asked me for

word of rebel movements and I told him that Cawnpore was already surrounded.'

Adam, then, had been alive the previous night — but so had many others!

Ram Singh was continuing, unaware of the thoughts jostling in her head.

'He told me to go to Parakesh to warn them that the rebels were at Cawnpore but I arrived too late. I don't know how many survived. The bazaar is littered with bodies — my own people but not, praise be, any of my family. Another runner was sent by Captain Channing to turn back the travellers on their way to Cawnpore — '

'We were ambushed,' Melody said.

'He arrived too late, then,' Ram Singh said.

'And Captain Channing?' She hardly dared ask the question.

'He rode to his house, I suppose, to take care of Meera,' Ram Singh told her. 'She is, after all his most precious possession.'

'Captain Channing has no . . . daughters, I suppose?'

'He has never been married,' Ram Singh said, looking slightly surprised. 'But, mem-sahib, your own hopes and wishes . . . ' He had paused, obviously embarrassed, looking at the two stiffening bodies on the floor.

'Captain Hallett was not the man I believed him to be,' she said shortly.

Later on she might find tears for buried hopes and dreams but now shock had numbed her emotions and she watched with a curious indifference as he took some sheets from the bed and covered the remains decently. When he turned to her again his voice had a fresh urgency.

'Memsahib, there is a possibility the rebels will fall back here when reinforcements reach Cawnpore. It is better for those few remaining to be gone from the compound.'

'But where?' She looked up at him helplessly. 'Where is safe now? Where should I run?'

'Some memsahibs are donning Indian dress and hiding among the native population,' he said.

'What good will that do when Indian is killing Indian?'

'There is madness abroad,' he said gravely. 'Best hide until it has passed.'

'Dressed as an Indian! Do I look like an Indian?'

'Some of the hill tribes are fair skinned but not yellow-haired or blue-eyed,' he admitted.

'Then I must take my chances,' she said wearily.

'I believe some in the compound hid in the cellars of the hotel,' Ram Singh said. 'I did not stay to enquire.'

'The Patels and their staff are safe,' she told him.

'So there are still those left alive in Parakesh,' he said.

The rebels, she thought, had been clever, splitting into two groups, one to circle around and attack those evacuating, the others to wait until most of the soldiers had gone, when they had swarmed in to kill and kill again.

'You look weary, memsahib,' he said.

'To the bone!' Melody tried to smile. 'I need several hours' sleep.'

'I will try to find Captain Channing,' Ram Singh decided. 'I think that later this day the rebels may return to occupy Parakesh. It would be well for you and the others to be away by then.'

'Away where?' she asked.

'The one place completely safe would be Captain Channing's house.'

'Why?'

'Because Meera is there,' he said and volunteered no further explanation.

Life, she thought, pulling herself to her feet again, had assumed the quality of a grotesque nightmare. She averted her eyes from the sheeted shapes on the floor and went out into the street again.

'Do not venture further here, memsahib,' Ram Singh said from the doorway. 'Go to the hotel. I will try to send word to Captain Channing — '

He broke off in mid sentence and Melody swung about in panic.

Coming from the direction of the bazaar two uniformed figures, their uniforms sadly the worse for wear, limped towards her.

'Sergeant Grant, ma'am!' The bulkier of the two saluted her smartly. 'Sergeant Trenton has a broken arm.'

'But you are both safe!' Melody exclaimed.

'Defended the watchtowers as long as we could and then managed to get away. Wholesale slaughter by then, Miss Craven.'

'Why are you . . . ?' Melody began to ask.

'When the devils attacked, ma'am, we fought them off as best we could but in the end they were swarming everywhere,' he said wearily. 'The colonel told us to break ranks and abandon camp. We marched most of the night. Found the evacuation column — dreadful slaughter — '

He broke off abruptly, the muscles of his jaw working.

'Both your wives are safe,' Melody said quickly. 'Both quite unharmed. We turned back and came into Parakesh by way of an old temple.'

'And now?' He looked towards the bungalow.

'Captain Hallett is dead,' she said steadily. 'Ram Singh returned here to see exactly what had occurred. There are people unharmed in the hotel but no military. The colonel . . . ?'

'Rode off to obtain further instructions,' Sergeant Trenton said. 'In my opinion he ought to be court-martialled when this is all over but he probably won't be.'

'I go to seek Captain Channing,' Ram Singh said. 'Memsahib, you must get back to the hotel.'

'Yes. Yes, I am going directly,' she promised.

Hotel, compound, bazaar — it made no difference. At that moment she wished herself most fervently back in England again.

She nodded briefly to Ram Singh, shook her head slightly since she had no adequate reply to Sergeant Grant's murmured condolences on the death of her fiancé and went ahead of the exhausted soldiers towards the main compound again.

From a bungalow at the end of the street a dishevelled figure, sari fluttering in the hot wind, came towards her, hands outstretched pleadingly.

'Olive?' She came towards Melody. 'Please, memsahib, I am ayah to Olive but there was not room for me when all left.'

'Olive is safe. Come with me!' Melody put

her arm around the woman and urged her into the passageway that led to the main compound.

'The mother of Olive? She also is safe?' the woman asked.

Melody shook her head wordlessly and the ayah began to weep afresh.

Overhead the sun was now high and hot, the bloodstains on the paving stones dark and dry.

'Melody! Are you all right?' Forgetting formality for once Mrs Grant hurried down the steps of the hotel.

'Perfectly all right,' Melody told her. 'Roger — Captain Hallett is dead.'

'My dear!'

'Killed apparently defending one of the natives,' Melody said. Such a report would give some consolation to his parents she supposed, even though he had never been a satisfactory son.

'I am very sorry,' Mrs Grant said.

'This is Olive's ayah.'

'Yes, of course! I recognize her now. Olive will find comfort with her now that she begins to realize fully that her mother is dead.'

'I go to her at once,' the Indian woman said, drying her tears and smoothing down her veil.

'Our ayahs are always devoted to their charges,' Mrs Grant said, and broke off suddenly, her eyes riveted to the two figures just limping into the square.

'Your husband and brother-in-law,' Melody said, glad of the chance to give happy news, 'are alive and only slightly hurt!'

'Sister!' Mrs Grant turned to shout but Mrs Trenton was already hurrying towards them, her face looking positively pretty.

Mrs Grant had checked herself and now deliberately smoothed down her dusty skirt and composed her features before she went more sedately to greet her husband.

'Well, Arthur!' Her voice rang out. 'You managed to do your duty and survive! Brother-in-law, I am glad to see you too are not seriously hurt. Sister, if you cling about him like that you will further damage his arm! Let us retain some dignity before our native people!'

Since the only native in sight was a bowing if somewhat flustered Mr Patel her remark struck Melody as intolerably funny. She found herself beginning to laugh but her laughter caught in her throat and suddenly she was seated on the hotel steps, weeping bitterly.

'What has happened?' Chloe Greenacre had run out through the main door.

'Captain Hallett is dead,' Mrs Trenton said.

'Oh, I am so very sorry!' Chloe paused, sudden anxiety in her face. 'Sergeant Grant, have you any word of my Barry?'

There was a horrible little silence. Then Sergeant Grant said heavily:

'My condolences, my dear, but I saw him go down in the first assault on the watchtowers.'

Chloe's already pale face had whitened into snow and her eyes were dilated with shock and horror. In a small disbelieving voice she said:

'It's not true. Please tell me it's not true. Please?'

Mrs Trenton put a comforting arm around the girl's shoulders and Mrs Grant chafed her hands between her own but it was clear that Chloe felt nothing, heard nothing, saw nothing but the loss of her young husband.

Melody turned and went up the steps into the hotel where several of the staff were busily clearing up the mess of broken glass and tipped-up chairs. Hardly knowing what she did Melody climbed the stairs and returned to her own room.

There was a tap on the door and Mrs Grant came in, her face drawn with tiredness.

'They had been married scarcely a year,' she said. 'Such a bright and promising young couple! This is a terrible time.'

'Yes,' Melody said dully.

'And Captain Hallett?'

'We had decided to break off the engagement,' Melody said.

'You discovered certain facts?' The tone was gently probing.

Melody nodded.

'There were always rumours,' Mrs Grant said. 'One tries not to give them credence. You are not wearing your ring.'

'It never felt like mine in the first place,' Melody said.

One day, if they survived, she would tell Mrs Grant the whole sorry tale, but for the moment she wanted only to forget.

'You must get some sleep,' Mrs Grant said, patting her shoulder. 'There is the night to get through. I wish Captain Channing was here. He is always a tower of strength with a cool head in an emergency.'

'Yes,' Melody said.

'And Ram Singh, the guide, is in the compound? He is loyal. There are many who are still loyal.'

But Ram Singh was only one man and there had been no word from Adam Channing.

'There is to be a meeting at dusk,' Mrs Grant said, patting her shoulder again.

'Another meeting? What good can it do?'

'My dear, Mr Patel and his staff escaped the carnage by hiding in the cellar. The rebels in their bloodlust never thought of there being cellars. There must still be people hiding in the bazaar. It must be decided where we are to go,' Mrs Grant said.

'You really think they will return here?'

'I know they will.' The older women spoke with a sad certainly. 'The water in the wells is very low because the rains are late but what water there is remains fresh and pure. Had they meant to abandon Parakesh for good they would have poisoned the wells. That they have not makes it certain they will return. Get what sleep you can, my dear, for there's a long night ahead.'

17

She hadn't expected to do more than snatch
a brief doze but once on her bed Melody fell
into a deep, exhausted sleep. The heat of the
sun piercing the damaged lattice, the sounds
of grief that drifted faintly from the direction
of the bazaar where those who had survived
the terror had ventured out to seek their
friends and relatives, didn't impinge on her
sleeping mind.

She woke to a brisk tapping on her door
and to Mrs Trenton's voice.

'My dear, dusk has come! Mr Patel is
preparing what refreshments he can find. Are
you able to rouse yourself to come down?'

'Yes, of course!'

Melody sat up somewhat dizzily, pushing
her hair out of her eyes.

'How is Chloe Greenacre?' she asked as she
began to put on her shoes.

'Heartbroken,' Mrs Trenton said sombrely,
and went out quietly.

But at least she had been loved, had known
the satisfactions of love, Melody reflected
sadly as she donned a plain dark dress and
sponged her face and hands with the small

amount of water remaining in the ewer.

She went downstairs to find the remnants of the community gathered round a series of small tables on which Mr Patel had placed pots of tea and, by some magic known only to himself, sandwiches of bread and sardines.

Chloe sat alone, encircled by her quiet despairing grief. It was clear that she was not yet ready to accept comfort. Sergeant Trenton, his broken arm in a sling, sat with his wife, and Mrs Grant, while seeking obviously to remain calm and cool, could not resist pausing now and then as she moved from table to table to send an almost maternal smile in her own husband's direction.

Olive sat on her ayah's knee. She had obviously been crying but now she clung to the Indian woman who fed her bits of bread and fish and murmured to her soothingly from time to time.

'Ladies and gentlemen! If you please?' Mr Patel clapped his hands commandingly.

Faces turned towards him. Ram Singh rose, his face impassive under his turban.

'I am of the opinion,' he said, 'that we must all leave as soon as possible.'

'And go where?' Mrs Grant asked.

'To the house of Captain Channing,' he responded promptly.

'But we've had no word from him,' someone objected. 'We don't even know if he is still alive.'

'If anyone remains alive after these present troubles I would wager on Adam Channing,' said Sergeant Grant.

'There has been no word,' his wife objected.

'He is hardly going to sit at his ease and write a letter, sister!' Mrs Trenton said.

'And he may have no way of knowing whether any here remain alive,' someone else said.

'If I may speak?' Ram Singh rose from his chair.

'Ram Singh?' Mr Patel waved his hand and bowed slightly.

'When rumour reached me of the attack on Parakesh I hastened here as quickly as I could, going first to the bazaar. The slaughter there has indeed been great but there are survivors who have been mourning their dead. Here, in the compound itself, with the watchtowers seized and those who were killed flung into the bazaar with the rest it seemed to me that no more evil remained to be done, but there are survivors and by now the rebels will have learned of them and will return to finish the business they began. I am almost certain they will return later tonight and before that all those remaining here must be gone towards Captain Channing's house. Whether he be alive or dead — and I firmly believe he is alive — his property is always strictly guarded, almost like a fortress. The mules and horses have been taken and it will be wiser to take a roundabout route to his property but I take it to be our only chance.'

When he had finished speaking there was a troubled silence and then a babble of voices.

'Forgive me,' one woman said, 'but Ram Singh is a guide not an official spokesman.'

'You are right,' Ram Singh answered. 'I also follow the faith of Islam and neither eat nor touch pork but while I would die for my faith I would not kill for it nor betray others of many different opinions to their enemies.'

'As we are officially under military discipline,' Sergeant Grant said, rising heavily to his feet, 'I am convinced that we must all leave and that Ram Singh be named as our official guide.'

'My husband,' Mrs Grant murmured audibly, 'always speaks good sense.'

'In that case,' Ram Singh continued, 'I ask that all be ready to leave in half an hour.'

There were general murmurs of agreement.

'Let us pack up what food remains and carry what water we can,' Mr Patel said.

Melody, having already put the few

personal possessions she cherished into a small bag, went upstairs to don a dark cloak and hood. The possibility of all of them reaching Adam Channing's property in safety struck her as uncertain, but at least Ram Singh was a reliable guide.

Outside, the darkness of evening was lit by flames that sprang higher and waved like banners of orange, scarlet and gold in the wind.

Without pausing to look further through the broken lattice Melody grabbed her bag and hastened downstairs.

'Ram Singh!' She touched his sleeve urgently, lowering her voice. 'I believe the rebels are here already and beginning to fire the compound!'

'The people are burning their dead,' he answered sombrely. 'It is customary with them but it may well attract attention elsewhere, memsahib. We leave now.'

He nodded towards Sergeant Grant who was marshalling the twenty or so survivors in the hotel into a column.

'Others will join us when their funeral rites are complete,' Ram Singh said. 'We must rely on them to catch us up. Come, memsahib!'

She was being guided into the column which already presented a somewhat motley crew with Olive clinging to her ayah, Mr Patel chivvying his family into line, others drifting in to join the exodus. Among them Chloe Greenacre seemed to move alone, wrapped in her own silent grief which, Melody decided, was best left for the moment without any offers of unwanted consolation.

They walked across the square and through the main gates, past the passage that gave on to the bazaar, behind the walls of which the funeral pyres were still crackling, past the narrow opening that led to the designated married quarters and the guardhouse where she had read the letter from her uncle and learnt the full extent of Roger's falsehoods.

Those joining them as they left their dead to burn had covered their heads and walked slowly as if reluctant to desert the ones they had loved and lost.

'I had all my muslins washed and starched last week,' Mrs Trenton said wistfully.

Melody felt a pang of conscience. She had hardly realized that for women who lived in the married quarters evacuating meant leaving their homes to the destruction that would certainly follow when the rebels arrived.

Mr Patel, an arm about his daughter, whose head had been carefully bandaged, spoke with determined optimism.

'The stone buildings will survive and the

rest can be rebuilt when the rebellion is over. We British do not allow a small mutiny to discompose us, goodness me, no!'

'We must gain the shelter of the trees as quickly as possible,' Ram Singh was saying. 'Here on the open plain they can pick us off one by one.'

The moon had risen, brightening as it rose, painting the yellow grass silvery white, outlining the shapes of those who made their way across it. Progress was slow — too slow, Melody thought, with a little clutch of fear at her heartstrings, but in places the grasslands dipped into steep slopes littered with the rocks and shingle she recalled from her first journey to what had been expected to be her future home, and then the men had to help the women down.

'We will rest here for a very short while,' Ram Singh said as they descended another slippery incline.

With both relief and trepidation the column broke up into smaller groups. Water was handed round to be sipped, the ayah coaxed Olive into eating some biscuits she had brought.

Melody thought almost longingly of the palanquin in which she had previously travelled. It had struck her as an uncomfortable mode of transport with its flapping covers and swaying rhythm but she would have given much to be riding in one now. Even the rickety carriage in which they had essayed their first attempt at escape shone in her memory as brightly as a state coach!

She moved a little apart from the others, finding a flat rock on which to sit, wishing for the umpteenth time that the removing of one's stays and rigidly hooped petticoats would not, as the other ladies appeared to think, disgrace the entire British Empire, when a slight sound, the scrape of a boot against stone, the long inward breath of someone pausing for rest, caught her attention.

Ram Singh had risen, finger to his lips, his other hand near his belted tunic where a pistol gleamed blackly.

A figure was approaching them, featureless in the moonlight, stumbling a little but holding itself upright in military fashion.

Among the now silent and motionless watchers one had risen to her feet, uttering a half-choked cry before, evading Ram Singh's restraining hand, she rushed forward to fling herself upon the advancing figure.

'Barry? Barry! You're alive! You're alive!'

She was laughing and crying at the same time, pumelling him with her shall fists. For that brief moment Chloe Greenacre had lost all sense of decorum.

311

The rest were crowding round as Lieutenant Greenacre sank down wearily on a large flat stone, half-embracing and half-restraining his wife while he spoke in the dull tones of one almost past exhaustion.

'I went down in the first attack on the watch tower, knocked out by some idiot's rifle butt. Then all hell broke loose. The sepoys were firing at random, slashing with their sabres. Someone pulled me out of the pile of wounded and then I was being force-marched along. I saw the flames in the bazaar and then the killing began again. Someone — a sowar — Lord knows who! — hit me over the head and I went down. I was half-stunned but I had the sense to wait, hearing the cries and the yells and the screaming all about me. I must have passed out then because when I came round the noises had stopped. I was covered in blood, not my blood but — well, no matter! I stayed where I was, even slept a while, and then I started back to the compound but it was deserted, so I decided to make for Channing's house. That's how I found you.'

'I would say Lieutenant Greenacre has a slight concussion,' Mrs Grant said in her best professional manner. 'Rest and quiet are the remedies.'

'Not until we reach Channing's property,'

312

her husband contradicted. 'We cannot run the risk of running into those murdering devils again.'

'Ladies present, sir!' Mr Patel rebuked.

'We ought to continue on our way,' Ram Singh advised. 'When the moon is full out we shall make fine targets for any lurking rebel.'

Wearily the group, with Chloe still trembling with excited joy, began to pick themselves and their bags up and reform the straggling column as it moved into the shadow of the trees. Melody, stumbling along, tried not to imagine as they penetrated the forest what dangers might lie in wait. It was fruitless anyway. She could only follow the rest and hope there would be some joy at the end of the trek. Such joy as Chloe was feeling was not, she thought sadly, likely to be her lot.

'Memsahib?'

Ram Singh had drawn level with her and now spoke in a whisper. Even though the moon glinted only fitfully through the branches of the trees the gravity of his face was apparent.

'Yes?' She answered him in the same whisper.

'I have only one bullet left,' he murmured. 'If we are set upon for whom shall the bullet be?'

Melody's eyes dilated as she took his meaning. Then she said in a voice that scarcely rose above a breath:

'In the last resort — the child, I think.'

'I think so too. Let us pray, memsahib, that it will not come to a last resort,' he said quietly and moved away from her side.

They plodded on through the undergrowth, the branches of the trees bending above them. Not a soul spoke but the soft crunching of the twigs and leaves underfoot could, she feared, be heard at some distance and in the confusion of darkness she heard, or hoped she imagined she heard, the treading of other feet, the listening of other ears.

'Ram Singh!' Mrs Grant had stepped to his side. 'We need to rest for a little while. The ayah insists upon carrying Olive but the poor woman is near exhausted and Lieutenant Greenacre needs an hour's respite.

'We will separate into ones and twos.' Ram Singh nodded. 'All together might not be wise — you understand my meaning?'

As Mrs Grant nodded Melody thought with an inward shiver, 'If we are all bunched together we provide sitting targets for any rebels who might be in the forest.'

The decision was passed in whispers to the rest, Mr Patel gravely shepherding people in twos and threes to the tiny glades between the trees.

Melody moved away quietly, pushing her way through a screen of long splayed branches thick with leaves until she found a comparatively clear patch of long grass where she could sit and lean her head against the trunk of an arching tree. How long they could dare to remain she had no notion and was suddenly too exhausted to trouble her mind about it. Instead she leaned with as much confidence as she could muster against the rough bark, forbade her thoughts to wander in the direction of snakes possibly curled in the upper branches and slept without even being conscious of her descent into slumber.

The sound that woke her was no louder than the creaking of a twig among the rest of the forest sounds, so that for an instant she felt only a vague sense of annoyance that such a little noise had disturbed her. Then everything went black. She tried to cry out, to pull frantically at the thick cloth that enveloped her head, but rough hands were dragging her to her feet, and then she was being lifted, flung across something, the air in her lungs becoming laboured and her breaths short and rasping. Her last thought before she lost awareness of time was that the bull in the park had been far less dangerous than either she or Mary had supposed!

Somebody was splashing water into her face, forcing the neck of a bottle between her lips. She swallowed the tepid liquid but her throat felt dry and scratchy. When she tried to lift her hand to push the bottle away she realized that both her arms were bound tightly to her sides, cords cutting into her flesh.

There was very little light. It came from a candle burning in its sconce on a ledge nearby, faintly illuminating a dark cave of some kind where half a dozen turbanned men, pistols and sabres at their belts, stood or sat about, their gleaming dark eyes fixed on her.

For an instant the thought of screaming loudly entered her head but though she felt sick and dizzy and more afraid than she had ever been in her life she retained the sense to remain mute, to stare back at those gleaming black eyes.

'You are Melody Craven?'

A short, thickset man who yet seemed to have the air of authority about him had addressed her, his accent barely discernible.

'Yes,' she said briefly.

'You do not beg for your life?' he resumed in an interested tone.

'No,' Melody said.

'That is wise,' the man said. 'What we shall do we shall do.'

But I'm not brave and I'm not wise, Melody thought in panic. I'm stupid and pigheaded and naïve and I rush into things without stopping to consider the consequences.

'You wish to eat?' the man said.

She nodded briefly.

One of the others stepped forward and sliced through the cords that bound her. The blood rushing back into her cramped arms made her bite her lips with pain.

Someone came forward and put a shallow saucer of lentils mixed with beans in her lap. There was a shallow spoon laid across them. She waited until the circulation in her hands had returned to near normal, then lifted the spoon, thinking hopefully as she ate the not unappetizing mess that it seemed likely they might not be going to kill her. Since they were living rough food was probably too scarce to waste on a potential victim.

When she had scraped the platter clean another stepped forward with a cup of what proved to be the same tepid water she had drunk before.

'You had best sleep,' the thickset man said.

'I am not tired,' Melody said coldly.

'Then lie down,' he said, not unkindly.

317

One of the others tossed her a blanket and then, apparently being under orders, took up his rifle and moved out of the low entrance that led, as far as she could make out, into a clearing in a hollow of the woods. Through the opening she could see the first pearly gleams of dawn.

Sleep claimed her again, though she felt, as she was roughly shaken awake, that it had lasted scarcely long enough for her to close her eyes. However, it was now full day and even here, within the dimly gleaming stone, she could feel the heat rising.

'We wait for your buyer,' the thickset man said as she pulled herself into a sitting position.

'My — what?'

The shock on her face evidently amused them as a couple of them laughed.

'Your buyer,' the other said. 'We need ammunition in order to join equal forces with our friends in other places. We sell you for guns and bullets.'

'To whom,' she asked indignantly.

'One who moves between the warring sides.' He grinned suddenly, observing as he watched her expression. 'I act as spokesman because, until quite recently, I worked in the Civil Service and am therefore more educated than my fellows. I speak English and

318

can read and write in that language also. Neither am I an ignorant sepoy though I am a good Muslim.'

'And a traitor to the Civil Service, which trusted you!' she could not avoid exclaiming.

'To the occupying forces who take the wealth of India while our people remain ignorant and poor, who trade with the princes who are themselves corrupt and cruel. We fight for our freedom from injustice. We fight for the religion that forbids us certain foods — a fact ignored by the British Government — '

'One foolish official who made a stupid mistake!' she interrupted.

'One mistake can be a key to freedom,' he said.

The figure of one of the others who had evidently been standing guard darkened the entrance. He said something in his own tongue and then stood aside, allowing a newcomer to enter the dim space within.

'This is an unexpected pleasure,' Adam Channing said as casually as if they had just met at a London theatre or garden party. 'I hope you had some hours of peaceful sleep?'

18

At a loss for an immediate reply she could only stare at him while thoughts jostled in her mind. His being one-quarter Indian in blood and perhaps more than that in upbringing would have given him a deep and wide understanding of his grandmother's culture but it had not prevented him from obtaining rapid promotion in the regiment. He had seemed to her to bestride two worlds and to occupy both with equal ease. Now however, in riding-breeches and belted tunic he had apparently crossed invisible boundaries, something that became even more obvious when he began to speak in what was obviously fluent Hindustani to the men now crowding around him.

There was a brief silence when he had finished and then half a dozen voices broke out in what sounded to her apprehensive ears like furious argument.

Adam spoke again, his tone measured, his stance casual though she noticed his hand strayed to the pistol at his belt.

There was a frowning silence when he had finished and then a huddle of urgent, unintelligible whispers during which he took the few paces that brought him to her side.

'They are demanding more money for your ransom,' he said in a tone as casual as if he were commenting on the weather. 'They will agree with my price in the end but every Indian likes to haggle over prices. When I nod to you rise and walk slowly outside without looking back. My horse is tethered there. Can you mount up in those ridiculous hoops?'

'Yes,' Melody said, equally curtly.

'The rest I will explain when we are clear of this place.'

He turned away, leaving her to wait anxiously as he joined in the discussion.

It was clear, she thought, that his arrival had been no surprise to them which could only mean that Captain Adam Channing knew more about the present revolt than he had admitted. Or was he a spy and, if so, for which side? The questions revolved in her mind as she sat stiffly on the mattress where she had already spent too many nerve-racking hours.

He turned briefly to glance towards her and she saw him nod in a casual, offhand fashion. Hardly daring to breathe she rose slowly and sauntered towards the entrance as unhurriedly as her fast-beating heart would allow.

The day's heat shot burning arrows down through the foliage of the trees. A saddled horse was tethered at a short distance.

Melody felt unreality close in around her. Her thoughts flew inevitably back to that long-ago day in the park when Mary had distracted the attention of the escaped bull and dragged Melody away, only to claim an almost impossible debt of gratitude.

'If I emerge from this alive,' she reflected, gritting her teeth as she prepared to mount the waiting horse, 'I wonder what impossible promise Adam Channing will expect from me.'

Somehow or other, her skirts flying up behind her, she gained the saddle, fixed her feet in the stirrups and leaned to untie the rope that had been fastened to one of the lower branches of the tree.

From the cave behind her came a series of furious yells, Adam's bargaining powers having evidently proved superior. The noise startled the horse which, from standing placidly still, reared up and then galloped off through the trees, Melody clinging to the reins, bent almost double against the saddle which was threatening to slip sideways and dislodge her.

This was no tame pony such as she and Mary had been accustomed to ride in the park but an Arab steed, highly bred and partly untamed. Its standing quietly while she mounted had been surprising but now, any training it might have received forgotten, it plunged through the forest and with equal suddenness stopped dead, almost pitching Melody over its head.

Shaken, she dismounted, clinging to the reins lest the animal decide to bolt again but it merely stood quivering for an instant and then, looking quietly satisfied at having dislodged an unwelcome passenger, began to crop the grass that grew thickly round about.

Melody, too exhausted to plan any further moves, sat down abruptly on a tussock of grass and tried to think what an earth to do next. Was Adam still bargaining with the rebels? Indeed, had he anything with which to bargain, or was it a gigantic bluff on his part, a move to help her make a bid for freedom? If so then she was very likely to be seized again since she had no notion exactly where she was!

In the grass near her where she had sunk down tiredly a flicker caught her eye. She stared at the movement which was no stronger than the ripple of a stray sunbeam across the back of a — Suddenly cold with terror, she saw the V-shaped markings, the sleek pointed head, the fluttering tongue.

A shot rang out, almost deafening her and as she turned her head she saw Adam Channing, pistol still in his hand, one dark eyebrow raised in simulated surprise.

'You might have waited,' he said reproachfully.

'You told me to mount up so what was I supposed to do?' she flared back. 'If the men had refused to accept your terms they would have recaptured me and the chance to escape would have gone!'

'Quite right!' he said placidly. 'However since it was rather a lot of gold I was offering they were not likely to turn it down. I'm glad you didn't decide to be a heroine.'

'A heroine!' Her pent-up anger and fear flashed out. 'Never was any girl less suitable to be a heroine! If I hadn't made a stupid promise to my cousin Mary I wouldn't be here now! I would be safe in London in a comfortable sitting-room helping my aunt to sort silks! As it is, I have learned that the man I thought I loved was false through and through! I have seen violent death at close quarters! I have been forced to walk for hours through forests and grasslands that are teeming with rebels and snakes and the Lord knows what else. This horse has done every mortal thing to dislodge me and succeeded! I have been kidnapped by rebels and calmly sold to a man who seems on excellent terms with murdering sepoys!'

'You seem somewhat out of sorts,' he said provokingly. 'The ransom, by the by, was hardly agreed calmly. They wanted more than the regiment was prepared to offer. I did some hard bargaining back there — had to add some of my own cash to sweeten it.'

'You mean the army arranged for a ransom?' Melody said blankly.

'You thought that I came galloping to rescue you like a latter day Sir Lancelot?' He looked wryly amused. 'I happened to be in the vicinity when your disappearance was discovered. It so chanced that a couple of my relatives — second or third cousins — formed part of the break-away faction which is having its own somewhat more profitable revolt and so I was deputed to go to your rescue while the rest of your party continued on to my house.'

'I still owe you thanks,' she said sombrely.

'Accepted with pleasure!' His smile flashed out again. 'You and I seem fated to bump into each other at stated intervals. When you have rested a little we will continue. We are some way outside the route to my property.'

'I don't need to rest — ' she began.

'No, but the horse does. I've ridden Sultan hard over the last few hours. He's weary.'

'I would never have guessed it,' she said tartly.

She expected a sharp reply but he merely looked at her with a gentleness in his gaze that made her feel suddenly small and ashamed.

'You've had a bad time since you came here,' he said at length. 'Roger Hallett turned out to be rather far from the ideal fiancé, didn't he? But his death must have shocked you beyond measure. Love can take a long time to die.'

'It was never love,' Melody told him. 'It was a silly girl's dream of happiness and it was also jealousy, I think. The fact is that he courted my cousin for the sake of her inheritance and at the same time pretended that I was the one he'd really wanted to marry. So when Mary fell in love with someone else we arranged the substitution without telling him.'

'I have often wondered how 'Mary' arrived and proved to be 'Melody',' Adam said.

'I thought it would be a wonderful surprise for him,' she said miserably.

'He seemed more shocked than surprised,' Adam said.

'And after a very little while I realized that I didn't love him at all,' Melody confessed. 'And then there was the girl, Lalika.'

'Many British officers take Indian mistresses.'

'I realized that, but she loved him and he'd promised her marriage. She had the bride-scarf all ready.'

'And you found them both,' Adam said gently.

'Yes.' Melody bent her head.

'When all this is over you'll be going back to England?' he asked.

'I wish I'd never left,' Melody said, drawing her hand across her lashes in a childlike gesture. 'I was safe there and life — well, it was boring sometimes — but at least I could be certain of still being alive the following morning!'

'I guarantee,' Adam said, taking both her hands and pulling her towards him, 'that you will wake up alive on many mornings to come! Now, are you ready to trust yourself on Sultan again? I will take the leading rein and we'll make our way, albeit slowly, to my property.'

'Yes,' she said simply.

He had spoken no warm words of sympathy but she felt stronger from the touch of his hand. He helped her to her feet and on to the horse which merely turned its handsome head and gave her a look of mingled disgust and resignation.

'Sultan has little patience with the ladies,' Adam said, taking the leading rein and moving towards a narrow path that twisted between the trees.

They moved in silence, the woods enclosing them. This, she guessed, was a roundabout route to his property. By now, barring misfortune, the rest of the fugitives would be safely installed in the remote and beautiful old house.

'I am taking a fairly untrodden route,' Adam said, after he had led the horse with herself perched aloft for some considerable time. 'There are scattered bands of rebel sepoys and sowars moving to join together and make concerted attacks on Delhi and Calcutta.'

'You are not in contact with them?' Melody ventured.

'You mean am I a double agent of some sort?'

To her embarrassment he dropped the rein and laughed heartily, the lines of fatigue fading from his face.

'I merely thought — ' she began lamely.

'That I could move safely anywhere I pleased? Melody, my grandmother was a Hindu but the idea of there being hatred between them and the Moslems never entered her or my grandfather's heads! To

328

them and to my parents all people are equally valuable as human beings and toleration makes for friendship. This stupid rebellion has its roots in a Government error which called forth many grudges secretly harboured by malcontents. It has nothing to do with the basic laws of civilized living! I employ Hindus and Moslems and Christians — my cook provides the correct foods for everyone — and I have moved all my life ever since I was a small boy without fear but with equal respect for everybody. I wouldn't lower myself to play off one group against another or to act the spy for the sake of further promotion in the East India Regiment! If that's what you imagined then you were greatly mistaken!'

He took up the reins again and walked on.

'I owe you an apology,' she said at last in a small voice.

'Indeed you do not!'

He had stopped again, turned to look at her, the anger dying out of his face. 'What else could you have thought when I entered that cave? The truth is that I came upon the group making for my house when my runners brought me word that fugitives were approaching. I rode out and found them hopelessly lost with most of them frantically searching for you!'

'I never meant to cause any trouble,'

Melody said contritely, 'but it was agreed that we should rest in ones and twos instead of being bunched together.'

'Ideas that are good in theory don't always work out in practice,' Adam said wryly. 'At the very least a guard should have been set. As it was, the idea of holding someone, preferably a woman, to ransom had already occurred to the gang. They are none of them rebels for any cause at all save obtaining as much money as possible with the least possible trouble to themselves! When I came upon the rest of your party I found them practically running round in circles wondering what to do about finding you when the most sensible action would have been to carry on to my house and raise a search party there.'

'People don't always think sensibly when they are in great danger!' Melody argued.

'Grant and Trenton should have taken command,' Adam said. 'I suspect their wives out-argued them and Trenton anyway has a broken arm. At least you are safe!'

'And you are somewhat the poorer for my rescue,' Melody said.

'There are some things that are more important than money,' he said.

There was a sudden warmth in his glance and his voice that made her heart beat faster.

She reminded herself quickly that it would be utterly foolish for her to lose her heart to another unsuitable man, not a cheat and a liar like Roger Hallett but a man who was already bound to the beloved Meera. Adam Channing was not the kind of man who abandoned the girl he loved for one to whom, as she suspected, he was momentarily attracted, and for her own part she was determined not to be the cause of another's heartbreak.

'I am sure,' she said stiffly as they continued their slow journey, 'that my uncle in London will be glad to reimburse you for the ransom you paid.'

'And I would be infinitely obliged if you never informed him of it,' he returned. 'In fact you would be wise simply to say that you wandered away in the forest and got lost. A white woman risks losing her reputation if she has been alone with Indian brigands.'

'But surely — !'

'You forget I was educated in England,' he broke in. 'At public school one learns the conventions of civilized living very quickly. We had best increase our speed. Nightfall draws near and I would like to be secure in my own territory before darkness is upon us.'

She nodded and he began to move in a loping stride that covered the ground more speedily than she would have believed possible.

Clinging to the pommel of the saddle she found herself jerking awake when she had not even realized that she had slept for a few minutes. The twilight had purpled into a sky across which the first faint stars were marshalling themselves.

'We are almost there.' Adam broke a long silence.

'How can you possibly tell?' Melody demanded.

She felt stiff and saddle-sore and the gnawing pain in her stomach reminded her that she hadn't eaten for many hours.

'We have been on my land this past half-hour,' he replied.

'And the rest of the party will be in your house?'

'I'm certain of it. If you can bear to stay in the saddle another few minutes we shall see my house as the trees thin out.'

They pressed on, Melody by this time so weary that when hanging creepers brushed her neck she no longer thought of snakes.

Then, almost without warning, they were clear of the trees and as she raised her head she saw the outlines of the large building ahead, saw the light from many lanterns in the windows and figures emerging from the wide entrance hall.

'Remember,' Adam said rapidly, 'that you lost your way in the forest and feared to shout for help lest rebels be lurking. I came upon you by chance.'

Melody did no more than nod when those emerging from the house were hurrying to surround her, voices raised excitedly in question and greeting.

'I found her hours ago,' Adam was saying cheerfully. 'Wandering around and hopelessly lost and not daring to call out lest rebels be lurking!'

He was helping her to the ground where for an instant she leaned weakly against him.

'My poor dear child!' Mrs Grant was exclaiming. 'What possessed you to lose yourself? We were quite frantic in our efforts to find you!'

'Though we dare not call out,' Mrs Trenton put in, 'in case there were rebels nearby. In the end we came on here on Captain Channing's advice and he found you! What a blessing and a mercy!'

The ladies had taken charge, between them guiding her into the house where all seemed to be bustle and stir, with Mr Patel hurrying to shake her hand fervently.

'Did I not insist that a young lady from our beloved British Empire would not vanish for ever? Did I not say and affirm in the strongest possible terms that Captain Channing would find her and restore her to the bosom of her friends?'

'You did indeed,' Mrs Grant agreed. 'Several times over!'

Instinctively Melody looked about her for Adam in order to share a moment's amusement. For a moment she failed to spot him and then she saw his tall figure, both hands outstretched to greet the slight, delicate Meera in her pastel-shaded sari who was looking up at him with the same worshipping smile that Melody was certain he would be returning in full measure could she but see the expression on his face.

Suddenly she was too tired to care, too tired to do more than pick at the food that was placed before her. She wanted only to sleep and forget and, if at that moment some genie had appeared to grant her dearest wish, she would have found herself in her own room in the Craven household in foggy, smoky London!

Someone took her arm and led her, stumblingly, into a small room she hadn't seen before. She had a vague impression of struggling out of her hooped petticoat and of someone pulling off her shoes and a little later of blankets being pulled up around her.

And then she slept, unaware of anything at all!

A chattering sound roused her. Opening her eyes she beheld something small and furry, seated on the edge of the low bed and gently patting her face.

'Kara!'

Suddenly awake Melody sat up.

'Please to wash. Memsahib?'

One of the servants, an elderly woman, was gesturing towards an inner door through which the steam of hot water mingled with the scent of perfume was issuing.

There were lamps burning still in the room but through the latticed windows crept a sullen morning.

Melody pushed the blankets aside and rose somewhat stiffly. Clean clothes had been laid ready over a chair nearby and large fluffy towels waited to envelope her. In a little while, she thought, she would be feeling quite human again.

Half an hour later, aided by the ministrations of the servant, she sat, wearing one of her simpler cotton dresses over a hooped and pristine petticoat, her feet encased in a carefully polished pair of low-heeled shoes while another servant brushed and combed her hair and she herself drank thirstily a cup of hot sweet tea.

'Captain Channing wishes to speak with you, memsahib,' the elderly woman said in hesitant English.

A glance in a long mirror showed that the rest and the leisurely toilet had banished the deathly pallor of fatigue from her face and that her hair fell in its usual bright curls. Not, she reminded herself, that her appearance made the least difference!

With Kara perched in friendly fashion on her shoulder she was conducted along a narrow passage into a room furnished more in the English style with books lining the walls and dark oak table and chairs. Adam, now back in uniform and looking as trim as if he were ready to go on parade, rose from a handsomely carved desk to greet her.

'There is bread, fruit and fish on the table. You need to eat something before we talk,' he said.

'There is fresh news?' Her eyes strayed to the pile of documents on the desk.

'Coming from all parts,' he said wryly. 'Colonel Smith is dead together with those who went with him in a last attempt to relieve Cawnpore. They were killed instantly and Cawnpore itself is said to be in flames. More rebels have occupied Delhi and are besieging Calcutta where many British have taken refuge. Meanwhile the British Government agonizes as to whether this is a rebellion or a mutiny since it originated in military ranks!'

'But many sepoys and sowars are still loyal?'

'Thankfully yes, but the conflict threatens to engulf India.'

'And Parakesh?'

'Will rise again on new foundations. What matters now is the evacuation of those still in the affected areas.'

He sounded brisk and businesslike.

'Queen Victoria will be unhappy,' Melody said. 'The newspapers at home often report how she regards the Indians as her own special favourites.'

'Having met at least a dozen of them in her entire life, I daresay,' he retorted cynically and suddenly, unexpectedly, laughed. 'Take no notice of me, Melody! I spent much of my boyhood in England and I learned when I came back here just how much the native Indians are appreciated by the British! Eat your breakfast and then you will tell me what decision you have taken.'

'Decision?'

'Will you return to your uncle's house or remain here? There are many English girls on the subcontinent — most of them looking for husbands.'

'The Fishing Fleet,' Melody said and found herself laughing.

'Yes indeed. What a pretty laugh you have!' he said unexpectedly. 'A pretty laugh and a pretty face and a stubborn nature! You will plough your own furrow, I believe.'

'Probably in Lisbon,' she said. 'My cousin Mary is settled there with her new husband and they would happily give me a home.'

'Maiden aunt to their blossoming children, I daresay! Melody, you are not a girl to be content with that! You came out here to marry a man who had offered for your cousin. That was naïve of you.'

'It was stupid of me,' she admitted.

'Well-intentioned,' he corrected, rising from his seat to join her at the table. 'Eat something! You must be famished!'

'I am wondering what happens next,' she said, helping herself to bread.

'The revolt will be contained,' he said with quiet assurance, 'but the simmering discontent will remain and the old trust between those of different faiths will be hard to regain. For India it will be an exciting time.'

He sounded suddenly boyishly enthusiastic.

Melody continued silently with her light breakfast, drank some juice that had been poured for her, and waited. For what she waited she had no clear notion.

'You have had some unusual experiences

338

since coming here,' Adam said abruptly.

'More unusual than I could have dreamed,' she admitted. 'I really thought that I was in love with Roger Hallett but the plain truth is that I was in love with the idea of being in love. If I had stopped to reason things out I never would have taken my cousin's place.'

'And now?' He asked the question suddenly, his dark eyes holding her own blue gaze.

'I have resolved,' she said steadily, 'never to fall in love with any man who has other claims on his affection.'

'Very sensible! Come up on to the roof. The whole household will be stirring very soon and I have something particular to say to you.'

Time seemed to run backwards as she climbed the steps on to the roof and looked down at the gardens below, the flowering creepers still veiled in morning mist.

'So you have determined to return to England?'

He asked the question casually but his expression was strained.

'I've no desire to join the Fishing Fleet,' Melody said, 'and single women in a foreign land must inevitably be at a disadvantage.'

'Next year,' Adam said, 'I hope to fulfil a dream I've had for a long time. I have a furlough coming and since I've no close family in England I intend to set off and explore what I can of Tibet. Few foreigners have ever ventured there but that land of high mountains and deep valleys and gentle people fascinates me. I hope to go with a companion.'

'With Meera,' Melody said. Despite herself her voice quivered slightly.

'Meera? Why would I take Meera?' Adam enquired.

'I assumed — it was said — she is beloved by you.' Her voice trailed away uncertainly.

'Most beloved,' he said. 'Meera is the daughter of a cousin of my grandmother's, born to parents who thought themselves past the age when they could conceive a child. And she was born at a particular time when local tradition, held by both Muslims and Hindus, tells of a young girl born under a particular bright star who represents a living goddess, a spirit of spring and loving kindness. She has spent her life here in this house that my guardian willed to me, and because of her presence here this property is respected, a sanctuary. Next year she will be of an age to marry a husband of her choosing and enter the real world as an ordinary person though Lord knows she is so sweet and good that she is much more than ordinary!'

'You will leave her behind when you travel to Tibet?'

'I will leave her with her husband,' Adam said. 'She is certainly beloved by me but not in any romantic sense. Muslims and Hindus alike respect her but she has chosen her husband and I was delighted to give my full approval. Ram Singh is a man of great integrity and — '

'She is engaged to Ram Singh?' Melody stared at him in astonishment.

'Ram Singh is respected and admired and one of the most reliable and intelligent guides in India. Meera and he have loved for a long time and he is the one person who can help her to adjust to the outside world when her years of solitude are complete.'

'Nobody ever said,' Melody told him.

'Not all customs, especially those held by Indians of all faiths, are divulged to the white man,' Adam said, smiling slightly.

'I see,' Melody said.

'Ancient traditions, legends carried on the breeze, superstitions if you like but strong in their antiquity and honoured by many who may not agree on other matters.'

'So peace might yet come?'

'If the ties that bind are stronger than the swords that separate. But Meera will make her own happiness with the man she has chosen. I wanted to speak of us, of you and me. When I first saw you I felt deep regret that you were engaged to Roger Hallett for I knew his reputation, knew he kept an Indian mistress and yet, military etiquette being as rigid as it is, I could say nothing to warn you! I was convinced your marriage would never work but it wasn't my place to interfere. I could only hope that his true nature would become apparent to you before the actual ceremony. Then the present troubles began and the rebellion occupied all our thoughts.'

'You sent Ram Singh to the married quarters?'

'To find out if the girl — Lalika was safe. He found both her and Hallett dead. Then you arrived and — the rest you know. I am sorry you had to find out in such a way.'

'I had already guessed,' Melody said in a low voice. 'By then I was beginning to admit to myself that Roger wasn't the man first Mary and then I believed him to be. I grew up very quickly.'

'When this is over, when my furlough comes, would you think about coming with me to Tibet — as my wife?' Adam asked.

'As anything you wished!' Melody exclaimed and blushed scarlet as he pulled her to him, saying between kisses:

'My wife, dearest Melody. Anything less would shock Mrs Grant and Mrs Trenton beyond anything. Will you be my wife truly?'

'Most truly,' she said softly.

And then he was kissing her again until her own lips took fire from his passion and to them drifted the ghostly scent of long vanished jasmine as the heavens opened and the long awaited rain began to fall.

Mrs Grant, hurrying out of the house, stopped short and stared up at the two figures entwined above her. For a moment her powers of speech seemed to have deserted her and then, turning to Mr Patel, who was struggling to open an umbrella for her, she said.

'They will be soaked to the skin!'

'We British,' said Mr Patel, his smile approving, 'are the most romantic people in the world, my dear memsahib!'

We do hope that you have enjoyed reading this large print book.

Did you know that all of our titles are available for purchase?

We publish a wide range of high quality large print books including:
Romances, Mysteries, Classics
General Fiction
Non Fiction and Westerns

Special interest titles available in large print are:
The Little Oxford Dictionary
Music Book
Song Book
Hymn Book
Service Book

Also available from us courtesy of Oxford University Press:
Young Readers' Dictionary
(large print edition)
Young Readers' Thesaurus
(large print edition)

For further information or a free brochure, please contact us at:
Ulverscroft Large Print Books Ltd.,
The Green, Bradgate Road, Anstey,
Leicester, LE7 7FU, England.
Tel: (00 44) **0116 236 4325**
Fax: (00 44) **0116 234 0205**

Other titles published by
The House of Ulverscroft:

VASHTI

Maureen Peters

Tansy Clark is intrigued by the newspaper items her father shows her, about two assistant curators who have died suddenly of gastric influenza at a time when no epidemic exists. She begins her own investigation which reveals illegal and dangerous goings on behind the respectable façade of London museums. Going undercover, Tansy takes a post at a museum founded by a reclusive millionaire. But then she is attacked whilst out walking . . . Soon she is involved in a thirty-year-old story concerning the statue of a biblical queen, Vashti. Tansy must endure shocks, intrigue and a danger that bears every hallmark of death . . .

TRUMPET MORNING

Maureen Peters

The Petrie family live on a farm in Anglesey, North Wales. Grandfather Taid is a Revivalist preacher; his wife, Nain, an Irish gypsy who casts spells to annoy her husband. Then there is the aunt who's sworn off men forever, and another always ready for a lark. Also an uncle married to a wife who doesn't fit in, another whose marriage will benefit the farm, and the youngest facing a darker destiny in 1940 with Great Britain at war. As eleven-year-old Nell prepares for grammar school, and the shadows of war creep closer, comedy and heartbreak mingle in this story of a most eccentric family.